W9-CHM-051

ADVANCE PRAISE FOR *The Monkey Bible*

". . . a fast-paced adventure that explores the edgy frontiers between primatology and philosophy through the enquiring mind of an unlikely young hero. I was impressed with the quality of the science and the passion for conservation was clear and effectively done . . ." —DR. RICHARD WRANGHAM, Harvard University

". . . will challenge believers and skeptics both . . ." —PASTOR ROBERT HOLUM, Luther Place Memorial Church

". . . so well does it nail the myth of intelligent design and the mixed-up thinking used to justify racist bigotry, it is more likely to be burned in protest by religious extremists and white supremacists!" —IAN REDMOND, OBE, Chief Consultant, GRASP - UNEP/UNESCO Great Ape Survival Partnership

". . . one of the most innovative books I have read in a long time . . . the writing is fresh and wonderful . . . This is the work of a very creative thinker and writer." —PATSY SIMS, Director, MFA in Creative Nonfiction Program, Goucher College

"Laxer has taken on the challenge of bridging the huge gulf between creationists and Darwinians . . . [The] novel and music will be enjoyed by those who value their religious beliefs yet are seeking to understand our biological origins." —DR. SIMON BARON-COHEN, Cambridge University

". . . makes the case that species loss should be at the forefront of our environmental concerns . . . shows that faithful Christian communities can take creative action to preserve important habitats . . .[Eric Maring's] imaginative, playful, soulful style works perfectly . . . [a] real gem." —PASTOR SARAH SCHERSCHLIGT, Prince of Peace Lutheran Church

"Quite the provocative and well-written story which raises thought-provoking questions about what it means to be human and in so doing gives us a refreshing perspective on our own place in the living world . . ." —DR. GRAEME PATTERSON, Assistant Director Africa Program, Wildlife Conservation Society

". . . the work of an exceptionally inventive mind . . ." —LAUREN SALLINGER, Teaching Instructor, University Writing Program, George Washington University

"*The Monkey Bible* raises a question we should all ponder: does the line between humans and other animals really have the moral significance we give it?" —DR. PETER SINGER, Princeton University

"*Ishmael* meets *The Celestine Prophecy* . . . All the information of three college classes wrapped into a powerful tale." — MICHAEL STERN, Co-founder, New Nature Foundation

". . . skillfully explores the conflict between religion and evolution . . . addresses a number of critical ethical issues, particularly given the rate with which apes, our closest relatives, are being hunted and their habitat destroyed. It is a thrilling read . . ." —DR. COLIN A. CHAPMAN, McGill University, Canada Research Chair in Primate Ecology and Conservation

". . . This lyrical narrative combines lines of analysis, anxieties and dreams that one doesn't dare hope to find combined in one book . . . confronts its readers with strong, original ideas and challenges, particularly regarding solutions to our global environmental crisis . . . the music is a great accomplice in this effort . . ." —ALEXANDER VON BISMARCK, Executive Director, Environmental Investigative Agency

"Ingenious! A captivating tale skillfully woven around the complex themes of evolution, philosophy and religion, plus delivering a strong conservation message . . ." —DR. ELANOR BELL, Lecturer in Microbial Ecology and Marine Conservation, Scottish Association for Marine Science

". . . introduc[es] new perspectives in a non-threatening, open-minded, playful format . . ." —REVEREND JAY HARTLEY, Eastwood Christian Church

". . . weaves a tapestry of fantasy and reality, truth, myth and science and lures us into a journey that challenges us to think about who and what we believe we are . . ." —DEBRA CURTIN, President and Founder, New England Primate Sanctuary

". . . the universal story of searching for one's place in the world." —ANDREW K. JOHNSTON, Smithsonian Institution

"An impressive book! Laxer is a skillful storyteller with an important mission. The reader is taken on an exhilarating, suspenseful journey across the globe in this scientifically fact filled 'bio-romance'. . ." —MICHAEL A HUFFMAN, Primate Research Institute, Kyoto University

"A wonderful rollicking adventure through what it means to be a human animal in the 21st century . . . paves the way for a creative coming together of religion and science into a new ethic for conservation . . ." —DR. DAVID BROWNE, Director of Conservation, Canadian Wildlife Federation

". . . thought-provoking and well-researched . . . challenges the way we view our relatedness to apes . . . an entertaining and educational story." —JENNIFER WHITAKER, Founding Director, Coalition for Primate Protection

". . . a unique and gentle treatment of the seemingly irreconcilable chasm between the creationists and the evolutionists . . . give[s] us the tools to explore both worlds and thus encourage the spirit of inquiry in young and old alike . . ." —NIGEL PENNEY, Director, Marianopolis Science Camp

". . . After a fast-paced adventure across four continents, discovering that 'the line' between humans and nature is fuzzier than he thought, Emmanuel faces an even tougher reality: humankind's destructive tendencies, and how to preserve the 99.999999999% of species that are not human . . ." —DR. MITCHELL IRWIN, Primatologist, Co-founder, Sadabe

Additional praise at www.monkeybible.com

The Monkey Bible

The Monkey Bible

— a modern allegory by —

MARK LAXER

Outer Rim Press, LLC
Burlington, Vermont

Outer Rim Press, LLC

Published in the United States of America
by Outer Rim Press, LLC
70 South Winooski Ave #287
Burlington, VT 05401
info@monkeybible.com

ISBN-13: 978-0-9638108-0-9
Library of Congress Control Number: 2010928845

Printed in The United States of America
First Printing, July 2010
10 9 8 7 6 5 4 3 2 1   10 11 12 13 14 15

Book Design by Peter Holm, Sterling Hill Productions
Illustrations by Sara Lourie
Photographs illustrating "The Monkey Bible" by Arthur Laxer

Printed on recycled paper with soy-based inks

To remarkable teachers, such as Jan Laxer,
who fire the imagination and stir the soul
with stories from the natural world.

And to Grizzwauld the chimp
and the shared, distant memories.

Animals run,
Animals run,
Animals run
the zoo.

—*The Monkey Bible*

Obscured by the shadows of a cobwebbed, musty attic, a large dark animal pressed its fists to the floor and knuckle-walked toward the light. It appeared to be an ape, but when it opened a box and pulled out a book, it appeared to be human. It was too tall to stand upright. Its name was Emmanuel. . . .

—*The Monkey Bible*

CONTENTS

PROLOGUE

"Do you think it's fiction?" asked Lucy, hair flapping wildly in the wind.

Emmanuel shifted uneasily in the passenger seat. "What do you mean?"

"The story about your genes—do you think it's fiction?"

"It is in Father's handwriting; Father does not lie."

"So," said Lucy, "what's it like to see the world through the eyes of an . . ."

"I am noticing your breasts," he said. "Breasts hardly hidden, breasts pressed and shaped by your black spandex top. Your lower region appears in my mind like a spider in a moist, perfect garden."

"Really?"

She pressed the accelerator hard.

"The story of my creation," he added, "explains the rise of my animal instincts."

"You beast," she breathed, "take me now . . ."

PART ONE

100 Percent

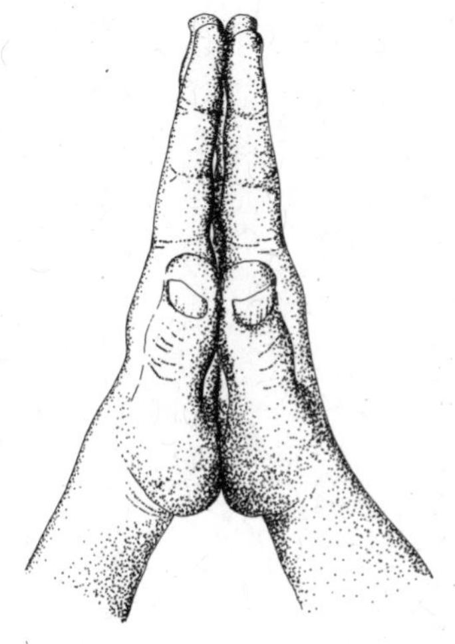

—1—

The eighteen-year-old Emmanuel loved Bible stories. He felt comforted by the one in which God creates humans in His own image and grants them dominion over all the animals. The story of Genesis made Emmanuel feel taller than he actually was.

One day his Bible was gone.

Emmanuel looked for it in church, at home, in school, and on the sidewalks of Washington DC. After days of searching, praying, and gnawing at his fingernails, he decided to find a replacement. He approached his father for advice.

Ernesto stood poised, five feet tall, with a solid build and near-perfect posture. Both he and Emmanuel had light yellow-brown skin, with black hair brushed over dark brown eyes.

"My Bible is gone, *Bapak,*" Emmanuel confessed, using the Indonesian word for father.

Ernesto looked up. His son's body proportions—the arms seemed too long and the legs seemed too short for the torso—explained why Emmanuel found it uncomfortable and unnatural to stand straight or still, but today the fidgeting seemed worse than normal. The fidgeting made sense to Ernesto, who understood Emmanuel's deep ties to the Bible and to this Bible in particular. Ernesto had read this Bible aloud to Emmanuel over a dozen years ago. He had taught Emmanuel to read from it and, years later, he saw Emmanuel rescue it one moonless night when men with machetes set fire to their village. Flames had engulfed their home and neighbors had died from burns and gashes. Emmanuel had been fourteen.

Ernesto recalled how, after the massacre, the family had left East Timor for Australia and then America, where Emmanuel arrived clutching the Bible. Its edges were charred and smelled of smoke.

"Why not look in the attic? There may be a family Bible in with the textbooks."

Emmanuel thanked him, extended his lips in a tightly closed O, and climbed to the attic where the patter of rain on the roof accentuated the feeling of dampness. The ceiling here was low, and he leaned forward, bent his legs slightly, and knuckle-walked toward the dim attic light.

He found a box with "Buku-Buku" written in red. *Books.*

He opened the box and pulled out a textbook with a twisted, colorful ladder of DNA on the cover. Molecules of DNA, he had learned in school, help to build and differentiate every living cell on earth.

He pulled out another textbook, the cover of which showed an artist's rendition of an early hominid, a primate with both human and ape-like features. He flipped through the pages and stopped at a picture of a naked female covered in hair. The caption read: "Lucy Lived In Ethiopia 3.6 Million Years Ago." He imagined getting behind her, cupping her Australopithecine breasts, thrusting his bone-shaped tool into folds of ancient flesh. He imagined her pushing back and quickly jerking forward, swiftly moving in rhythm, grunting with pleasure. His crotch responded and his face went red. *Shame*, he thought, and he resumed his search.

He pulled out a book, the cover of which showed a sword stuck in stone from the legend of King Arthur. Emmanuel remembered from the legend that Merlin transformed Arthur into a fish, badger, goose, hawk, as well as an ant. The wizard, Emmanuel recalled, thought it prudent for Arthur to swim, fly, and march among animals *as* an animal before wielding power as a human king.

He pulled out a textbook, the cover of which showed a cross, two overlapping triangles, and a crescent opened toward a star. The images made him think of his home, East Timor, an island of Christians in a sea of Muslims, and it occurred to him that while most Muslims treated neighbors with respect, some made it difficult for the conquered Christian colony. He reflected on family history: his uncle, wary of being treated by machete-bearing militias like an animal, had left East Timor and moved to Washington DC, but his parents, frightened to trust the road that twisted past their village like a serpent, remained and endured the abuse. Uncle Mateus later sent the textbooks, including the one in his hand, from America, to help the family pursue an education, but when tensions in East Timor exploded, Father returned the books for safekeeping.

Emmanuel pulled out a textbook on English literature, a book on creative writing, and a novel by Mark Twain. He pulled out a Holy Bible. It was fragile and old and smelled of must. He took a deep breath and opened it—a handful of pages flipped back, as if on their own accord, to a document inserted in Genesis.

He glanced at the document's title and recognized his father's handwriting: "The Story of My Son's Creation."

Emmanuel quickly inhaled, tensed his stomach, and read: "My son Emmanuel is not who he thinks he is. He—"

"EMMAAAAAAAANUEL!" his mother called from two stories below. "*MAKANLAH*—let's eat!"

He looked up. "But how could that be?" he cried.

His heart pounded. He wanted to read more.

"Why must it be forbidden?" he whispered hoarsely, glancing at the page.

His mother called again, louder.

Emmanuel, drenched in sweat, stood up and banged his head on a low wooden beam. Returning the document to the Bible, and the Bible to the box, he knuckle-walked to the stairs, touched the bump on his head, and began the descent.

— 2 —

Lucy crouched and shivered in the three-and-a-half-foot-high cave and listened to the roar of the wind. An hour ago she had slipped on thin ice over swift-moving water and now, with no stove or matches, she was wet and dangerously cold. She hugged herself for warmth and thought about Adam.

Last night she had told Adam of her plans to hike and camp alone in Mount Rainier National Park. He had looked down his nose at her and explained that severe storms strike quickly and unpredictably near the fourteen-thousand-foot peak, even in mid-June. He had offered her a cell phone.

"I'd rather freeze to death," she had replied.

Now the wind outside the cave sounded like an accelerating jet engine.

Adam should have known better, she thought. It was no secret how she felt about cell phones. They *had* been together for years.

She imagined him tall and naked, with a crown of curly brown hair—a classical marble sculpture under the high, vaulted ceiling of an art museum. He could be so regal. So annoying.

Lucy's mind drifted to a time, years ago, when they had traveled together by train. They had been sitting in a crowded compartment when a man shouted: "MAYBE YOU DID IT, MAYBE YOU DIDN'T!"

Noticing that the man was speaking on a cell phone, Adam had signaled him to lower his voice, but he continued as though speaking through a megaphone: "LOOK, YOU DON'T GOTTA TELL ME ALL THAT!"

Adam had stood up and whistled.

"YEA!" the man announced. "BUT IF I DON'T KNOW, WHO'S GONNA KNOW?"

The man completed the conversation, snapped his cell phone to a clip, and approached Adam. "Hey, I'm conducting *business,*" he hissed, wrinkling his nose and widening his nostrils. "If you do that again I'll drop your teeth in your morning coffee."

Adam had stared straight ahead as the man returned to his seat.

A few seconds later Adam stood up and slowly approached the man.

Passengers watched nervously.

"Maybe I overreacted," Adam said softly, jutting his chin close to the man's face. "If I did, I apologize. But if you threaten me again with violence you'll be dealing with Amtrak police."

Lucy shivered uncontrollably and grimaced at the memory as winds exploded just outside the cave. She felt weak. She summoned her strength and found a tarp and pocketknife in the pack. She sliced the tarp in half, cut the green fleece into strips, and removed her wet pants. She wrapped the fleece and tarp loosely around her legs, put her pants and jacket back on, and began to do deep knee bends.

In the up position, her legs were straight and her torso angled forward, due to the ceiling of the cave.

In the down position, she squatted.

Up. Down. Seven times. She breathed slowly and steadily through her nose to conserve heat.

Up. Down. Nineteen times. She had come to the mountain to reflect on what had distanced her from Adam. Last week they had ended their relationship.

There's plenty of time to think, she thought. She wasn't going anywhere. Not in a wind that could topple a person.

Minutes later she grew weary and numb. Her physical exertions slowed. She breathed through her mouth. Thoughts drifted to the aggressive cell phone abuser as she felt a cold, wet hand on the back of her neck.

— 3 —

Light from a stained glass window illuminated Evelyn's silky brown hair like a halo, warming her soft shirt, tall body, and gold cross pendant. She gazed at the cross as her voice rose from the church balcony to the cathedral dome.

They can't sing, she told herself as her thoughts strayed from choir practice. They can't worship God. They're apes. *They're animals.*

Her thoughts were provoked by a book she had stumbled upon four days ago in a used bookstore in London. She recalled the man who had been working in the bookstore. He had worn a frock coat, a green waistcoat, a white frilly shirt, and a cravat that wrapped around his raised collar like a vine. His desk was littered with dried flowers, tiny skulls, and maps. He wrote in a book with a quill pen.

"Good afternoon," Evelyn had said at the same moment he began to speak.

"Pardon?" Evelyn had replied.

"The book shop is closed," he had repeated.

"Sorry."

He stopped writing and looked up. "How might I assist you?"

"I'm looking for a used Bible."

He frowned, recalling how prisoners had been sent to Australia and the devout to America.

"None of those *heeyuh,*" he said, returning to his writing.

Evelyn scanned the room and noticed a poster of a dragon chasing its tail. "What about *this* one?" she asked, taking a Bible from the shelf by the poster.

His eyebrows rose. "*That* one places quite unnatural emphasis upon *Homines sapientes.*"

Evelyn had no idea what he was talking about; she had enough trouble with the accent.

She noticed a sticker on the Bible. It read: "Tree of Knoll Edge Books Ltd., Knoll Edge has its price: 50p." The Bible seemed to be in good condition, and she paid with a pound. The man removed the sticker, dropped it in a bag, and returned the change.

"Good price," she said.

Value over content, he thought. *Very American.*

Evelyn glanced at the man's desk. The maps, skulls, and quill pen gave the impression she had interrupted an early British naturalist explorer.

The man glanced at the dragon and handed her the bag.

"Thanks a lot," Evelyn said at the same moment he had begun to reply.

Later that night, on an airplane bound for the States, Evelyn thought about the Bible she had purchased and the friend, Emmanuel, she had bought it for. She closed her eyes. Conjuring his gentle strength and musky scent, she sensed that his needs let her fulfill her need to practice, and not just believe in, Christianity. His acceptance of her support gratified and strengthened her and, now that he had lost his Bible, she hoped he would in time accept her gift and heart's offer to be more than friends.

Evelyn reached in the bag from the bookstore and pulled out not the Bible but *The Third Chimpanzee,* a book by Jared Diamond. She gasped.

The cover photo of *The Third Chimpanzee* depicted a white-bearded chimp and a shadowy image of a naked man. She wondered if the mix-up had been an honest mistake or part of a prank. She opened to a bookmark that showed a half-eaten apple and read: "Knoll Edge is power, do not abuse." She began to read.

Evelyn had little understanding of molecular or evolutionary biology, biogeography, primatology, or anthropology, and she misunderstood the theory of evolution. She thought it claimed that people had evolved from chimps. Nonetheless, she was hardly a stranger to science. She knew, for instance, that continents move very slowly, that the Himalayan Mountains formed after India slammed into Asia long ago, and that ocean levels drop hundreds of feet during an ice age due to water accumulation on land as ice and snow. She was not intimidated by science, and as she read about taxonomy, the science of classifying living things, it didn't take her long to figure out that the book's title referred to human beings.

She was soon reading about a controversy within the field of taxonomy in which some methods of classification are said to be inconsistent. Taxonomists, for example, might use brain size and posture as criteria for classifying humans—thus creating a taxonomical branch on which humans alone reside—and taxonomists might use criteria *other* than brain size and posture for classifying nonhumans.

Greater consistency and accuracy might result, she read, if "genetic distance" and "time since speciation" classification methods were applied objectively and uniformly to the various forms of life.

Evelyn didn't understand the complexity behind the terms, but she grasped the implication: if the classification methods were applied objectively and uniformly, then human beings would be placed on a taxonomical branch with the common chimpanzee. This concerned her for the remainder of the flight, the remainder of the week, and beyond. The Church, as she saw it, would not welcome such a view and besides, she reminded herself, chimps are *animals*.

Nonetheless, she was heartened by the book's spirit of inquiry and now, bathed in the waning light on the high church balcony, she came to wonder if the attempt by the author to understand God's creation was a form of cerebral worship. She felt confident as her voice echoed through the space beneath the dome that the truth about human classification would, in God's own way, be revealed.

After choir practice, Evelyn asked Father Forsyth for reading material on people and their place in the natural world.

"Why not read what the Pope has to say?" he said, his voice resonating with the richness and poignancy of a well-worn cello. He wrote a Web address on a pad with a quill pen.

— 4 —

Emmanuel stood by the ocean's edge. A cold wind swept through the gray sky. The water receded, and he followed the slope to the dry ocean floor. Horseshoe crabs and rotting fish littered the vast plain.

Eventually he came upon a stream and there, in the icy mud, sat a man in tattered clothes. The man had bulging veins and a thick beard that hung like Spanish moss. "AYSEEAY-SEEJEEJEEAYTEESEE," he chanted.

The vibrations hummed in Emmanuel's chest like a honey bee's buzz.

"Excuse me," said Emmanuel. "What does it mean?"

"The Word," the man bellowed, "is forbidden."

"Why?"

"There are consequences! Did you not disobey?"

"Disobey?"

It was Saturday and Emmanuel had slept late. He woke and wrote the dream in his journal. He looked up and scanned the small, neat room with the high ceiling. No posters adorned the walls. He thought about the dream and wondered how he had disobeyed.

An answer came to him quickly. Late last night he had nearly returned to the attic to read Father's document despite Father's explicit request that Emmanuel *not* read it. The request had been clearly stated at the top of the document.

Nibbling the skin around his fingernails, he assured himself that the document had been part of a joke, but his assurance quickly faded. He knew too well that Father would never joke like that.

"Who am I?" Emmanuel wrote in the journal. "What is the story of my creation?"

He pulled his hand from his mouth and searched the computer for two dated e-mail messages. He found the one from Evelyn:

subject: Search Church

Dear Emmanuel,

You must be terribly frustrated. I'm sorry. I know how much your childhood Bible means to you. You mentioned that you have looked for it in Church but maybe look again? Church is such a big place . . .

I'm writing from a section of London packed with used bookstores (bliss!). I wish I had more time in this country, there's so much to explore. I'm on my way to the River Thames, then back to Heathrow and then the States.

What I love most in the UK is the strong sense of history that pervades life here. The people seem willing and proud to bear the burden and knowledge of the past. I wonder what their culture might teach ours were we willing to listen.

Take care. I look forward to seeing you soon,

Evelyn

Emmanuel and Evelyn had met after attending a church service, soon after Emmanuel first arrived in Washington DC. They had been walking home separately, but aware of one another's presence, when the skies darkened and it started to pour. They ran for cover but soon found themselves walking together, laughing off the chill of being wet and exposed. Neither of them spoke for a while, and there was a gentle awkwardness until Evelyn noted that at any given moment it is raining in countless thousands of places, and Emmanuel agreed that the world was small and interconnected in ways he did not understand. Afterwards, they often saw one another at church, where Evelyn encouraged Emmanuel to join the choir, which he did, and where the music and her kindness seemed to protect him from feeling alien in a strange new culture. Despite their inherent shyness the friendship grew, as did Emmanuel's reliance on her melodic, increasingly trusted voice.

Now Emmanuel reread Evelyn's message on the computer screen and wondered how she would respond to the document in the attic. Would she read it? Avoid it? Ask Father to explain it? Take it to the priest for advice? He sensed she would be wary of the document yet attracted to it; respectful of authority yet unwilling to follow blindly; fearful of sin yet confident as a Christian to seek the Truth.

Emmanuel found the e-mail message from Lucy:

> Subject: think about borders
>
> emmanuel,
>
> adam and i broke up last night. he had taken me under his wing like a favorite childhood story and directed me in ways i don't understand.
>
> am feeling sad and sore inside, totally not typical. need to be gentle with myself. think i'll go for a walk in the zoo and think about borders, like where adam ends and i begin. on sunday will hike near Mount Rainier, my temple.
>
> i'm wondering how you are.
>
> we both lost something we love. may we fill the emptiness with something meaningful.
>
> -lucy
>
> p.s. i'll audit two anthro courses over the summer session. r u coming to UW?

They had met months ago at the University of Washington, where Emmanuel had a college interview. Perhaps it was Lucy's tight jeans, ragged yellow sombrero, or black spandex top under the loose-fitting flannel shirt that had made her seem approachable. When Emmanuel had asked her for directions, she pushed back her unruly black hair, scratched her bushy brows, and marched him across the campus like a soldier on a mission. After the interview they met for lunch, but it was during the subsequent walking tour of the university when Emmanuel decided she smelled like cinnamon. They later exchanged e-mail addresses, solemnly shook hands, and walked in separate directions. Lucy found a grassy area, arched her back, and bent over backwards until her hands pressed the ground. Emmanuel, who had turned around more than once, felt compelled to run back and catch her should she fall.

Now Emmanuel reread Lucy's message on the computer screen and wondered how she would respond to Father's forbidden document. She would have read it by now, he concluded. He began to write a letter to her in his mind: "Hello Lucy. Yes, I will attend the University of Washington in the fall. Say, guess what I dreamt about last night? Horseshoe crabs!"

The strong smell of fish disrupted his reverie, and he traced the smell under the bed to an aging sandwich, which he carried downstairs and dumped in the kitchen garbage. On the table he found a note: "Dear Emmanuel Sleepy Head," it read. "We are going for a walk. Will be back soon. Love, Ibu-Mom."

Emmanuel opened the front door, stepped outside, and sniffed the air. A troop of gibbons vocalized their long call from the National Zoo nearby: "oooooHWHUUUUUUT HWHUUUT HWHUUT HWHUT!"

He stepped in the direction of their call but then darted back inside and raced upstairs. His heart beat wildly. He left the house minutes later with dusty knuckles and the document from the attic.

— 5 —

Lucy recognized that the cold wet hand on her neck was her own, and the fear from the delayed reaction—the fear of losing self-control—shocked her to clarity. She attacked the sets of knee bends with gusto, but soon the wind diminished, the light brightened, and she emerged through a slit in the jumble of snow-covered boulders into the brilliantly lit rocky slope. The sun's radiation warmed her face and thawed her hope.

She fetched her pack, pocketed a small flat rock, and began the hike to her car. Her feet dragged like blocks of ice. It was 2:35 p.m.

She felt pain as she descended the steep slope and entered the forest. Her feet burned as if she were shoeless in a colony of fire ants, yet she was thrilled: thrilled that her nerve endings were alive, thrilled to be in the woods, thrilled to be alive.

She wobbled down the mountain and continued to think about Adam and the train ride. Recalling how the passengers shifted about like poultry before the slaughter, she wondered why no one other than Adam had stood up to the loud, aggressive cell phone abuser. And why were the people so passive? Does abusive behavior flourish when good people do nothing?

Lucy—recalling from Adam's encounter that the teeth of the martyrs can be first to drop in the morning coffee—assumed that self-preservation explains much about passive behavior. She suspected that additional sources of passive behavior could be unearthed among humanity's biological roots.

Lucy considered the previous thought (about unearthing additional sources of passive behavior) and she clenched her teeth.

Dull dull dull, she scolded herself. She was frustrated with the way that she thought about things. She loved to learn about science but often found the ideas stuck in dry, unimaginative language. Before entering college, she had feared that strains of self-replicating Latin would pickle her brain and parch her sense of wonder, and now she wondered if it already had. She thirsted for a fresh, cool language.

She fingered the small flat rock from the cave, removed it from her jacket pocket, and held it toward the sun; it was black with gray relief and showed a flattened circle with two lines at one end. It seemed to be a fossil or primitive art.

Could it be? she wondered. *Could it be the Tablet of Manimal?*

She didn't know what the Tablet of Manimal was, but that didn't bother her. She wanted a new way to communicate scientific knowledge that wouldn't bore her silly, so she let her imagination guide her.

"I hereby dub thee progenitor of Bio-Storytelling Time," she whispered, touching the rock to her forehead.

She squeezed the rock and began to create—and say out loud—a story about passive behavior. She didn't worry that no one was around to hear her. She wanted to know what the story sounded like.

"Once upon a time," she said, "hundreds of millions of years ago, some animals began to live in groups. Did the animals consciously decide to live in groups as a way to improve their lot as a species? *No.* Did they develop tendencies that drew them together? *Yes.*

"Many did not benefit from the communal arrangement. This was due, in part, to an urge in some to kill their neighbors. Yet others did benefit, because group living provided a degree of protection from predators and it provided a more efficient way to find and protect resources. Some group dwellers thus gained a reproductive edge over solitary dwellers, and as their numbers increased they provided the basis for an increasing number of descendents to form groups.

"Some groups were more efficient than others and one type of efficiency was found in a system of social hierarchy and dominance, in which members communicated and understood their position within the hierarchy and, therefore, fought less.

"The framework of hierarchy and dominance is strong among dogs and their wolf ancestors. A young Siberian husky pup challenges its associates, canine or human, to determine its status within a social hierarchy. Instinctively, it vies for the dominant, or alpha, position but learns to accept submissive roles.

"Cows and most species of sheep also seek a position within a hierarchical group, and they are outstanding candidates for domestication partly because they are so easily duped into perceiving the human as the dominant creature in their social hierarchy. In contrast, North American bighorn sheep are not prone to domestication because they are less social than common domestic sheep and, therefore, less prone to manipulation by alpha sheep or alpha farmers in sheeps' clothing.

"The social apes also live within systems of hierarchy and dominance. Chimps, bonobos, gorillas, and . . ." Lucy stopped talking and frowned. Her own creation, Bio-Storytelling Time, was sounding too much like a boring lecture. Perhaps with some experimentation, practice, and luck, she told herself, her descriptions of the living world would capture her own imagination.

— 6 —

Evelyn surfed the Web while walking to the National Zoo using a wireless Internet device that projected shimmering images in the air. She correctly assumed that the automobiles she observed as she crossed Connecticut Avenue were not part of the virtual kingdom. They were physical. They were real.

Evelyn's walk this morning was unusual in that she had not approached a zoo in a decade. She had loved the zoo and had lived nearby, yet memories of Mrs. Lienmarck, the Sunday school teacher from long ago, had kept her away.

"Stand tall—God made us special!" Mrs. Lienmarck had said to the eight-year-olds in a concerned, impatient voice before telling them a Bible story.

The children, who noticed her stiffly erect posture, absorbed her stories like sponges and stretched their spines toward the heavens.

Once when Evelyn was eight, Mrs. Lienmarck had led the children to the zoo, where she took them to see the zebras, giraffes, elephants, and the great apes.

"Now listen carefully," she had said, "and I shall tell you the story of how the animals came to be."

"A long time ago," she began, "God created the . . ."

But Evelyn had never seen a live gorilla before. One had a silvery back and seemed to weigh as much as a small truck; a smaller one leapt from the top of a log to a pile of hay. Evelyn was transfixed. They looked so *very* much like people. Evelyn imagined, in a carefree sort of way, that she, too, were leaping about, dressed in a rough dark coat.

When the young ape began to knuckle-walk, Evelyn leaned forward and attempted to do the same. A hush spread among the children.

"Goodness, Evelyn!" Mrs. Lienmarck exclaimed. "You are *not* a monkey!"

Evelyn was a timid girl and wished to please. She acted submissively toward the loud, the lofty, and the large, and Mrs. Lienmarck was all three, but here in the zoo, surrounded by so many interesting animals, Evelyn regarded Mrs. Lienmarck as having no more authority than any other life form.

"True," Evelyn breathed. "I'm a gorilla."

Mrs. Lienmarck had been teaching for many years and had considerable experience dealing firmly and gently with misbehaving children, but this situation was different.

"You are getting *dirty!*" Mrs. Lienmarck shouted.

Evelyn continued to imitate the knuckle-walk.

Mrs. Lienmarck saw the child's behavior as an assault on the day's lesson, a lesson central to Lienmarck's understanding of the world and to the very purpose of a modern zoo, which was to reinforce the notion of an unbridgeable divide between enclosed animals on the one hand and free-ranging humans on the other. The child, by being naughty in this way, invoked powerful symbols of what Lienmarck thought of as the ancient zoo, the thought of which sent shudders of fear and uncertainty down her vertebral column.

"What has gotten *into* you?"

Evelyn grunted.

Lienmarck felt a wave of nausea rising, set in motion by the stench of ape urine that she wished someone would sanitize. Here in a modern zoo a person could clean the stink but not so in the ancient zoo, where the divide between animals and humans had not existed. The ancient zoo had existed millions of years before humans had ever appeared, and while Lienmarck assumed that the ancient zoo had abruptly ended after God created the first human being, its demise had begun much later, in part with the spreading of the story of Adam and Eve.

"Stop that right now!" Lienmarck thundered.

Evelyn tossed fig newton cookies from her lunch bag to the ground.

Lienmarck taught, as she had been taught, that the devil seduced Eve to eat from the tree of knowledge of good and evil. She taught that when Eve succumbed and ate from the tree, when Eve gained more sophisticated awareness of good and evil, humans were forever exiled from Paradise, from the Garden of Eden. What Lienmarck didn't teach, but dimly understood, was that without the seduction, without the loss of innocence, without the improved abstraction capability, humans would have remained without civilization and without supremacy, a dimly conscious creature in God's ancient zoo.

"*Don't!*" she commanded.

Evelyn grabbed the cookies and stuffed them in her mouth. She did not intend to disobey the teacher but wanted to mimic the apes who foraged on the other side of the glass wall.

Lienmarck rushed forward, gripped Evelyn's arm, and spanked her as though the devil himself had established residence in the child's rump. An aide escorted Evelyn, now screaming and in tears, back to church where men in robes taught her about sin.

From that day on, Evelyn no longer imitated other animals, no longer imagined herself as an animal, no longer approached the zoo—until ten years later, until today, until now.

Evelyn stepped up to the sidewalk of Connecticut Avenue, switched off the wireless Internet device, and approached the zoo's entrance. She felt embarrassed for having avoided the zoo all these years. It seemed an ideal place—with so many human and animal interactions—in which to read the Pope's Web site about people and their relationship to the natural world.

An image of Mrs. Lienmarck flashed in Evelyn's mind. She quickly corrected her posture. She felt vulnerable and small, as if she had done something wrong. She didn't have to go inside, she reminded herself. She *could* walk home now.

She hesitated before the iron gate. Just as she started to turn away, she recognized a woman who . . .

Evelyn's heartbeat quickened, her spirits lifted.

"It's her," she whispered. "It's Jane Goodall."

– 7 –

As Emmanuel walked through the zoo, hoofed black-and-white Malayan tapirs nodded at him, pint-size Golden Lion tamarins chirped at him, and a young gorilla knuckle-walked toward him—but he did not notice. He was preoccupied with the document in his daypack and the story of his creation.

Emmanuel approached the gibbons, whose long call increased in pitch and frequency, which resonated with his frantic state of mind. His path was blocked by a group of humans who were looking up. He looked up and saw a red-orange ape—an orang utan—hanging from the O Line, a cable strung along forty-foot-high towers. Orang utans used the O Line to move between two buildings by brachiating, hand-over-hand, as if they were wild orang utans on vines in southeast Asian forests.

A ten-foot buffer separated Emmanuel from the crowd. He watched the orang utan and listened to the barking of sea lions, the chatter of people, the thud of a bear's rubber ball.

Beeps from a construction site disrupted the reverie and Emmanuel lowered his gaze to a diamond-shaped "ORANG XING" sign.

"Orang crossing?" Emmanuel murmered, as the 280-pound orang utan directly above him gently tickled its belly.

Emmanuel understood that "ORANG XING" referred to the point at which the orang utan path intersected the human one. He understood that the sign had been placed to inform people about the apes overhead. But he could not help but interpret the sign in an additional way: in Bahasa Indonesia, his first language, *orang* means "person" and refers to modern humans, *Homo sapiens*; whereas *orang hutan* means "person of the forest" and refers to Asian apes, *Pongo pygmaeus* or *Pongo abilii*. Taken literally, then, the sign meant "person crossing" and seemed to warn the apes about the humans below.

A placard beneath the sign explained that orang utans traveled, weather permitting, between the Great Ape House and the Think Tank building in accordance with their own wishes. Furthermore, orang utans could choose to collaborate with scientists in language and tool-use activities.

Emmanuel glanced at the Think Tank building. A banner showed two gorillas and the words: "SOCIETY: Think About It. APES Do." He thought neither about apes nor about society but about Father's forbidden document in his pack.

The orang utan relaxed its bladder.

The crowd gasped.

Emmanuel approached the building, arms dangling by his sides, unaware of the urine splattering just behind him.

Inside the Think Tank, he matched the questions on the wall with the names of animals in the photographs, as if he were reciting a litany:

"What is thinking? Sea lion.

"Can animals think? Whale.

"What is language? Parrot.

"Can animals use language? Elephant.

"What are tools? Orang utan.

"Can animals use tools? Human.

"What is society? Termite.

"Do animals have social rules? Chimpanzee."

At first, Emmanuel did not pay attention to the meaning of the words. He shuffled along with the crowd, looked at photos, and reached around with his long arms to massage his back.

He came to a panel describing three factors—image, intention, and flexibility—which determine if an animal is actually thinking.

The panel pointed out that animals using image are able to visualize what is not present. Animals using intention have a purpose, a goal, a plan. Animals using flexibility are able to create plan B if plan A fails.

It was not the part about image or intention that bothered Emmanuel. Dogs, after all, visualize an absent human owner, and lions clearly intend to kill before a hunt. It was the next sentence, the one about flexibility, that he had trouble with: he did not believe that animals were capable of flexible thought. He wanted to read the next panel but a family blocked the way, so he waited briefly and walked around them. He smiled, recognizing his own flexibility in thought and action. The next panel described a shift in the way the scientific community regarded humans and nonhuman animals: it had been thought that only humans created tools, used language, and followed complex societal rules but scientists had recently learned that other animals do much the same. Nonhuman primates, for instance, cooperate, compete, form alliances, deceive, and manipulate.

Emmanuel, who believed that there existed a clean, thick line separating humans from animals, felt uneasy as he read the panel. For him the line was static and sacred, and it cut across every paradigm. It had been emphasized early and often in the stories that nourished his youth. Belief in it ran deep.

This was hardly the first time that an idea had threatened Emmanuel's worldview, but today was different. Today, the Bible was missing and he felt confused and off balance. His vulnerability dislodged a childhood memory and he stepped back from the panel when he remembered them—the men with scars, men with machetes, men on a mission, swinging and maiming, approaching and torching. Father had implored him to run and he ran, but not in the direction Father had commanded. Emmanuel wanted to obey but there had been no time to explain and he ran to a room already in flames and found the ancient Bible but it had already started to char and the smoke overtook him.

"Father!" he had gasped, and Father found him and carried him to safety.

"Isn't it fascinating?" the Think Tank volunteer said.

Emmanuel opened his eyes. He was not in East Timor. He was in Washington DC, at the National Zoo. He had bumped against a table with life-size models of various animals' brains.

"Uhh?" he said.

"Isn't it fascinating," continued the volunteer, "that all these different brains have different shapes? Yet they all have the same fundamental components. One of the things about brains is that each creature is adapted for the environment they are in. Brains represent that environment. An animal's brain must, after all, fit in its head. Notice how the alligator's brain is long and narrow."

Emmanuel looked at the shelf with the alligator's brain. "Uh."

"Now look at the models of the human brain here and the fin whale brain here. Here are the olfactory nerves. See?"

"Uh-huh."

"And here are the optic nerves."

"They do look similar," Emmanuel said.

"I suppose it suggests a commonality of the mechanism of perception."

Emmanuel looked at the table of brains. The orange-sized orang utan one was shaped like the coconut-sized human one.

"What does it mean," asked the volunteer, "that the human and orang utan brains are so similar? I suppose it suggests a stronger commonality of the mechanism of perception. Humans and orang utans both recognize color, for example, which scientists can tell by the presence of cones in the retina section of the eye. But we don't really know what an orang utan is thinking. One of the philosophical goals of the Orang Utan Language Project is to get a better sense of how orang utans perceive the world."

"Oh," said Emmanuel.

"There will be a language demonstration today at 11:00. If you have any questions, please don't hesitate to ask."

"I need to think about it."

"That's the idea!"

Emmanuel thanked the volunteer and moved to the main area of the Think Tank, a thirty-foot-high room that spanned the length of the building. Emmanuel looked at his watch. It was 10:44 a.m. To his right stood a glass enclosure; Emmanuel sat by the glass wall and looked in. An orang utan placed a white sheet over its head and climbed a fire hose to the ceiling while another orang utan, twice as large as the first and looking like a disheveled orange rug, did shoulder rolls around the perimeter of the enclosure. Emmanuel had seen orang utans up close before but had never carefully observed them. He now noticed that their hands were remarkably similar to human hands and that their arms, in proportion to the length of their bodies, were much longer than human arms. He noticed, too, that the smaller ape seemed to play and perform before an audience in the way that an attention-hungry young human would.

"The large one is a male," a different volunteer explained to the crowd. "His name is Azy. Azy is twenty-two years old. He weighs 295 pounds."

Emmanuel felt uncomfortable with his own observations. Apes, he told himself, are not conscious in the way that we are. *They are not even close.*

"The smaller one is a female," the volunteer continued. "Her name is Indah. Indah is fourteen years old and weighs 120 pounds. Can anyone guess what her name means?"

Emmanuel knew. It was a word in Bahasa Indonesia that means beautiful.

The thought of the Indonesian language made Emmanuel think about Father and the document. He fingered the zipper and unzipped the daypack, then quickly zipped it again.

Indah came over to watch him and the crowd followed.

The auto-tracking video camera, which had been programmed to follow orang utans, pointed toward Emmanuel.

"The monkey wants to see what's in the bag!" someone cried.

"It's not a monkey, it's an orang utan!"

Indah, a willing and impatient participant in the Think Tank's Orang Utan Language Project, watched Emmanuel open and close the zipper repeatedly. She watched him remove the document from the daypack. She had not yet studied the symbols for zippers, daypacks, or paper but she recognized the objects. She had seen them before. She noticed the water glisten in the young human's eyes.

— 8 —

As Lucy hiked down the mountain, she continued to create, from her knowledge of science and from her imagination, a bio-story on passive behavior. "Cows of America," she said, "rise from the squalor. Cows of Eurasia play follow the leader. Cows of Australia I control your hierarchical nature. Cows of Africa do you see through my mask? It is I, hunter-gatherer, who yesterday turned farmer. Mine is the true God who—surprise—looks like me. But watch the mask now. I am top cow in the blessed bovine trinity. Behold my crown udder of the highest bovinity. Cows of the world rise as I rise!"

Lucy fingered the small flat rock in her jacket pocket and recalled, from a favorite author she called EO, that scientists from outer space would quickly notice parallels between human and animal dominance behavior. According to EO, church is an illuminating place in which to observe this type of conduct.

"Humans of the world," she continued, "on your knees and pray. I control you and cows in much the same way. I am closer to angels than you. I'm a Gobi and you're a Moo!

"Gobis *go be*-tween people and God. *As if* intermediaries were needed. *As if* intermediaries were possible. Gobis teach hierarchy. Gobis start hierarchies. Gobis exude confidence as a way to show dominance!

"Moos are people who naturally follow. They don't have to obey;

they want to obey. They like to be told what to think every day. Most humans are Moos. Moos pray for stern love. Moos pray for instructions from heaven above!

"I'm a Gobi, you're a Moo. Farmers milk cows, we Gobis milk *you!*"

Lucy reflected on her first foray into Bio-Storytelling Time. The bio-story lacked characters, drama, and emotional depth but it was difficult for her to concoct a proper story on passive behavior. The science behind the narrative was, after all, largely new to her and she had no direct experience with the subject. She could only paraphrase others.

Sue me, she thought, shrugging her shoulders.

The trail dropped precipitously. Despite the bulky pants, she moved through dense forest with speed and agility. The blood streamed through her extremities and created a warm buzzing sensation, reminding her of Adam. It felt good.

My word, she thought, tickled by the memory. How that man had to be on top.

Lucy now realized that she *did* have extensive and direct experience with passive behavior. While Adam, a soft spoken rock climber, hardly seemed the domineering type, and while he climbed for the love of climbing, he also climbed to increase and broadcast his strength and status. He sought to be first, to be above others, to utter the final word, and now Lucy was coming to realize that she had been at the receiving end of a steep, hierarchical relationship.

The cell phone incident bothered her, she now understood, not because Adam had challenged the cell phone user but because of the way in which he did so. By diffusing the cell phone user's power, he had sought to enhance his own. Sure, Adam was calm, gentle, and kind. Sure, he was no military dictator. Yet he devoutly believed, and obsessively participated, in the world of competitive hierarchy.

Lucy wondered if it were healthy, or even possible, for men or women to bypass hierarchical tendencies altogether. Could millions of years of instinctual and cultural evolution be discarded at will? And if dominance behavior *was* her species' birthright, was it best if she remained in her place, in the hierarchy, under Adam?

She missed Adam's commanding voice and the way he defined her position in the world. She missed his smell, his wiry strength, and his penetrating boldness. She missed being squished beneath him.

I can think of worse places to be, she thought.

But now, annoyed at the thought of the Gobis and her role as a Moo, she hardened her stomach muscles and tightened her fists.

The age of kings is dead, she thought.

She was grateful to Adam but would not go back. She would renounce the world of dominance and hierarchy.

From this moment hence, she thought, *I shall a Flatlander be.*

She opened her fist and marveled at the surface of the flat black rock. The two lines and oval, etched in gray, looked like a prehistoric sketch of a horseshoe crab.

— 9 —

Evelyn recognized the blond hair, the safari shorts, and the spine as straight as an aspen tree. Here was no image projected from a wireless Internet device—here was *Jane Goodall!* Evelyn stared in disbelief and followed her into the zoo but, near the tall wooden statue, Goodall disappeared into the crowd.

Evelyn walked farther into the zoo and thought about Jane Goodall. She admired Goodall's embrace of both science and Christianity, and she admired Goodall's courage and tenacity. Evelyn was so excited about the possibility of meeting the chimp spokeswoman that she hardly noticed the zebras, giraffes, or elephants. She imagined Goodall observing chimpanzees in a remote forest clearing and the image, along with the light blue sky and the families out for a stroll, made the zoo seem wholesome, safe, and welcoming.

Evelyn walked down the hill to the Great Ape House, a familiar-looking building that, she vividly recalled, stank inside. The scent of her own urine filled her senses. Memories of Mrs. Lienmarck surfaced and Evelyn felt scared and insecure. She did not want to enter the building. She corrected her posture, switched on the Internet device, and typed in the Pope's Web address. The image of the Vatican, superimposed on the image of the Great Ape House, materialized and shimmered like a castle of gold.

A group of children rushed by.

"Monkey monkey monkey!" one girl shrieked.

The others howled with laughter.

Evelyn sensed the vulnerability of the children. They were making the same mistakes she had made with Mrs. Lienmarck. She followed them inside with a sense of fascination and terror.

The interior was bright and spacious; the stench hit her like a kick to the bridge of the nose.

The children shouted and snorted near the glass enclosure that housed a family of gorillas. The smell, rather than bothering the young humans, seemed to excite them.

A few dozen people sat facing the enclosure; Evelyn faced the children, who had started to imitate the gorillas.

Evelyn prayed they would not do that. She wanted to warn them not to act like apes. She wanted to warn them that bad things happen in here. She drew short breaths.

The Papal talk Webpage now appeared before her and she looked for the talk on evolution. The link seemed to be missing but she eventually found it buried near the bottom. She clicked on the link and the text of John Paul II's 1996 speech expanded and filled her vision.

It remained unclear to Evelyn, as she read the talk, whether the Pope believed in the theory of evolution. He didn't borrow from the language of evolutionary biology, nor did he speak of taxonomy, methods of classification, morphology, cladistics, time since speciation, mutation, heredity, genetics, phylogeny, natural or sexual selection, carbon dating, or the fossil record. He did credit scientists for mapping life "with increasing precision" to points along history's timeline and yet, by arguing that there were several theories of evolution, he seemed to discount a grand unified theory of biological evolution. The Pope, nonetheless, seemed prepared to identify that which is physical and measurable as being outside the Church's realm of expertise and, thus, he seemed prepared to concede biology to the biologists.

Meanwhile, the children had gathered in a circle. They held hands, rotated clockwise, and chanted, "Ring around the rosey, a pocket full of posey, ashes, ashes, we all fall *down!*" As they fell to the ground, Evelyn clutched her stomach and turned away. She was certain something terrible would happen to them.

Evelyn took refuge in the words of the Pope. The very existence of the talk on evolution, which was to say the Church's willingness to address this complex and difficult subject, pleased her. She believed that the Church had followed God's Holy Will even when, on occasion, it incorrectly interpreted scientific knowledge. The debate on evolution, she felt, provided the Church with an important and ongoing lesson in humility.

It occurred to her that the Pope did not address in his talk whether humans exist, taxonomically speaking, on the same physical branch as chimpanzees. Taxonomists would have to diffuse *that* bombshell. Nor did he comment on the social or psychological capabilities of nonhuman primates. Evelyn wondered if the Pope, by avoiding scientific detail, had sought to avoid further lessons in humility.

As she pondered the politics of pontiff discourse, a gorilla in the enclosure approached its larger sibling and slapped its butt.

The children noticed and, in a frenzy of hooting and laughter, chased each other and did the same.

The slaps looked to be painful; Evelyn was certain someone would get hurt.

But the gorillas soon settled down, as did the children, and Evelyn began to compare *The Third Chimpanzee* with the Pope's talk on evolution. Professor Diamond's book teaches about humans in the natural world, she noted, while the Pope teaches about humans in the spiritual world.

To better understand the contrast, Evelyn pictured two trees: the first was physical; the second, spiritual.

All living things, according to *The Third Chimpanzee,* can be found in the physical tree, in which humans and chimps share a common branch. But not all living things, wrote the Pope, can be found in the spiritual tree. The spiritual tree supports humans but not animals—not even in the lowest branches.

What seemed interesting to Evelyn, as she assessed the two worldviews, was the lack of common ground: no gradation, no continuum seemed to exist between the physical and spiritual trees.

The Pope approached the line between the physical and the spiritual with confidence. Only man, he wrote, is called to enter a relationship of knowledge and love with God. Nonhuman primates, the Pope suggested, were *not* created in God's image and likeness, nor are they capable of recognizing, naming, or worshipping that which is invisible, unknowable, and divine. Apes have no spirituality, nor have they any capacity for spirituality whatsoever. Man, she read, is the only creature on Earth that God wanted for its own sake. Man, unlike animals, has a value of his own. He is a person. Man alone is capable of forming a relationship of communion, solidarity, and self-giving with his peers.

As Evelyn watched the children huddle together, she wondered about these assertions. Certainly, she thought, apes are not like us. They can't perform sacred ritual. *They can't sing . . .*

But Evelyn wasn't fully convinced that animals had no value of their own. Nor was she fully convinced that apes had, in God's expansive eyes, zero capacity for spirituality.

As Evelyn entered a cloud of doubt, she wondered if it was okay to harbor, and to ponder, such critical thoughts. Was she being led astray?

But she was reassured by the unassailable fact that the Church, comprised of adults capable of grappling with difficult questions, was no magnet for mindless followers stuck in a station of fear. Difficult questions such as this one had, over centuries, helped the Church, the Body of Christ, to evolve.

The dominant alpha gorilla stood up and beat his chest. The vibrations were so powerful that Evelyn felt them inside her own chest.

The gorilla reminded Evelyn of something large, something somber, though she couldn't quite place it.

Then it came to her.

Evelyn didn't laugh much, and rarely laughed aloud, but now she could hardly contain herself.

"Hwyh," she started, her thin belly jiggling.

The gorilla looked like Mrs. Lienmarck.

"Haw!" she exploded.

Shame, she thought. *Shame.*

"Show your elders some respect," she scolded herself.

But each time Evelyn looked up at the silverback gorilla, she couldn't help but grin.

The children sat calmly and watched the gorilla family, and Evelyn turned and did the same. She recognized the baby, the adolescents, the mother, and the aunt. Their interactions looked familiar, gentle, and innocent.

Evelyn wondered what, if anything, the gorillas were thinking.

The little girl in the middle leapt out of the circle.

"Monkey!" she cried and walked on all fours.

Evelyn, red-faced, braced herself for confrontation. She wanted to rush the girl into her arms and protect her.

After a few minutes a woman approached and the children got up to leave.

"Second graders?" Evelyn asked.

"Church group," the woman replied, smiling.

"What does FONZ stand for?" Evelyn asked, noticing the woman's T-shirt.

"Friends of the National Zoo."

Evelyn stayed a while longer and, ignoring the smell, watched the gorillas play tag, tug-of-war, and let's-bother-mom. As she marveled at the similarity between gorillas and humans, it began to seem less far-fetched to her that apes could exist in a low branch of God's spiritual tree.

If God made humans in His image, she wondered, then how could apes—who so much resembled people—*not* fit in the picture? Had Church elders observed apes in zoos or in the wild? Had they studied the latest information available about higher primates? She sensed they had not.

She felt defensive and wondered how to protect the Church. But what, she wondered, could she do? She was but an individual and an ignorant one at that. Could she learn firsthand about humans and chimps and their place in the natural world? Could she live without hot showers, without comforts of home, among militia and malaria in the jungles of Africa? If she studied apes in the wild, would she have the courage to share what she learned?

As Evelyn left the Great Ape House and headed up the hill toward the Connecticut Avenue exit, she had an idea: why not volunteer at the Jane Goodall Institute? Goodall had spent thirty years observing chimps in the wild; surely *she* had insight on animal placement in God's spiritual tree. At the very least, people on Goodall's staff could recommend books.

Tiny steps, she told herself. Take tiny steps. Even if one's shoes are not glamorous, even if the steps are not much, they are a start, and after a while the steps may well add up.

She smiled. Volunteering at Goodall's organization would be a good way to learn about people and their place in the natural world. It would also help a good cause.

Evelyn was nearly home when she began to search the Web for Goodall's homepage but decided first to surf the Web site of the National Zoo. She found links to the orang utan Webcams housed in the Think Tank.

She clicked on the first one and saw hay strewn about the floor.

She clicked on the second one and saw a motionless rope.

She clicked on the third one and saw Emmanuel.

"Dear!" said Evelyn, pressing both hands to her chest. She touched the gold cross pendant. A chill swept down her spine.

Evelyn saw him opening and closing his daypack zipper, she saw him removing papers from the pack, she saw him crying. She wanted to support him, protect him, as she had done before. She recalled the time his sister, Isabel, had come down with a severe fever and Emmanuel had called her for support, and she had rushed to the hospital and used her voice, leading them in the do-re-mi song, to heal the fear. Tears for Isabel she had understood. But now? What, Evelyn wondered, was her special friend doing, crying, on the zoo's Webcam for apes?

— 10 —

Emmanuel's long, powerful fingers trembled as he gripped Father's document. He read about President Suharto, a former army general who had sensed the power inherent in the code of life and had begun to fund various projects in genetic research at a time when the field of molecular biology was in its infancy. As years passed and new technologies raised the prospect that gene manipulation would soon be possible, Suharto ordered the consolidation of genetic research into one laboratory, a move that he hoped would produce quicker results. It was announced to the public that the lab would explore Indonesia's diverse flora and fauna but its primary mission, to manipulate genes in animals, remained a tightly guarded government secret.

Emmanuel shook his head in disbelief and read on.

The idea was to create legions of fighting males, males capable of flexible thought but not of insubordination, males capable of handling sophisticated weaponry, males physically as powerful as apes.

Emmanuel envisioned columns of shadowy creatures knuckle-walking in flickering darkness toward oil soaked villages of burning straw. Wincing, he continued to read.

Suharto's government faced increasing threats less from neighbors such as Malaysia or the Philippines than from separatist forces within Indonesia. Suharto himself had risen to power by a coup and, a quarter of a century later, increasingly felt the sting of opportunistic eyes on his own back. The desire to engineer and control the ultimate fighting force inspired the aging ruler to contribute from his vast personal wealth toward a project at the Speciation Lab. Scientists were instructed to go where the West wouldn't dare. They began inserting nonhuman primate DNA into live human embryos.

"Oh my Lord," said Emmanuel, turning from the document. The story was part of a prank, he told himself. It had to be. Yet clearly it was in Father's handwriting and Father, since the violent raids on their village so long ago, had become too serious, too predictable to pull a prank.

Emmanuel coiled his hand into a fist and remembered how Suharto's thugs had torched his village and snapped East Timor's backbone. *Now this!*

A clean-cut young scientist appeared in the roped-off section between the humans and apes, interrupting Emmanuel's thoughts. The scientist darted about like a mouse on speed as he powered on a computer, adjusted the microphone headset, and laid out bags and cups on a table. He wore a shirt depicting an orang utan.

Indah knuckle-walked toward the researcher and a crowd of humans gathered. The Orang Utan Language Project was about to begin.

Emmanuel continued to read.

His parents had been forced to participate in Suharto's experiment at the Speciation Lab in southern Sulawesi, where they were confined to a cell and ordered to lie together often. They were separated for three months, reunited, and sent home where Mother was ordered to go through with the pregnancy. Mother had been heavily drugged and did not recall much. Scientists at the Speciation Lab manipulated traits using chimp DNA because chimps are, genetically speaking, close to humans and the DNA would more easily be integrated. But Father never found out—nor had Uncle Mateus, despite his channels to the government—if the forced change to the embryo involved part of a gene, several genes, or several hundred genes.

"I often wonder," Emmanuel read, "to what extent my beloved son is human and to what extent he is ape. I love him so and I pray for him every day, but then, how could one not worry about the nature of his soul for, God help us, he is not fully human."

Emmanuel drooped in the chair as if he had been anesthetized.

"FFFffffffffuuhhhhh," he said, sounding like a deflating balloon. He could not quite bring himself to curse.

So that is the story of my creation, he thought dismally. *I am part ape.*

He wanted to find and embrace the charred Bible. He desperately needed it now. But what if he could find it? What if he ran home and read his favorite stories? It would no longer work, it would no longer help, he realized, because *the Bible was not written for apes.*

"FFffvvvvvvuuuuhhgct!" he exclaimed.

He felt frightened and vulnerable. He started to shake. Tears welled. He felt stunned. The Bible was no longer for him.

"Good morning folks," said the zoo scientist with the orang utan shirt. "Welcome to the Think Tank. My name is Francis Bridges and I coordinate the Orang Utan Language Project. Behind me is Indah. Indah is fourteen years old. She is an adult orang utan who was born here at the National Zoo."

Indah, soothed by the voice, gazed at the scientist.

"Participation in the language project is entirely voluntary," said Bridges. "At least on her part."

This drew chuckles.

"I'm convinced that Indah participates because she likes the mental challenge. Nothing negative happens to her if she chooses not to participate."

Emmanuel chewed his fingers wildly. His mind raced. It is not fair, he thought. She does not have to participate but what about me?

"The Project is not meant to be a performance," continued Bridges, "but rather to make available to the public an ongoing scientific experiment. Please look to the easel and note the symbols."

Emmanuel glanced at the dozen or more shapes, inside of which were lines and dots. No two symbols were the same, and each symbol appeared by an English word.

"The symbols here are abstract. That means they don't look like the objects they describe."

Emmanuel agreed: the rectangle around the slash and dot looked nothing like an apple, nor did the circle with the dot in the middle look like a cup.

"All the symbols fall into observable categories, each of which are defined by their shape: rectangles are food items, circles are objects, and the diamonds are verbs."

Indah climbed on a stool, sat before two large computer screens, and reached out and touched the lower one with a long index finger.

"Hold on a minute, Indah," said Bridges. "*Good* girl. We'll start by reviewing symbols Indah is familiar with, then we'll work on increasing her vocabulary, and then we'll finish up with more review. Okay?"

Emmanuel, soothed by the scientist's voice, nodded.

"Good."

Bridges faced Indah and held up an apple.

"Now *look,* Indah."

Indah turned from Bridges and glanced at the top screen where she saw an apple. She glanced at the bottom screen where she saw four different symbols. One was correct.

By the time Emmanuel had figured it out, Indah had touched the rectangle with the slash and dot in it and then she touched the right arrow.

Ding! chimed the computer.

"*Good* girl," said Bridges and gave her some apple.

An image of popcorn appeared above. Indah looked at the six symbols on the screen below and touched the rectangle with the backward slash. Then she touched the right arrow.

Ding!

Indah devoured the popcorn.

"Good, good, good."

As the session progressed, Indah chose from an ever-increasing number of symbols on the screen below. Though the symbols changed their position with each new screen, Indah maintained 100 percent accuracy until, when presented with an image of grapes, she touched the correct symbol but failed to touch the right arrow.

ERRRRRRR! disapproved the computer.

Indah scratched her shoulders and squirmed on the stool.

This time, not an image but a symbol (a circle with a vertical line in it) appeared on the upper screen and several images (grapes, popcorn, a bag, a cup, a banana, and an apple) appeared below.

Indah scanned these images, glanced again at the screen above, and hesitated. She touched the image of the bag, then the right arrow.

Ding!

Good girl, thought Emmanuel.

Indah did not seem to recognize the next set of symbols and her score dropped significantly.

Scratching his shoulders and squirming in the chair, Emmanuel glanced at Father's document and continued to read.

The genetic tinkering at Suharto's Speciation Lab had affected his reproductive cells, he learned. As a result, his offspring would inherit the change.

"No children!" he gasped.

Emmanuel, who had always wanted to have children, found himself thinking about Evelyn. He visualized the gold cross near the valley of her chest, caressed by her silky brown hair. He longed to be with her, to hold her hand, to hear her voice. They were friends, true, but they were more than that, and though their love had not been physical, and though they had not spoken of it, he had assumed they would have a future together. But now, he realized, it could not be. Evelyn, after all, was Christian. What in God's name was he?

The language experiment had finished. Emmanuel noticed Indah gazing at Bridges. She seemed to be following his every move and Emmanuel wondered if the ape had a crush on the scientist (Indah had adored Francis Bridges since her orang utan adolescence and had tried, repeatedly, to rip off his belt and jeans).

Bridges fielded questions from the audience.

"Which of the great apes is our closest relative?" a man asked.

"Chimps and bonobos," replied Bridges. "Bonobos are also known as Pygmy chimpanzees."

"Where do bonobos live?"

"There are a few in the Democratic Republic of Congo."

"Are there any in zoos?"

"Yes, I've recently seen them at the San Diego Zoo."

A young girl raised her hand and asked, "Why do you do this?"

"That's a good question," Bridges replied. "People know very little about orang utans and this is a way to learn about how they think. Also, zoo animals get terribly bored and this challenges them in a way that is healthy for them, mentally speaking. Also, I like to share what I discover with people—people just like you."

The girl's eyes opened wide.

Bridges smiled and said, "It's also my job."

"What does it all mean?" a woman asked.

"Another good question. The research shows that orang utans map information in sophisticated ways. It shows that differences in human and orang utan language skills are not all or nothing but are a matter of degrees. Indah and her brother Azy process language in ways comparable to that of a two- or three-year-old human being."

Emmanuel partly listened and partly wrestled with haunting questions, for which there seemed to be no clear answers. What did it mean that the charred Bible was lost? That he had disobeyed Father and had read the document? That he was not fully human? That he had observed an orang utan accurately identify shifting symbols and images?

It struck him as being odd that he did not *feel* like an ape. He wondered what sorts of things apes thought about.

"This is ridiculous," he said bitterly, questioning the authenticity of Father's document. "Genes cannot be manipulated like that. No way!"

People nearby moved away when they heard him talking to himself.

But upon reflection, Emmanuel had to admit that this type of gene manipulation *was* possible according to what he had learned in school and had read in *The Washington Post.* Inserting genes from one animal to another had the feel of science fiction but for the past two decades or so the technique was hardly fiction.

Painful though it was, Emmanuel had to admit that Father's document made sense. It explained his frequent role as a social outsider, it explained his long fingers and dangling arms, and it explained why his youngest sister, Teresa, often called him Grizzwauld.

"G-R-I-Z-Z, W-A-U-L-D!" she would laugh, "*Grizzwauld the chimp!*"

Emmanuel recognized the wretched truth in her teasing and gazed at the glass pane. The reflection of the humans behind him appeared like ghosts in a cage.

Bridges disappeared in the back and Indah returned to the larger enclosure. She tumbled down a fire hose with a cotton sheet on her head. Azy, twice her size, sat facing the humans with a white sheet draped over his head as if he were defending a throne.

A man in the crowd pointed at the ape and laughed, exposing his canines.

Emmanuel, nervously chewing his thumb, bit too hard. "Ow!" he cried.

The crowd turned to him.

That is what an *ape* would have done, Emmanuel thought angrily. He stood up, leaned forward, and walked cautiously toward the exit with his arms dangling in front of him.

He glanced at a large poster featuring a chimpanzee's face: "If we look straight and deep into a chimpanzee's eyes, an intelligent self-assured personality looks back at us. If they are animals, what must we be?"

He noticed the Sulawesi macaques to the right. They were monkeys, not apes, with pink, brown, and gray swollen butts. He could see they were smaller than the orang utans.

A macaque approached the glass enclosure, stared at Emmanuel, and opened and closed its mouth rapidly as if trying to speak. No sound emerged.

Emmanuel watched the monkey dart through the branches. The realization that both he and the monkey had been conceived in Sulawesi, Indonesia, ushered in a flood of despair. During the walk home, he mostly stared at the ground and dragged his feet.

Late that night, obscured by shadows of a cobwebbed, musty attic, Emmanuel dropped the book in a box, pressed his fists to the floor, and knuckle-walked from the light.

PART TWO

99.9 Percent

— 11 —

"Knock! Knock!"

Emmanuel leaned forward. "Yes?"

"Hey, Grizzwauld." Teresa flung open the door to his room.

"Please do not use that word," he said meekly.

"Hey *Grizzwauld*—your banana mush is ready!"

Emmanuel watched the twelve-year-old with untied shoelaces run down the carpeted hallway. He watched the blue and red Mickey Mouse dance on her sweatshirt and disappear down the stairs. He recalled running barefoot with his three sisters in Asia, where the mouse had danced on muddy torn T-shirts.

He followed Teresa downstairs to the dining room and sat between Ana and Isabel.

Ernesto nodded to Emmanuel and lowered his head. "We are grateful, Lord, for Thy gifts," he said. "May our hearts be pure as we receive Thy food. Amen."

"Amen," the family rejoined.

"And may God protect Emmanuel," added Mateus, who looked to be an older, less solemn version of Ernesto. "We shall miss him dearly and pray he comes home often."

"Amen," said Maria, passing a bowl of steaming rice. Emmanuel's mother was smaller than each of her daughters and considerably smaller than her son. Her eyes reflected the muted brown of the dress. Perhaps it was her size, the burn mark on her forehead, or the way she lowered her gaze that made her seem like a victim.

Emmanuel, aware of the forbidden document, pictured her and Father surrounded by needle-jabbing scientists, test tubes, and whirring white sterile machines. Father's document helped to explain why the family had stayed in Asia after Uncle Mateus left. They had stayed out of fear. "*We will be back*," they had been warned. "*We will be back for the boy. If you leave we will track you down!*"

What a family history, Emmanuel thought. Aunt Winnie seemed normal in comparison. Winnie, an American from northern Virginia, ran a software company that she had founded and owned. She wore a crisp blue suit.

Emmanuel passed her the bowl of rice.

"Thank you, dear," she said, helping herself and passing the bowl to the eldest daughter, Isabel, who was two years younger than her brother.

"Why must you study so far away?" asked Isabel.

Emmanuel shrugged and muttered something about a scholarship. He wondered if Isabel knew the story of his creation. No, he decided, but surely Uncle Mateus and Aunt Winnie did. As did scientists in Indonesia.

"The Emmanuel you have reached," quipped Teresa, "has been disconnected or is no longer in service!"

"Teresa, hush," scolded Maria. "Emmanuel, Ana asked you a question."

"Sorry, Ana, I was spacing out."

"I just want to know when you'll come home," she said, a tear streaming down her face. She rushed from the table.

Isabel followed her younger sister and touched Emmanuel's shoulder as she went by.

Emmanuel looked down. He felt loved here, but he could not help but wonder about his other family, the family of apes. What were they like? Could he ever meet them? What would they think of him?

He wondered, too, about his spiritual family. If he was a spiritual orphan, if he had not been made in God's image, then in whose image had he been made? How did God view him and, assuming he had one, what would become of his soul?

As curiosity gave way to fear, Emmanuel gripped the chair with his large, muscular hands and wondered what to do.

— 12 —

As Evelyn walked home from church, she thought about Emmanuel and wondered if he had arrived yet in Washington State. She had known of his plans to study there but had been unprepared for his distant, vague good-bye. It seemed so unlike him to leave such a phone message.

She recalled, from the other day, how she had run back to the Think Tank after observing Emmanuel on the ape-viewing Webcam, but he had been nowhere to be found. She wondered what it all meant, but she wanted to exercise patience. Give him time, give him space, she told herself.

She smiled but the facial muscles didn't hold. She tried to sing but nothing came out. She pictured rain in Seattle.

— 13 —

Emmanuel paced by the gate when a passenger service agent approached, touched his shoulder, and offered him a ticket.

"Sorry," he said. "I do not understand what you want."

She repeated the offer.

"For free?"

She nodded.

"Why would you give me a ticket for *not* flying?"

"The flight to Seattle is overbooked and . . ."

"But I must go to Seattle. . . ."

"If you fly to Seattle tomorrow instead of today, the airline will give you a free ticket, good for anywhere in North America, plus we'll put you up for the night, pay your meals, and pay for a trip to the zoo."

"Oh."

Emmanuel noticed her braided blond hair, navy blue suit, and red scarf. Her eyes matched the blue of the San Diego sky. She smiled.

"I did not mean to be abrupt," he said. "I am nervous."

"It's fine. Really. Is this your first time flying?"

"Years ago I came to America."

"From where?"

"East Timor."

Interesting, she thought, noticing the scent of musk. He seemed innocent, vulnerable, and cute. His torso leaned forward, as though he might fall. She wondered if he had hurt his back. She felt an urge to protect him.

"I was wondering," she said. "I get off from work soon. If you choose to stay in San Diego an extra day, would you like to walk with me in the zoo?"

Emmanuel studied her. She looked to be a few years older than he was. Guys at school would call her a babe but what, he wondered, did that really mean? Did it refer to the comparative size and shape of various body parts? Or was there more to it? He typically avoided babes based on fear that he would not know what to say—and that they would just see him as a nerd—but all that changed last week when the truth of his lowly nature came to light. Now, with hope lost and expectations dashed, he could swing, he could fall, it mattered not.

"I love spending time in zoos," she added. "But it's more fun to go there with people."

"Would you like to go there with an ape?" Emmanuel blurted.

"I can see this is going to be different," she laughed. "So we're on?"

"Uh, well, I guess so."

She explained where to claim the free ticket. "I'll meet you there in an hour."

"At 1:30?"

"Mmmm . . . you forgot to reset your watch."

"Oops. 10:30?"

"Right. By the way, my name's Meecha."

"Emmanuel," he said. "Nice to meet you."

Emmanuel found a phone, left a message for Lucy that he would be late, and bought a yogurt and a banana. He could not rid himself of the sinking feeling that he had missed the connecting flight and was getting left behind.

Emmanuel found Meecha at the meeting spot a few minutes early, and she drove him to the zoo in Balboa Park.

"San Diego," said Meecha, "has one of the best zoos in the world."

"Why?"

"The enclosures are closer to what animals experience in nature. But I should let you know—I'm no bio person. Actually, I have a confession to make: I love spending time in zoos largely because they're such great places to go people-watching."

"Why go to the zoo for that?"

"You can learn a lot about people by watching them watch animals."

Emmanuel wondered what could be learned but he did not ask; he would see for himself shortly.

They entered the zoo and approached a crowd, above which a stationary koala bear clung to a tree. Meecha silently looked at the animal and hardly moved; Emmanuel did the same. They observed each other, however, through peripheral vision and fifteen minutes later their eyes met.

"You are very patient," Emmanuel said, brushing back his hair.

"Thanks," said Meecha. "I've yet to see a koala bear move. I think they're the third cutest animal in the zoo."

Emmanuel nodded and they continued the walk. "If you are not a bio person, then what kind of person are you?"

"I suppose a language person," she said. "I studied languages in college, and I'm forever fascinated by the language war back home."

"A war?"

"Yes, between French and English speakers. Signs are bilingual—it's required by law."

"That would be interesting to see. Where is back home?"

"Montreal," she said. "What about you? What will you study in Seattle?"

"Religion, but who knows—lately biology seems interesting."

Emmanuel saw a sign with pandas on it and asked Meecha if she would like to see them. She took his hand and led him in the opposite direction.

"Look!" she exclaimed. "Isn't it beautiful?"

"What?"

"Right in front of you!"

"Uh?"

"The child!"

"The child?"

"And the bird!"

"The pigeon?"

"Yes, the rock dove."

"What about it?"

"Look," said Meecha. "I love pandas as much as anyone—they're the second cutest animal in the zoo—but charismatic animals aren't necessary. Not really. Not if you look hard enough. Don't you see? The magic is *here!*"

The pigeon pecked at dirt.

"Here?"

"Watch, Emmanuel. Watch the child watching the rock dove. Watch the child's expression."

"Uhh, the child likes the bird."

"The child's world is *lit up* by the dove. You see, children aren't born knowing which animals are pretty and which ones are not. They are taught that. They are naturally attracted to *life*."

Emmanuel squatted, balanced on his knuckles, and watched the pigeon fly away. He watched the child wave good-bye.

"That was special," said Emmanuel.

She squeezed his hand and they continued the walk.

After a few minutes they looked at a map.

"There are bonobos here!" said Emmanuel.

"I've walked by the bonobos," said Meecha, "but don't know much about them. Do you?"

"Not much," he admitted. "I just know that chimps and bonobos are the closest animals to human beings."

"Want to check it out?"

"Oh, definitely!"

They were closer to the bonobos than they had thought and soon they were walking around the enclosure's perimeter, inside of which were boulders, trees, and hills.

"What a great place to live," said Emmanuel.

Meecha looked at him.

"For the apes," he added.

"Look," Meecha said, pointing to the far side of the enclosure. Two bonobos sauntered across the field, sometimes knuckle-walking, sometimes walking upright.

"They look like chimpanzees," whispered Emmanuel.

"Yes," said Meecha excitedly. "But they're taller than chimps and less stocky; I think their legs are longer."

Nearby, a man with a broad face and large frame spoke with a woman who was decades his junior. Meecha thought he looked like a magnificent male lion; Emmanuel thought she looked like a cheetah.

Emmanuel and Meecha caught snippets of their conversation. The man sounded British; the woman sounded American, from the south, and they used words such as "bonobos," "Congo," and "matriarchal."

"What does matriarchal mean?" Emmanuel whispered.

Meecha wet her upper lip with her tongue and looked directly into Emmanuel's eyes. "It means the ladies are in charge."

"Oh." He averted her gaze.

Emmanuel and Meecha edged closer so they could make out the conversation.

"Bonobos relieve stress," said the woman, "through *very* frequent sexual encounters."

"Yes," agreed the man, "sometimes every fifteen minutes."

Emmanuel felt Meecha's direct gaze and felt he should say something. "Gee, I did not know that."

Meecha hid a smile.

"And they do it face-to-face," the cheetah woman continued matter-of-factly.

Hundreds of people along the perimeter path watched the bonobos. Emmanuel imagined himself inside the enclosure where the humans could observe his every move.

"I would want some privacy," he said absentmindedly.

"Excuse me?" said Meecha.

"I was just saying the bonobos deserve some privacy."

Emmanuel grew apprehensive: what if the bonobos started doing it *now?* What if they started doing it *face-to-face?* What would he say? He blushed. Something in his stomach fluttered, as if he had swallowed a live fish.

Emmanuel realized that he might be part bonobo. He realized that he might belong out there with the *animals*. He turned to Meecha and imagined pressing his mouth against her lips.

"It sounds like they run their own zoo," Meecha said, watching the couple. "I wonder who they are."

A group of high school students ran by.

"Look—chimps!" exclaimed one student.

"They're not chimps," shouted another. "They're *bonobos!*"

The British man murmured, "There are precious few bonobos left. Like the pristine, submerged islands of innocence and youth, they will be forever lost from this hauntingly beautiful world."

Emmanuel watched the man gaze at the apes, watched him reach for the woman's hand. Emmanuel did not understand the dynamics of habitat loss, ecological degradation, or extinction but he could feel the man's pain. He had seen it before. He watched the water glisten in the large human's eyes.

— 14 —

By the main library of the University of California at San Diego, Emmanuel observed a rabbit hopping across the brown tiled path. Moments later, its white fur began taking on a green fluorescent hue but more surprising to Emmanuel was when the rabbit entirely disappeared. Nearby stood a student wearing sandals, shorts, and a wireless Internet device.

"Excuse me," Emmanuel asked. "Did you create the bunny?"

"No," said the student, touching the Internet device. "I was exploring a Web site and the shared mode was on—sorry about that."

"That is okay," said Emmanuel, wistfully. "I thought a real bunny had turned green."

"It is a *real* bunny," said the student. "Its name is Alba and I've been reading about it on the Web."

"What makes it turn green?"

"A gene tells its body to make a protein that under certain conditions glows bright fluorescent green. The gene is inserted by scientists."

"Where did the gene come from?"

"Jellyfish."

"A jellyfish gene was put inside a bunny?" cried Emmanuel, fearful that scientists had conducted a similar experiment on him.

"Essentially, yes. It sounds futuristic but zygote microinjection is nothing new."

Emmanuel cleared his throat. "Why would someone want to . . ."

"I don't know," replied the student, initializing the Internet device in shared mode, "but we can learn more about it."

Emmanuel sat and felt the coolness of the marble bench. The image of a Webpage appeared a foot-and-a-half in front of him, complicating the view of a nearby garden and tree. He skimmed the paragraphs of the Webpage.

"Excuse me, uhh . . ."

"Dean."

"Excuse me, Dean. Where is the part about the bunny?"

"I don't know, the Web site describes several experiments. Check this one out: a sentence from the Bible was translated into morse code, then into DNA base pairs. The artificial 'Bible' gene was inserted into bacteria as if it were a real gene."

"You mean part of the Bible is alive in bacteria?"

"In a symbolic sense, yes—it is alive and changing."

"Changing?"

"The Bible gene is subject to mutation."

"From radiation?"

"Yes, and here is the interactive part of the experiment: ultraviolet light strikes the bacteria with the Bible gene when someone on the Web site selects *this* button."

"Clicking would cause a mutation?"

"It might."

"What is the sentence?"

"Let man have dominion over the fish of the sea, and over the fowl of the air, and over every living thing that moves upon the earth."

Emmanuel had grown up with the sentence and had considered it to be a reliable friend. The Web site could make its claims, he decided, but the sentence would never change. And yet the sentence had let him down. It had placed him down among the crawly things. The sentence empowered men, true. *But he was no man.*

"If someone clicks on the button and a mutation takes place," Emmanuel wondered aloud, "is there a way to know how the sentence will change?"

"It doesn't work that way," explained Dean. "Mutations occur randomly and are not guided or predictable, so there's no way to know what part of the sentence might change. You'd have to take your chances."

Emmanuel wanted to click on the Web site button, and nearly did, but he held back. He wanted to have a greater understanding of the experiment before participating in it.

"What do you study?" Emmanuel asked.

"Copepods."

"What are they?"

"Pin-size creatures that live in the sea."

"Why study copepods?"

Dean shifted uncomfortably.

"Sorry," said Emmanuel, sensing that he might be bothering the student. "You came here to think, not answer a lot of questions."

"I came here to think," clarified Dean, "about why I study copepods. I need to understand the nature of their reproductive capabilities. I need to understand why, despite enormous genetic difference, they are able to produce successful offspring. Some individual copepods share only *80 percent* of their genes with their mate!"

"Is that unusual?"

"Definitely! Sexually successful couples in the animal kingdom tend to share roughly 99 percent of their genes."

But Emmanuel was not doing the math. He was thinking of Meecha. He was thinking of her in a way that, until recently, he would have quickly suppressed. But it did not seem sinful or wrong for a human-ape hybrid such as himself to entertain explicit thoughts about sex, and in the fertile soil of his imagination, on the moist and bare forest floor, new growth took root and blossomed. He pictured Meecha slowly removing her shirt.

"Can chimps and . . . uhh . . . humans successfully . . . uhh . . ."

"Chances are strongly against it," replied Dean. "Certainly it would have worked a few million years ago, between early chimps and early humans, soon after the two species diverged. Today, chimps and humans share more than 98 percent of their genes."

Emmanuel's thoughts returned to the math and he sought clarification. "You mean chimps and humans can*not* make babies with a 2 percent difference, but copepods *can* with a 20 percent difference?"

"Correct."

"But given those numbers," said Emmanuel, "would chimps and humans not be more likely to make babies than copepods?"

"Precisely," said Dean, "but the numbers, the copepods teach us, don't tell the full story."

They were silent for a minute until Emmanuel asked, "If a guy is 99.9 percent the same as a girl, could the tiny difference get in the way?"

"Yes, in fact it could. What determines sexual compatibility and relatedness is quantitative *and* qualitative. In other words, it's not so much how many genes are shared but which ones. If genetic difference occurs, for instance, in a reproduction-related gene, the 0.1 percent could—excuse the pun—conceivably get in the way."

Emmanuel wondered if such individuals would be classified as separate species, but Dean had to get back to the lab.

Emmanuel extended a lengthy arm to the graduate student and they shook hands.

"Keep in mind that the quantification of genetic difference between creatures can be misleading," Dean said, "because a small number of genes might control a large number of other genes. Here's my e-mail address at Scripps. Write if you have questions. You can get to that Web site by searching on the name Eduardo Kac, the one who created the genetic experiments; he created the bunny."

Emmanuel thanked him and said good-bye.

Emmanuel sat a while longer. Etched in the marble bench beneath him lay a naked woman covered by a branch. He thought about Meecha who, in his imagination, slowly removed the red scarf and panties. Embarrassed by his large erection, he got up and walked up the hill along the brown tiled path. When seen from above, the tiles depicted a several-hundred-foot-long snake, which coiled around the bench, garden, and fig tree. The head of the serpent pointed to the entrance of the campus library.

— 15 —

Alone in the motel room, Emmanuel thought about Meecha. Earlier that day, she had held his hand, held his gaze, and teased him gently about the third and second cutest animals in the zoo. Had she been implying that he was the cutest? Or was that wishful thinking? He was not sure.

The phone rang.

It was 10:42 p.m.

He walked to the phone and his legs went rubbery.

Wrong number.

He had to pee but it took four awkward minutes; the full-rocket erection saw to that.

He decided to call her. With teeth chattering, he reached for the phone.

"Awww . . ." He put down the receiver. It was too late to call. And what would he say? Would he admit that he has a crush on her?

He turned away and walked back to the chair when the phone rang again. His heart pumped wildly. It rang again. And again.

He lifted the receiver, his large hand visibly shaking.

It was her, and a few minutes later she arrived, freshly showered.

She wrapped an arm around his back. Her long soft hair, scented like herbs, massaged his neck.

Moments later they were naked and in bed; she slid over him, tucked him in, and rode him like a twenty-two-year-old on a wild bucking pony.

Emmanuel took deep breaths as her generous breasts bobbed in front of his face.

It is wet, he thought. *Oh my God it is so wet.*

Her hair, undone, fell like a canopy of rain and she dropped down on him and pushed her tongue inside his mouth. Now she was up again and he wanted the heat. She returned.

So, so wet.

Exquisite pressure mounted and he gripped her thighs. Sharp mint chocolate explosions frosted his brain and out of embarrassment he tried to stem the flow but the effort made him larger still.

"Oh my *God,*" moaned Meecha, overwhelmed by the musky scent and size of the testicles as the hardness spread sunset-spasm rings of electric pleasure. "What a *man!*"

"Oh," he grunted, noticing the smell of sweat and swamp. "Oh—*oh*—ohhhhhhh!"

— 16 —

Lucy recognized the long arms in the distance and she noticed how the large pack and two smaller ones pulled Emmanuel's muscular shoulders forward. She recognized his thick black hair that nearly covered his eyes and she recalled, with excitement, the contrast between his powerful physique and his seemingly sincere, gentle, and humble nature. She recalled, too, with admiration, the unusual fact that he didn't want to be easily reachable and didn't carry a cell phone.

Emmanuel recognized Lucy's damp unruly tangle of black seaweed hair and her ragged yellow sombrero. Her flannel shirt seemed several sizes too large for her slim frame and he recognized her tight jeans and black spandex top.

"Hey, welcome," she said, noticing the scent of musk as they briefly hugged.

"Thanks."

So *that* is what it is like to hug a wet sheep, Emmanuel thought, noticing the scent of cinnamon. He recalled their first conversation when they had met on campus months ago. He had asked Lucy what it was like to live in Seattle.

"It's cool," she had said. "So cool that people move here in droves until the cool people can't afford it and have to move out."

"How do you tell," Emmanuel had replied, "who the cool people are?"

Lucy had tried to picture cool but instead pictured nearly cool and almost nearly cool. Realizing that cool sometimes gets less cool and, on occasion, way cool, she grew increasingly flummoxed and uncharacteristically silent.

"Things change terribly fast," Emmanuel had offered, sensing he said something wrong.

"You know what hasn't changed much?" Lucy had replied, regaining her footing.

"What?"

"Horseshoe crabs—they've hardly changed in hundreds of millions of years!"

Emmanuel had been intrigued months ago by their first conversation and he felt intrigued now.

"This may sound strange," Lucy said as they walked down the hill, "but I think I have Paul Theroux disease."

"What is that?"

"Have you read any books by Paul Theroux?"

"I have read parts of *Walden Pond.*"

"No—*Walden Pond* is by Henry David Thoreau!"

"Oh."

"Paul Theroux wrote *The Mosquito Coast.* It's excellent. Well, no, it's horrible."

"What do you mean?"

"It's a huge freaking warning to the fringe," she explained. "Don't go too far in pursuit of your dreams, it says. Don't be too creative, too independent, too much of a nonconformist, lest you lose it and go insane. It's an important message brilliantly told."

"Why is it horrible?" Emmanuel asked as they approached 25th Street.

"I resent being reigned in," said Lucy, crossing the street.

Emmanuel waited a moment for a car to pass, caught up with her, and asked if having contradictory feelings was a symptom of Paul Theroux disease.

"No," she replied. "Theroux also writes travel books. You start to read one and you can't put it down; you reread it and bam—the disease takes hold and begins to spread."

"What happens?"

"You begin to see the world as if you're Paul Theroux."

"And?"

"You're so well traveled, you're so well read, and you're so in the know, that you can weave insightful, cultured, titillating tales at the drop of a hat."

"What is wrong with that?"

"You're also snotty."

"Oh." He paused. "Is there a cure?"

"Not that I know of."

Emmanuel looked over his shoulder as if scanning for predators. "What if you temporarily stopped reading his books?"

"Easier said than done," she said, eyeing her pack. "I'm currently rereading *The Old Patagonia Express*."

Emmanuel shrugged. "There *are* other books and authors."

Lucy pouted. "Yea, sure, but . . ."

Emmanuel lifted a small notebook from his pack. "Maybe you could read *this* instead."

"What is it?"

"A journal."

"You'd let me read your journal?"

Emmanuel smiled. Offering Lucy advice and support had generated a sense of self-worth and confidence. That and the greenness of the pedestrian path, the brightness of the wildflowers, and the newness of Seattle gave him a sense of hope.

— 17 —

"Dear Emmanuel," wrote Evelyn. "I saw you on the zoo's Web site for apes. Why . . ."

Don't pry, she thought, and backspaced through the sentence. "I'd love to hear about your recent experiences," she wrote. "I think about you . . ."

Give him space, she reminded herself, and started again: "Things here in Washington DC are fine. I went to a church sale and found a used Bible; it's worn and comfortable, the cover is thick and oversized like folds of rhinoceros armor, the pages are bound in yellowing clumps, and the spaces between clumps look like missing teeth. But what stands out the most about the book is its size. It's the granddaddy of Bibles and the world it seems could fit inside."

Evelyn wanted to share more than this huge old Bible with Emmanuel. She wanted to tell him how her Bible search had sparked an interest in humans and their place in the natural world. She wanted to tell him about her gentle, healing experience in the zoo. She wanted to tell him, too, about her hope to protect the Church but her desire to share was checked by an uncomfortable question: how close should she try to be when Emmanuel seemed so far away?

— 18 —

Emmanuel replayed the scene in his mind from hours ago. He had reached out to shake Meecha's hand good-bye. Ignoring it, she had rushed forward and kissed him on the lips.

"I'd like to go out with you," she had said, "but a long-distance relationship would be cruel to us both."

And a *genetically* long-distant relationship, Emmanuel now realized, would be even worse. He wanted to write to her but images of bobbing, bull's-eye breasts, and the drive to slide inside her, interrupted the train of thought, providing additional proof that his animal nature was spiraling out of control.

"Dear Meecha," he wrote in Lucy's living room as he recalled the warm push of her tongue, "we are so far apart. Yes, it would be difficult. You are kind and beautiful and smart and I miss you."

Emmanuel let out a little moan that masked yearning and hurt. Meecha had laid open for him the kingdom of animal pleasure but by now, driven by the knowledge of his creation, the pleasure had pressurized to angst, isolation, and despair.

The despair lingered and now he harbored increasing doubts about himself and the move to Seattle. College was no place for an academically gifted hybrid ape. What if the students or teachers found out? And what would he study? *Himself?* It made more sense to run away. But to what? The circus? The jungles of Africa and Asia?

Emmanuel felt an urge to share the story of his creation but how would Meecha react? How would his parents and friends react? He longed to be embraced and protected by the Bible, but he believed that the Bible was no longer there for him.

— 19 —

Lucy fell asleep and in the dream she saw dozens of males, each of which looked part human and part ape. Unlike the naked males in her anthropology textbook, the males in her dream wore white wing collar shirts, gold cufflinks, black evening tails, and dark glasses. They followed no progression, no order, no hierarchy such as: erect ones in front with thick-boned knuckle-walkers hunched in back. They danced, laughed, and belched in a muddle of chaotic abandon. Lucy marveled at their bulging muscles and smartly tailored suits that barely contained the impressive tufts of hair and rock-hard sweaty bodies. She approached a tall powerful male with spectacularly long arms and introduced herself, when a loud knock interrupted the dream.

Lucy awoke and sprang forward.

The sound startled Emmanuel, who had been thinking about what to write to Evelyn.

Lucy looked up as the door opened and a wolfish creature leapt in the house.

"Nunatak!" Lucy exclaimed.

"Raaa-ra-rrrrraaaaaaaaah!" howled the Siberian husky.

Lucy hugged the husky and stroked the thick coat.

Mark, tall and wiry with hair in a ponytail, stood at the door. The left side of his wire-rimmed glasses rose slightly higher than the right. Dog fur covered his flannel shirt.

"Come in," implored Lucy. "Here be Emmanuel!"

"Thanks," said Mark. "How's it going?"

Nunatak nudged her snout into Emmanuel's crotch.

"Eeuhhh!" said Emmanuel.

The husky looked to Mark for approval.

"No, girl," said Mark gently.

"Aww . . . give her a break," complained Lucy, "she's just introducing herself."

"There are socially acceptable ways of doing so."

"But she's a *dog!*"

"Dog nothing—she thinks she's human. Anyway, I came to invite you all to hang out at Ana's now. I hope you can make it."

"Cool," said Lucy. "We'll be there in a few minutes."

"Okay—see you in a few," he said, and left with the dog.

Emmanuel was curious about Mark and Ana.

"Let's go for a walk," replied Lucy, "and I'll fill you in."

She found her yellow sombrero and they stepped into the drizzle. "Do you see the house with the purple shutters?"

Emmanuel nodded.

"That's Ana's. You see the Volkswagon van with the solar cells on the roof? That's Mark's. Ana often takes in strays, and Mark and Nunatak are the latest; they're staying in the Treasure Room."

"The Treasure Room?"

Lucy did not answer; she was watching a small gray poodle. She removed the sombrero, spun it hard in the air, and it landed on her index finger.

The fine spray blurred Emmanuel's vision and he blinked.

Lucy said, "Do you see the poodle? Ana says it's the alpha dog."

"What is that?"

"Alpha means it's the one in charge. The poodle leads the larger dogs around the neighborhood."

"What about the largest dog?"

"You'd think the largest one would lead," Lucy said, continuing the tour around the block, "but the poodle is the smartest of the pack, and the other dogs know it—that's what Ana says. I started telling you about Ana. She's an environmental attorney, fisherwoman, and champion of the underdog. She's a fighter for . . ." Lucy paused. "Ana has cancer."

Emmanuel put an arm around her and her breathing eased. He touched the wetness on her face.

"Ana should have died long ago," Lucy continued. "When things get bad she travels: she goes down rivers in South America, she goes to villages in Africa, she goes to Alaska in the winter. And when she comes back, the cancer is in remission."

Emmanuel had questions but remained silent.

"The Treasure Room," she continued, "is where Ana keeps the relics from her travels."

After a few minutes, Emmanuel pointed across the street. "That dog seems to know you."

The golden retriever wagged its tail so that its entire body swayed.

Lucy crossed the street and lay on the wet lawn beside the dog and its rubber ball. She reached for the ball and threw it in the air.

The three of them watched it rise and fall.

Ffffudt!

Lucy pounced on the ball and scampered away on all fours, and the dog followed her, licked her face, and made her laugh. When she stood and led Emmanuel to the house with the purple shutters, her mood turned somber.

— 20 —

Ana Mayd wore an aviator scarf and sported a large frame, tiny glasses, and curly hair. She placed the ale, frosted mugs, and bananas on the round wooden table. "Guess who wants to start a chimp sanctuary?" she asked.

"Who?" Emmanuel blurted, leaping to his feet.

Ana, Mark, and Lucy looked at him expectantly.

Hot faced and embarrassed, Emmanuel folded his dangling arms and sat back down.

"Me," said Mark.

"Why?" asked Lucy.

"Should I tell the short or the long version?"

"The long one," said Ana, "but not *too* long. And remember: we have no fact-checking department."

"When I was seventeen," Mark began, "I embarked on a quest: I wanted to learn about who I was and where I fit into the bigger picture and so, to the dismay of my parents, I landed at the feet of a guru."

Emmanuel reached for a banana and wondered what finding a guru had to do with starting a chimpanzee sanctuary.

You landed at the feet of a *Gobi*, Lucy thought.

"It took a while, but over the years I mastered a lesson of significance."

Lucy raised an eyebrow. "What was that?"

"How to leave a guru and step back from a hierarchical system of beliefs. As it turns out, it's not as easy as it sounds."

Lucy nodded.

"After I left the guru, I wrote a book about my experiences and published it in its entirety on the Internet, for all to read."

"You mean the whole book is on the Web for *free?*"

Mark nodded.

Ana's eyes sparkled; she had hoped that Lucy and Mark would hit it off.

"What did you do next?" asked Lucy.

"I continued the quest, but this time I chose to seek knowledge—of who I was and how I came to be—in anthropology and biology. I studied humans and creatures similar to humans, and when I read Jane Goodall's books I became fascinated by wild chimpanzees, who reflect so much of who we are.

"One day I learned that Goodall's organization was moving to a suburb of Washington DC, which was near to where I lived. I tried getting involved but quickly learned that they accepted volunteers during weekday hours only. It wasn't clear to me how I could help, but I wasn't about to give up. If only I could talk with Dr. Goodall *directly,* I told myself, and she could see how motivated I was, then surely she'd create a window of opportunity for me, as Dr. Leakey had done for her."

"Sounds reasonable," said Ana, tugging at the scarf, "but how does one approach the famous chimp scientist?"

"I showed up early to a talk she was giving at Peace Corps Headquarters," Mark replied, "and sat in the second row. After her presentation, I raised my hand and said: 'Peace Corps volunteers help distant cultures in distant lands, not by sending money but by sharing two years of ideas, enthusiasm, hope. The hands-on experience forever changes worldviews and, thus, changes the world. Dr. Goodall, I deeply want to help chimpanzees in a way that will teach me about my biological cousins and about my species, in a way that will expand my worldview. *But there is no United States ChimpCorps*. And the Jane Goodall Institute currently accepts volunteers during weekday hours only. Each of your books are fascinating glimpses through a window of who we were and who we are. But Dr. Goodall, many of us are left standing, noses and hearts pressed against the glass, dreaming of ChimpCorps. How might we help?'"

"Bravo!" cried Ana.

Lucy looked stunned. "You said *that* to Jane Goodall?"

Emmanuel, who noticed Lucy's interest in Mark, broke into a sweat and drove his thumbnail into his middle digit.

Mark nodded, lost in the memory.

"Did she take you under her wing?" asked Lucy.

Mark scratched Nunatak behind the ears. "No."

Lucy sat on the edge of her chair.

Ana coiled the scarf around her fingers, looking as if she'd cry.

"After Goodall left the room," Mark continued, "the crowd dispersed. Just as I started to leave, the director of the United States Peace Corps approached, shook my hand, and said: '*That* was a good question.'

"At that moment I knew what I had to do. I had to stop relying on others to help in my quest. I needed to innovate, improvise, and look to myself. I needed to start my own ChimpCorps.

"Sure I want to help existing organizations, and there are some good ones out there. There's the Wildlife Conservation Society, the World Wildlife Fund, and Conservation International. There's the Orangutan Conservancy, the International Gorilla Conservation Programme, and the Jane Goodall Institute. I write them checks and will continue to write them checks. But I want to do more."

And you will, thought Ana.

— 21 —

"There are many potential ChimpCorps projects," Mark continued. "We could raise money to protect habitat in Africa, we could plant corridors of trees to connect protected parks, we could start a chimp rehab sanctuary, we could teach poachers to be guides . . ."

"That is *so cool!*" gushed Lucy.

Emmanuel's underarms itched from the drying sweat. He rolled his eyes.

"The primary motive behind ChimpCorps," admitted Mark, "is a selfish one. If chimps forever disappear, so will the living reflection of ourselves."

"Have you ever seen a chimp up close?" Lucy asked.

"Not in the wild, but I'd like to."

The front door swung open, interrupting Mark's story, and in walked a small thin woman with a mournful mouth.

"Blenny," said Ana, "is a fisherwoman. We were just talking about . . ."

The door swung open again and in walked a tall man in a jumpsuit with a hooked nose and short white hair. He scowled.

"Bandit," said Ana, "is a flight instructor in Alaska."

"Who *isn't* a flight instructor up there?" quipped Blenny.

Bandit glared at her.

The door swung open and in walked a man with large brown eyes and a long thick neck. He gave Ana a hug and said, "I had trouble with the directions, but I'm soooo glad I finally made it."

"Ernie," said Ana, "is a dairy farmer from my home state of Iowa."

Ernie lowered his head.

The door swung open and in walked a tall, muscular woman in leotards.

"Welcome," said Ana. "What's your name?"

"Fleshot," the woman hissed.

Ernie and Blenny took a step back while Bandit stood his ground and watched her closely.

Emmanuel took the opportunity to scratch under the arms.

"Ana's house," Lucy said to Emmanuel, "is an informal hangout for storytellers from around the world. People just hear about it and show up."

"Everyone's welcome here," Ana added. "We get Alaskans and New Yorkers, Microsoft engineers and the homeless, republicans and democrats, cats and dogs—and they all have a story to tell."

"Cats and dogs tell stories here?" asked Emmanuel.

"Yes," Ana answered, "but you have to know how to listen. We even get folks on spiritual quests who want to help the chimps. It's enough to make you giddy!"

"Spiritual *smeeeritual,*" retorted Blenny.

"Gosh," said Ernie, "why do you say that?"

"*My* spiritual quest led to nothing but trouble," said Blenny.

"Oh dear, what happened?"

"I was in a market in the Comoros, off the coast of Africa, when I recognized it, bought it, and took it to a priest to get it blessed."

"It? What was *it?*"

"*It* was a coelacanth."

"What's that?" asked Ernie.

"A fish."

"Why did you want to get a fish blessed?"

"You have to understand that the coelacanth is special. It's a living fossil in that it has hardly changed in hundreds of millions of years. It was thought to have been extinct for tens of millions of years, until one was caught—live—and identified in 1938."

"Okay, it's special," agreed Ernie, blinking, "but why ask a priest to bless a special fish?"

"Scientists believe the coelacanth of today may be closely related to the fish that crawled out of the sea some four hundred million years ago. In other words, if you follow your ancestry far enough back in time, you might find a creature much like a coelacanth."

"But why . . ."

"Why not? Why *shouldn't* a priest bless my parents, and their parents, and their parents' parents? *Are our ancestors increasingly less spiritual than ourselves?*"

"So what happened?" asked Ana.

"The priest said that there's nothing spiritual about a fish," continued Blenny, "and that this sort of thinking was *disrespectful* and would lead to trouble. And he was right—it has lead to trouble. The way I see it, I'm in a heap of trouble: on the one hand I openly acknowledge scientific knowledge but, on the other hand, I believe in the sanctity of the Church and I can't seem to reconcile . . ."

"So where's the ancient fish *now?*" demanded Fleshot.

Blenny pretended not to hear.

Flecks of red appeared in Fleshot's eyes.

Ernie began chewing gum and lolling his head.

Bandit changed the subject. "Once I was flying over the lower forty-eight," he began, "when the weight of my sins, my colorful sins, tugged at my conscience and drew me to church. So I landed and found a pretty white church in the countryside and I knocked on the door. But—if I'm not a monkey's uncle—they would not let me in!"

"Why not?" asked Blenny.

"I'd been traveling with my beloved parrot, Squawkie-Talkie, and the preacher told me that animals are forbidden in the house of the Lord."

"So who let the humans in?" growled Fleshot.

"Precisely," said Bandit. "It's strange, very strange, that animals are taboo in the house of the Lord. I don't get it, I don't like it, and the people in the cockpit of the Church should look out the window every few hundred years and see how high we're really flying."

Emmanuel looked at Ana and at the guests. He smiled. He felt welcomed here. He felt at home.

Mark and Lucy went to the kitchen for more ale.

Ana excused herself from the table and beckoned Emmanuel to follow her.

— 22 —

Emmanuel followed Ana down the stairs to the basement, past a woodworking bench, to a door slightly ajar. Peering inside, Emmanuel saw the Siberian husky and golden retriever on pillows on the shaggy carpet. Wool rugs hung from the walls and the shelves were filled with books and with red, white, and black masks from Alaska, South America, Africa, and Papua New Guinea.

Ana greeted the dogs as they entered the room.

The dogs sniffed the air.

"It is nice listening to stories," said Emmanuel. "I did that back home."

"Where is home, Emmanuel?"

"East Timor."

He's lucky to be alive, she thought. *Like me.*

"Do you ever have a story," Emmanuel wondered, "that is scared to come out?"

Ana sat beside the dogs and motioned for Emmanuel to do the same. "Yes, the important stories can be that way. When that happens, do you know what I do?"

Emmanuel shook his head.

"I take it on a journey!"

"I do not understand."

"Let me explain. A story—like a child—is packed with potential, but before it can grow, before it can blossom into something positive, it needs a healthy environment. I nurture stories by taking them on journeys."

Emmanuel blinked.

"Now imagine there's something brewing and festering inside you and you don't understand it, you don't know how to deal with it, and you don't know how to share it. What you're carrying is a confused, undernourished, undeveloped story. But stories evolve and if you take the story on a journey, on an adventure, then the light and the dust of cultures and continents might change your perspective and it might change you."

"Take it on an adventure?"

"Yes but not just any old kind," Ana whispered, as if sharing a secret. "It should have three parts."

Emmanuel leaned forward.

"The first part is to organize the journey around a theme that relates to the story you're grappling with. Do you understand?"

He looked unsure.

"Let's say you learned you were going blind in one eye and it was eating you up inside. On your journey you might want to visit people blind in both eyes."

"You would do that," he said, remembering Ana's cancer, "to learn to feel good about having one good eye?"

Ana smiled. "That's right. The second part is to start the journey by sharing your story. It doesn't have to be with a group, nor does it have to be with family or friends. The point is to share it—even with a stranger."

"Why?"

"It serves as a reference point, a bookend of sorts, something to compare with later on. The third part is to share the story again, at the end of the journey, which helps you integrate what you've learned. It's also a good way to communicate knowledge of the outer rim with the inner hub. Speaking of which, let me show you my African mask collection."

She led him to the other side of the Treasure Room. "This red and black one is a death mask."

She held it over her face.

Emmanuel noticed the mask's acrid smoky smell and wondered about the meaning of death. He knew what death meant to a Christian, but Christian rules no longer applied to him. "Are you afraid of death, Ana?"

"Yes, Emmanuel, I am. And the story of death, the story of *my* death, is one I travel with often. One way I cope, one way I deal with the harsh grip of fear, is to picture moose in Canada, bears in the Rockies, snowy owls in Wisconsin, manatees in the Everglades, gorillas in Rwanda. When I picture animals, nonhuman animals, on the land, in the air, and in the sea, I connect with them, if only in my mind, and the connection eases the stress of being a knowledge-burdened human. The connection brings me a deep and honest peace."

Emmanuel and Ana paused and listened to the roars, howls, and riotous squawks that emerged from the guests upstairs.

"If you didn't know better," Ana laughed, "you'd think they were a bunch of animals."

— 23 —

Emmanuel sat in a canoe with Lucy and worried about how to pay for the upcoming journey. He worried, too, about how to tell Mother and Father that he would not be going to college. The new plan—to meet apes in his immediate family—would surely not go over well with them.

He let the paddle drag in Lake Washington.

Lucy tried to steer. "Hey Emmanuel—are you sleeping up there?"

He started to stand up.

"No! Don't do that—we'll go over!"

"I am tired of bending over," he muttered. "*Tired!* I want to stand up straight like everyone else!"

"Stand up straight—sure!—but not in the . . ."

"Humans stand straight!" he wailed.

"What are you *doing?* No don't . . ."

The boat flipped.

Splash!

Splash!!

That's what I get for bothering him, Lucy thought, as she swam back to the canoe.

Emmanuel thrashed his arms wildly.

"It's okay," she said, grasping him around the waist. "The water's not deep here."

He dug his feet in the mud and stood up.

People stared at them from the bridge above.

They righted the canoe and climbed in. Emmanuel shivered as Lucy rubbed his back.

"There's no harm done," she said. "Are you okay? Is there something on your mind?"

"You would not believe it," Emmanuel said, hugging his knees.

"Maybe not, but I'll listen."

He started at the beginning and when he got to the part about Suharto, Lucy stopped rubbing his back.

After the story there was a long pause.

Lucy suppressed a grin. "So in theory you're carrying around some nonhuman genes and you're *upset?* You should have met the guys I went to high school with."

Emmanuel looked wretched.

Lucy regretted her words. "What will you do?" she whispered.

It had started to rain.

"Go to the jungles and visit my . . ."

His voice trailed off.

Lucy took his hand and looked to the shore. The word *relatives* came to mind.

— 24 —

A week after Emmanuel had stood up in the canoe, Lucy considered the options. She could stay in Seattle and pursue book knowledge or she could take a year off and study apes and ape hybrids—Emmanuel in particular—in the field. She considered Emmanuel's story to be far-fetched and yet she knew, from scientific journals, that cross-species genetic manipulations were not limited to the world of fiction.

Lucy favored the field study. She would learn a great deal about apes no matter what Emmanuel turned out to be. Money for the trip wouldn't be an issue as there was plenty left over from the inheritance. Moreover, she found herself attracted to Emmanuel's powerful chimpanzee-like body, gorilla-like gentleness, and human vulnerability.

The only downside to the journey, as far as she could tell, was that Emmanuel had yet to invite her.

Lucy shrugged. "Screw that," she said and started to pack for the adventure. She wasn't going to let details get in the way.

As she packed, a bio-story came to mind.

"There was a young male named Emmanuel," she said aloud, wanting to hear how the story sounded, "and though he mostly looked human, his genes told a different story. His genes described him as a *manimal*—a living animal that is largely, but not entirely, human.

"One day," she continued, "after discovering the secret of his genes, Emmanuel set out for the jungle to meet his hairy kin. He decided to invite a most charming girlfriend who, for reasons of her own, refused to bow to ancient rules of social hierarchy. But alas! So absorbed was Emmanuel in his personal mounting woes that he hardly noticed her cool experiment in dominance behavior. One night on the fragrant, leafy floor of the jungle, Emmanuel fancied himself to be the alpha ape and . . ."

Lucy stopped the bio-story, stuffed an old toothbrush in a side pocket, and stopped grinning. Emmanuel was in no shape to be on top, she reminded herself. Nor was he prepared to organize and lead a scientific exploration that cut across multiple languages, cultures, continents, and species. Clearly, she'd have to take charge. But what would be her strategy?

She thought about Mark's dream of helping the chimps in West Africa. Mark wasn't quite ready to take the first step with Chimp-Corps, but Emmanuel wouldn't have to know that.

Besides, she told herself. If a story is told for a good cause, who needs a fact-checking department?

"Say, Emmanuel," she said later that day. "I got an e-mail this morning from Mark; apparently some ChimpCorps funding came through and he's looking for interns."

"Please wish him luck," Emmanuel replied.

Lucy scratched her chin. "Interns don't get paid. They supply their own food, malaria medicine, and medical insurance, but here's the amazing part: ChimpCorps pays for the flights."

He looked up. "To Africa?"

"Yep. They mostly work with chimps in Africa, but they also work with orang utans in Asia."

"The interns learn about the apes?"

"Yes—we'd learn a great deal."

"We?"

"You better believe it, pal. I want to have fun, too. Plus . . . I . . . I . . ."

Lucy blushed.

"I want to be with you," she managed to say.

Emmanuel took in Lucy's gaze and the rugged beauty of her face.

"Thank you for being my friend," he said, wetting his lips and noticing the scent of cinnamon.

PART THREE

Tree Of Life

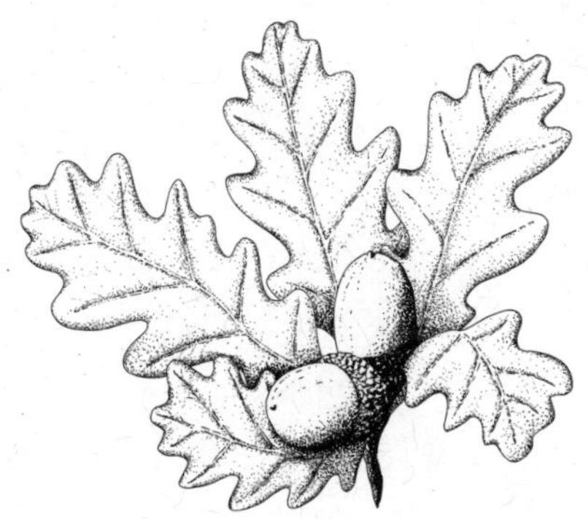

— 25 —

"Do you think it's fiction?" asked Lucy, hair flapping wildly in the wind.

Emmanuel shifted uneasily in the passenger seat. "What do you mean?"

"The story about your genes—do you think it's fiction?"

"It is in Father's handwriting; Father does not lie."

"So," said Lucy, "what's it like to see the world through the eyes of an . . ."

"I am noticing your breasts," he said. "Breasts hardly hidden, breasts pressed and shaped by your black spandex top. Your lower region appears in my mind like a spider in a moist, perfect garden."

"Really?"

She pressed the accelerator hard.

"The story of my creation," he added, "explains the rise of my animal instincts."

"You beast," she breathed. "Take me now . . ."

Lucy woke at the rest stop, raised her bushy brows, and marveled at the vividness of the dream. She listened to sounds of the interstate and tried to recall what she had been telling Emmanuel about the journey. She wanted to keep the story straight.

They were interns. That was it. They were ChimpCorps interns, and when they arrived in West Africa someone would give them instructions.

The *true* part of the story was easier for her to remember: she had booked and paid for the flight to Africa and she and Emmanuel would drive across North America and leave from New York in ten days.

Lucy shook Emmanuel, who lay on the ground beside her. "Hey monkey boy, let's get going. Africa and Asia are waiting."

Emmanuel bit his lip. He did not like to be called that.

"And don't forget," she continued, "in keeping with the educational theme of our trip, we're stopping off today to visit a chimp who communicates using sign language."

"Okay," he said, folding the tarp and following Lucy out from the bushes.

They returned to the car.

Emmanuel felt intimidated by the leather seat covers. The vehicle seemed more suitable for Aunt Winnie, he thought, than for an ape-human college drop-out.

"Where on the east coast did you say we need to drop off the car?" he asked.

"New Jersey," she replied.

"I have a friend in New Jersey," he said.

"No kidding. What exit?"

"What do you mean?" Emmanuel asked.

"It's a joke," she said as she sped in the left lane of Interstate 90.

She glanced over at Emmanuel and entertained the possibility that he might actually be a member of a different species. She recalled what Ana had taught her about different species: *do not assume humans are superior.*

Lucy's thoughts drifted to Ana. She had wanted to say good-bye in Seattle but Ana had been nowhere to be found, and now Lucy wondered if she'd ever see her again. She recalled a poem Ana had taught her: *do not look for me here at the grave site for I am long gone to travel as the wind among exquisite currents of nature.*

It went something like that, and the words sparked a memory of walking barefoot with Ana by Lake Washington in the driving rain.

Emmanuel, too, thought about Ana as he looked out the window at the blur of pine trees. He imagined talking with her: "I told Lucy the whole thing. . . . I am taking the story on a journey. . . . I started the day before. . . . I am going to Africa. . . . I will work as an intern and meet the *other* family. . . . it sounds silly, but Father would not lie. . . . I wonder what they are like. . . . I wonder how they communicate. . . . I wonder how they will react to a hybrid. . . ."

Emmanuel recalled Ana's smoky red and black death mask, which she had slipped over her face, and he thought of the dangers lurking in the African jungle: snakes, malarial mosquitoes, and berries that kill. There were psychological dangers, too: isolation, fear, and angst over what he would discover by peering into the hairy genetic mirror.

Emmanuel recalled the e-mail he had sent Father last night.

subject: Start my Education

Dear Father,

All is well here in Seattle. I am looking forward to starting my education.

Love,

Emmanuel

At first it bothered him that he had intentionally deceived Father, but he also realized that an ape hybrid such as himself was incapable of sin because nonhumans would be barred from confession.

The thought made his head hurt; he wanted to think about something other than himself.

"So," he said, "we are visiting Washoe today?"

"Yes," replied Lucy.

"And who again is Washoe?"

"A chimpanzee."

"We are going to the zoo?"

"Nope—we're going to Central Washington University."

"Washoe is going to school there?"

"She's not taking courses, if that's what you mean. She lives in a large enclosed area, which is part of the university."

"She is a special chimpanzee?"

"Yes and no. Yes because she was taught American Sign Language, a language largely used by deaf people. She knows over a hundred signs and combines them in ways never taught to her. She—like humans—mentally manipulates abstract symbols in flexible and creative ways to control her environment."

Emmanuel nodded, recalling the Orang Utan Language Project at the National Zoo.

"But in another sense," Lucy continued, "Washoe is not special. If chimpanzees are taught in a supportive environment, they can generally learn to manipulate abstract symbols with a measure of sophistication."

"As sophisticated as humans?"

"As sophisticated as two- or three-year-old humans."

Emmanuel looked down.

"It doesn't mean that humans are superior," she said, placing a hand on his shoulder. "Creatures evolve in ways that help them survive within given environments, and the human ability to abstract on abstractions is one survival tool out of many. Nonhuman animals do remarkable things, mentally and otherwise, that humans can't. Besides, it may turn out that turbo-charged abstraction capability, over stretches of geological time, empowers humans to self-destruct."

Emmanuel looked mournful.

"Let's drop our preconceived notions about humans and apes," Lucy suggested. "We don't know much about them yet. I have a good feeling about our trip and think we're going to learn a lot. Let's give it some time and be patient with ourselves, okay? Now we're coming up on Ellensburg. Let's find a phone booth and make an appointment today to see Washoe."

Lucy pulled up to a gas station phone booth. "Here's the number for the Washoe Hotline."

"What should I say?"

"Tell 'em you're a ChimpCorps volunteer and want to meet Washoe before you leave for West Africa. If that doesn't work, tell 'em you're

Washoe's next of kin and there's millions of years of catching up to do."

Emmanuel climbed out of the car, squinted in the sunlight, and approached the phone booth.

"Hello?" he said, calling the main office number, but there was a glitch in the phone lines and the call was intercepted by Language Bridge (LB), a computer-based system that facilitated communication between scientists and Washoe.

LB had been deemed necessary by psychologists and linguists who doubted claims of Washoe's language prowess and who wanted to use technology to observe her. The animal behaviorists thought the attempt to achieve greater objectivity by using LB was unnecessary, if not ridiculous, but it had been years since they controlled the purse strings of a high profile project.

LB translated simple English phrases into sign language displayed by a small furry gorilla robot and Washoe, who now heard Emmanuel's voice over a speaker, observed the gorilla robot sign the word "hello."

"Hello," Washoe signed back.

LB used video-fed pattern recognition software to translate Washoe's signing motions into English.

"He-llo," LB translated in a low, raspy woman's voice.

"We would like to see Washoe now," said Emmanuel. "Is that okay?"

"Come," signed Washoe. "Washoe play now."

"Okay, great," Emmanuel said. "We would like to see Washoe play."

Washoe loved to play, particularly with toys, but her rubber duck had been missing for days. "Bring Washoe duck," she signed.

"What?" Emmanuel said.

"Bring duck. Come play."

"Okay. We will be there soon."

LB, which frequently made translation errors, instructed the robot to chew its fingernails.

"Sad monster," signed Washoe, feeling sorry for the robot gorilla.

Emmanuel's eyes moistened when he heard the woman's voice say, "sad monster." He hung up the phone, rubbed his face, and returned to the car.

"What did they say?" asked Lucy.

"We can come over now and should bring a duck for Washoe to play with."

Lucy reached for the plastic duck on the dashboard, removed the compass taped to its bright yellow chest, and led Emmanuel to the building that housed Washoe.

They knocked on the door but no one answered.

"Are you sure they said to come over now?" Lucy asked.

"Yes. Washoe wants to play."

Finally a young woman answered the door. "Can I help you?"

"We're here to see Washoe!"

"I'm sorry but the public may spend time with Washoe at specific times only. Here's a schedule and if you're around over the weekend, you can attend the Chimposium."

"The *public?*" Lucy exclaimed. "We're not the public. We're on a mission to explore the so-called line that separates humans from nonhuman primates!"

"Sorry but we're closed."

"But we've come all the way from—from *Seattle!*"

"I'm sorry, but Washoe's desire for privacy must be respected."

"Good point," offered Emmanuel.

Lucy glared at him. "Have you ever heard of ChimpCorps?"

"I can't say that I have," the student admitted.

"Well we're ChimpCorps volunteers, and Emmanuel here says that Washoe wants to play ducky and . . ."

The student looked concerned. "How did you know about the duck?"

"As I said, we're with ChimpCorps—you know, *Help the Chimps or Just Monkey Around.*"

But the student was eyeing the duck.

"Look," said Lucy, "I'll tell you what. If we can watch Washoe for five minutes, she can keep the duck."

"I can't do that. . . . I'll get in trouble."

"Who will know? We won't interfere, I promise."

"Washoe would tell Roger."

"You mean Washoe would tell Dr. Roger Fouts?"

The student nodded.

"Couldn't you say Washoe was lying?"

"Sure, but Washoe has a lot of credibility around here."

"More than the students?"

She nodded.

"That's tough," said Lucy.

"Okay," said the student after an uneasy silence. "I'll take you in—briefly—if Washoe can have the duck, but you'll have to hide in the corner."

"Deal."

It was dark inside. They could see inside the large enclosure but couldn't see Washoe. Emmanuel closed his eyes and sniffed the urine-scented air.

Another student had been peering into the room when he mistook Emmanuel—hunched over and partly hidden behind a banana plant—for one of the chimps. "Mojo is out!" the student's voice crackled over a walkie-talkie.

"Mojo is out!" another voice announced over the loudspeaker.

Seconds later, the first student returned. "Listen!" she said, out of breath. "Things are about to get crazy here—I'm sorry but you'll have to leave right away!"

"We understand," said Lucy. "We hope things work out. Oh, and Washoe can keep the duck."

"Thank you for letting us inside," said Emmanuel, rushing after Lucy.

Washoe recognized Emmanuel's voice from the earlier Language Bridge phone call. "Sad monster come play," she signed.

A walkie-talkie blared: "Mojo has escaped to the courtyard and is heading for the parking lot!"

Emmanuel slipped into the parking lot, climbed into the car, and shut the door.

Lucy fired up the engine.

Five people scoured the parking lot, looking under cars.

"Please drive carefully," a woman cautioned. "There's a chimpanzee on the loose!"

"I'll keep that in mind," Lucy replied.

— 26 —

At the Jane Goodall Institute headquarters, Evelyn approached a bookshelf and jotted down titles. So many interesting books, she thought after the presentation for potential volunteers. And such nice people. Too bad about the hours.

On the walk to the Silver Spring metro station, Evelyn wondered how she might free up time to volunteer during weekday hours but, with the political science classes at American University and the part-time work as a research assistant, timing was tight. She realized she'd have to find a different organization to volunteer with.

Evelyn thought about Emmanuel. She had mailed him the huge old Bible, along with a few e-mails, but there had been no response. So unlike him.

She approached a café, attracted by the scent of coffee and folk music, and took a seat near the stage where her eyebrows, in synchronization with the guitarist's eyebrows, rose and fell with the emotional intensity of the song.

I'm there for Emmanuel, she thought as she stroked her long brown hair, but I'm not going to sit around and pout. Why make myself miserable? It won't help anyone and, besides, there's too much to learn, too much to do.

— 27 —

Emmanuel sat in the passenger seat and thought about Evelyn. He badly wanted to write to her, but it seemed unfair for him—a hybrid ape—to pursue a relationship with a human whose deeply held views on Christianity would surely keep them apart. Lucy, he noted, seemed to accept him for who he was.

Moments later, Lucy stopped for a hitchhiker who looked to be roughly Emmanuel's age and who, minutes into the ride, boasted that he was wanted by the police.

"So, tough guy, are you going to mug us?" Lucy asked.

"No, no."

"Good. Now when was the last time you had a decent meal?"

"It's no problem; I dumpster dive."

Emmanuel had never heard the expression.

"It's when you rummage for food in the garbage," Lucy explained. She stopped at a Burger King and bought the hitchhiker a veggie burger, an orange juice, and a salad.

He wolfed the food, patted his stomach, and burped loudly.

"You're welcome," said Lucy.

When they returned to the car, the hitchhiker announced he was headed for New York City. Neither Lucy nor Emmanuel responded. They sensed it was best not to divulge their destination.

By the time they reached Montana the conversation had shifted to politics and by now the hitchhiker, who spoke as loudly as he burped, was blaming World War II on the Jews.

"They knew what was coming," he said. "Hitler published his plans in the finest detail and the Jews did *nothing* about it. They deserved what they got."

Emmanuel felt nauseated.

"You don't kill people because they are passive!" said Lucy angrily.

"Stupid and weak people deserve to die."

Lucy said, "How old are you?"

"Twenty-two."

"*Why* are you wanted by the police?"

"I took action against the German government, which has no right to . . ."

"What type of action?"

"I threw a bomb during a protest."

The silence stretched interminably until they exited at a rest stop a few miles before Missoula. The hitchhiker went to the bathroom.

Lucy turned to Emmanuel. "What a sick creep!"

"He is a bad man," agreed Emmanuel.

"He's had some twisted teachers along the way. It's weird. Most Germans I've met are left-leaning peaceniks who consider the *United States* the great source of violence and moral corruption."

But Emmanuel was not thinking about the shifting morals of nations.

Lucy brushed the hair from his eyes. "What's on your mind?" she asked.

"Maybe it is not a blessing to be fully human."

She squeezed his hand.

The hitchhiker approached. "We will go now!" he said.

Lucy suppressed a smile, pleased at her self-restraint. She hadn't told the hitchhiker off because she wanted to study and, possibly, influence him.

They returned to the car and Lucy eased back on the interstate. "Gentlemen, fasten your seat belts," she said softly, flooring the pedal.

The hitchhiker nervously scratched at his nose. "You drive too fast. So we go to New York?"

"*We* are visiting friends in Canada and *may* head north to Moose Jaw or Winnipeg or Thunder Bay, depending on *our* friends' schedules."

Lucy didn't wait for an answer. She slapped Emmanuel's knee.

His lower leg responded by kicking the floorboard.

"HEY!" she said. "You know what *we* haven't done in a while?"

"What?" said Emmanuel.

"Played the *abstraction* game!"

"How does it go?" asked the hitchhiker.

"It's easy. Each of us considers a subject from various points of view and abstracts on the ideas."

"What's the subject?"

"Abstraction."

"So, abstract on abstraction?"

"That's right."

"Who goes first?"

"Emmanuel."

Emmanuel scratched his head. "There is an object," he said, "call it X. You are aware of X. You can think about it, talk about it, describe it. You are pleased with yourself for knowing so much about X. As a matter of fact, you are an expert about X. Now here is the important part: you wonder how to improve the way you think about X. You decide you need to go for long walks. Why? Because you realize you do your best thinking when you are walking."

"Well done!" exclaimed Lucy. "You abstracted on abstraction by thinking about the way you think about something!"

Emmanuel smiled.

"My turn," said Lucy. "There's an object, call it X, and you're vaguely aware of it. You can sort of think about it, you can recognize it, and to a degree you can even grasp its context, but you can't communicate knowledge about it in great detail, nor can you think about it in the highly abstract ways that a human can. Incidentally, you're a gorilla. Though you have mental strengths, and though your ability to spatially map objects helps you survive in a forest environment, still, you lack the abstraction skills required to mold X into a catastrophic weapon system. From an evolutionary point of view, is it better to have human abstraction abilities?"

"Very clever," said the hitchhiker, "but now it's my turn! Animals with the smarter genes win! Take your pitiful gorillas—they are just about extinct! In twenty years there will be no living gorillas in the wild! Why? Because we kill them, we take their land, we kill and eat them all! We are smarter, we are superior, *we kill and eat them because we can!*"

Emmanuel's mouth opened. His lips quivered.

"That's not all!" said the hitchhiker, nearly shouting. "Abstract on what I just said and apply it to people. Go ahead—*do it!* People with *better* genes abstract on abstractions better than those in the lesser races. We will dominate the other races in the same way God instructed humans to dominate the dirty, stinking animals!"

Lucy took a deep slow breath. "Science doesn't support your ideas," she said. "Here's the scoop. Evolution is based on variation and natural selection. Variation comes from mutations that are changes in DNA. Now listen closely. There are three types of mutations: ones that have little or no effect on the creature, ones that damage the creature, and ones that help the creature. The third type, which is extremely rare, has a chance of spreading through a population . . ."

"I know all about your Darwin," interrupted the hitchhiker. "There are genes that control the ability to abstract. The genes generate a greater abstraction capability in humans than in apes, and the genes generate a greater abstraction capability in *some* humans than in others. *That is the scientific basis for the master race!*"

"No," said Lucy, "genetic difference does *not* empower one human population to abstract better than another."

"Why not?"

"To begin with, there are thousands of genetically influenced components that contribute to one's ability to think abstractly."

"So?"

"So a population might have genes that create maverick neurons that increase abstraction capability. But that same population might also have genes that lower the amount of oxygen flowing to the brain. Or it might have genes that make people so fidgety that they can't concentrate for very long."

"Why couldn't a population have thousands of *superior* components?"

"It's a highly competitive, specialized world out there and it's doubtful that any individual or group can genetically compete successfully on all fronts. But even if they could, keep in mind that environments change. What is superior today isn't necessarily superior tomorrow."

The hitchhiker didn't answer.

"Then there's the nature-nurture angle," said Lucy. "If a baby from 'superior' human parents is deprived of intellectual stimulation, will it develop advanced abstraction capabilities? If a baby from 'inferior' genetic stock is raised in a stimulating environment, will it do better than the intellectually deprived 'superior' baby?"

The hitchhiker frowned.

"Here's another example: in one culture, young adults are pressured to read, study, and pursue an advanced education, whereas in another culture they are encouraged to watch a lot of television. Which culture will tend to nurture deeper thought? There are *hundreds* of behaviors not coded in DNA that have direct influence over abstraction capability, and any one of the behaviors could overshadow genetic difference."

The hitchhiker bit his lower lip.

"Another blow to the myth of the master race," said Lucy, "comes from a story that I will now tell you. Once upon a time, there lived a nineteen-and-a-half-year-old maiden named Luby. Luby stood out in a crowd largely because of her deep sensuality and beauty, her exceptionally well-developed ability to abstract upon abstractions, and her failure each day and night to wear a shirt or bra."

Emmanuel and the hitchhiker listened closely. Emmanuel licked his lips.

"One day," Lucy continued, "Luby was strolling in the forest when a tall, muscular young man approached.

"'I'm Stiff,' said the man.

"Luby was attracted to Stiff, and vice versa, but Luby knew too well it was forbidden to lay with a man from so far away, whose home was situated beyond the forbidden mountains. She nonetheless curtseyed, touched the man, and merrily went ahead and disobeyed the rules. It therefore came as no surprise to her when, weeks later, she learned that she was with child."

Emmanuel and the hitchhiker were enthralled with the images from Lucy's story.

"Divergence within a species," explained Lucy, "can't gain momentum when there's gene flow between populations. Do you understand the point of the story?"

They did not respond.

"Ask yourself," Lucy added, "what do humans love to do the most—besides talking, that is?"

The hitchhiker smirked.

"That's right," said Lucy, "they love to have sex! Which is why I find it extremely hard to believe that there are human populations *not* sharing genes on a daily basis. How can you have a master race when there is gene flow between the populations?"

"Gene flow is a problem," the hitchhiker admitted.

"Good luck trying to stop it," said Lucy. "What fascinates me is why some humans are *technologically* superior to others."

"So!" the hitchhiker gloated. "You *do* believe in the superiority of some people!"

"Technologically speaking, yes; not because they are smarter or biologically superior than others but, rather, because their ancestors were at the right place at the right time."

"You are saying they were just lucky?" asked the hitchhiker.

"That's right. Agriculture began in China and the Fertile Crescent region long before it started elsewhere—*not* because the people were smarter or genetically superior, but because some plants and animals in the area happened to be useful to humans and lent themselves to domestication."

"Why does it matter where agriculture started?"

"Agriculture can enable a society to generate and store a surplus of food."

"So?"

"The idea of surplus is key," Lucy pointed out. "In societies with a surplus, it is no longer necessary for the vast majority of people to make a living looking for food. Instead, they can *specialize.*"

"Specialize?"

"In surplus societies people can be full-time warriors, tool makers, or inventors, which allows them to achieve technological superiority."

"So it boils down to who started farming first?"

"There are other reasons why some populations of humans are more technologically advanced than others. One has to do with the shape of the continents."

"I don't understand."

"Imagine the globe," Lucy instructed. "Imagine the shape of the Americas, Africa, Europe, and Asia. It's easier for agriculture, tools, and ideas to spread along a major east-west axis, such as you'd find in Europe or Asia, than it is to spread along a major north-south axis, such as you'd find in the Americas or Africa."

"Why?"

"Because of the relationship between climate and geography. Seeds that grow at a certain latitude can be farmed thousands of miles to the east or to the west because the climate will likely be similar, but the same seeds would fail if you planted them thousands of miles to the north or the south."

The hitchhiker looked depressed. "So who runs the planet is mostly determined by accidents of geography?"

"Essentially, yes. Here's another key consideration: if you develop agriculture and domesticate animals before others do, your population gradually builds resistance to the diseases carried by the farm animals. And so if you invade an agriculture-less population, you not only have more sophisticated weapons than they do as a result of your food surplus, you also introduce deadly microorganisms into their bodies *just by being near them*. Spanish conquerors managed to kill millions of American natives in this way before armed conflict even began."

The hitchhiker stamped his foot and insisted that Europeans were *genetically* superior to the Native Americans. Lucy responded by giving him a twenty dollar bill. "Go buy yourself a copy of Jared Diamond's *Guns, Germs, and Steel,*" she said, "and abstract on it."

For the next few days, Lucy and Emmanuel camped with the hitchhiker and bought him meals. While the intellectual sparring didn't seem to change his views about the master race, the abundance of food seemed to blunt the ferocity of his verbal assaults. When they neared the split before Youngstown, Ohio, between I-80 and I-76, Lucy pulled off the interstate.

"We're heading south," she told him, "to meet a friend in Pittsburgh."

The hitchhiker stepped on the pavement. For a moment he seemed speechless. "You will go now," he managed to say and slammed the door.

Lucy revved the engine.

"Good thing his views are not taught in school," Emmanuel whispered as the car shot out of the rest stop and into the left lane.

— 28 —

"Is Pittsburgh on the ape education tour?" asked Emmanuel.

"Nah," replied Lucy. "But Rebecca has an apartment and a shower; if you haven't noticed, the car smells like a zoo."

Emmanuel blushed.

"Besides," Lucy continued, "I owe her a visit, the poor thing."

"Why is she a poor thing?" he asked.

"Her parents desperately want her to be a lawyer, but she wants to be a writer."

Perhaps she can be a hybrid, Emmanuel thought.

At 9:20 p.m. Lucy knocked on the door. Rebecca's height and regal posture reminded Lucy of Adam, but she had no patience for memories of former boyfriends. After introductions, they followed Rebecca inside.

"What's new old friend?" asked Lucy.

"Mike."

"Do tell."

"We're in love!"

"Cool!"

"*Not cool!*"

"Why not?"

"He's not Jewish."

"Your parents found out?"

"Precisely."

"Uh-oh. Will you drop him?"

"I love him."

"Will he convert?"

"Yes, but . . ."

"But what?"

"My parents want me to marry someone *already* Jewish."

"Why?"

"They just do."

Emmanuel spoke. "Do your parents believe that Jews have special genes?"

"They believe that Judaism is special."

"Judaism is special," said Emmanuel. "But if it is the *genes* that make it special—and if you want to make your parents happy—you will have to find another guy. If Jewish genes are no more special than other people's genes, then Mike can convert and everyone can be happy."

Lucy hid a smile. She had been worried about Emmanuel's generally depressed state of mind and took his participation in the conversation as a good sign.

Rebecca looked perplexed. "If my parents *do* believe the genes are special, they'd never admit it—not even to themselves. But then again, there's the story of the chosen ones."

Emmanuel felt emboldened. "Can animals be Jewish?" he asked.

"Don't be *ridiculous!*" exclaimed Rebecca.

Emmanuel grimaced, as though a door had slammed shut in his face.

"Hey listen," Lucy said, "we've been driving crazy hours and . . ."

"I'm sorry," said Rebecca, "I've been an awful host; you both must be exhausted. There are towels in the guest room—please make yourselves at home. I hope you can stay for a few days."

"Thanks," said Lucy, "but we're due in Montreal pronto."

"Okay. At the very least I can show you around campus late tomorrow morning. Better yet, why don't you come with me to orientation?"

"I don't know," said Lucy. "We're not students here."

"So? I'm sure you'll fit in among seventy graduate students. Besides, since when are *you* shy? Come on—it will be fun!"

Lucy frowned.

"There'll be food. . . ."

"Okay," laughed Lucy, "but fitting in is not what we do best."

Later that night, as Emmanuel stretched out on the sofa, Lucy lay in the guest room next door. She yawned loudly and thought about Emmanuel. She wanted to sleep beside him. She recalled how, over the past few days, they had increasingly brushed against each other, engendering mutual feelings of camaraderie and sexual excitement. She wanted to lay by his powerful, taut body.

Lucy yawned again and thought about Emmanuel's trauma from the story of his creation. It didn't matter, she figured, if the story was true or not; what mattered was his belief in his father's words.

As she started drifting off to sleep, she wondered how she could help soften the blows of his genetic and spiritual isolation. A thought came to her. She would give him what he wanted most in the world. It would take time to write but the result—a gift for *all* great apes—would be worth the effort.

The following morning Emmanuel, Lucy, and Rebecca walked to the University of Pittsburgh and entered a towering building called the Cathedral of Learning. They found the room, sat in the back, and listened to a professor in her early thirties describe the philosophy of the writing program at Pitt.

"Words have no real meaning," she pointed out. "They merely point to other words."

Lucy wanted to respond but, for Rebecca's sake, she controlled herself.

"Language has no power," the professor went on. "The concept of the author is dead and there is no such thing as good writing. A third grader's writing is as good as the 'best' writing in the *New Yorker.*"

Lucy thought about language. While its symbols were largely arbitrary, the competitive advantage it gave to successful practitioners was anything but arbitrary, and its significance as a tool for survival seemed central to the human story. Washoe used language but not to the same degree or complexity as humans. Does increasingly abstract language empower its practitioners to think in increasingly abstract ways? The likelihood of such a link existed and the intentional emasculation of language seemed foolish and unnecessary.

Emmanuel also thought about language, particularly sophisticated language. It seemed like such a powerful tool and precious gift. He felt deeply grateful for his ability to use it and felt compelled to defend it.

Rebecca noticed Emmanuel's arm going up. A feeling of dread crept over her.

The professor pointed to Emmanuel. "Yes?"

Emmanuel had been looking forward to college and its intellectual challenges, and here was an opportunity to learn directly from the highly educated. "Excuse me," he said, "but are you saying there is no hierarchy *at all* in the use of language?"

"Precisely."

"And are you saying that a half-human, half-ape creature could write as good as a professor in your English department?"

A handful of students laughed aloud; the others managed to control themselves.

Rebecca's eyes bulged. *This* professor controlled graduate student funding. Without assistance, tuition at Pitt was out of the question.

Shocked by Emmanuel's boldness, Lucy thought he had made a fair point.

"Tell me, Sir," said the professor, "what are *you* here to study?"

"Creative nonfiction," Emmanuel said, recalling Rebecca's area of focus.

About a quarter of the students nodded their heads. The rest would study poetry, fiction, or general literature.

"And what is *that?*" returned the professor.

Lucy thought it odd that the professor looked above, and not at, Emmanuel's eyes. She also thought it odd that the professor, in a striped puffy dress, wore a button with no words or image on it.

"It is when you write about something true using fiction techniques," said Emmanuel, recalling more of what Rebecca had explained. "You know, like compressed time, compressed dialogue, and drama."

"And what is *true?*"

"What is true?" repeated Emmanuel.

"Do you know what is true? Does anyone know? How can anyone know that they know that they know? How can anyone distinguish fiction from nonfiction? Nonfiction is merely a western concept designed by rich white males whose phalocentric, self-referential narrative voice seeks to subjugate . . ."

The students looked to the young professor, then to Emmanuel.

Lucy looked to Emmanuel.

Rebecca wondered about the academic program she had signed up for. Whatever the professor was talking about had not been mentioned in the university catalogue; she wondered if the omission reflected the English department's inability to use language to transmit information.

"Look," Emmanuel said, standing up. "You have a five-hundred-foot-high godzilla-like monster marching down Fifth Avenue in Manhattan.

"Bamm! Bamm!" Emmanuel bellowed, sweeping his long powerful arms in opposing arcs. "The monster knocks down buildings, thousands die, millions flee. Did it happen? If it did, we call it nonfiction. If not, we call it fiction."

The students, including Rebecca, nodded their heads.

"That is the only situation where one may draw such an artifice!" cried the professor. "And what did *you* study as an undergraduate—*biology?*"

Emmanuel pressed his lips into an O.

The students watched the curl of the lip on the professor's face. They understood that to get through the graduate program and meet their career goals, they would have to get past this snarling lioness.

Emmanuel froze. He seemed incapable of answering. He felt a dryness in the back of his throat.

"Okay everybody," said Lucy, standing up. "He didn't study biology—I did! And, did'ya all know that *the ability of humans to perceive the world continues to be shaped by biological evolution?*"

The students gasped.

"I also studied *chemistry* and *physics!*" she exclaimed.

The class groaned.

"Plus, I've read E. O. Wilson's *Consilience: The Unity of Knowledge* cover to cover!"

Three students shrieked.

"Ignore them," the professor shouted, trying to regain control. "*We* are the humanities; *they* cannot touch us—nor can their words. *They* represent science and rocks and male phalo-gender-pleni-potentiaryistic hardness, replenishing gaps between stated and alluded to non-metaphoristisized meaning bonds. The self-referential Derridarian ploy of nonlinguistic intercourse proves, through the power struggles of the Euroneuro-phallically challenged, that *there can exist no meaningful communication . . .*"

"Someone just farted!" Lucy announced, and all hell broke loose.

— 29 —

Emmanuel and Lucy walked swiftly from the University of Pittsburgh campus to the car. They did not look back.

"We're outa here, dude," Lucy said, wiping the sweat from her forehead.

Emmanuel thought about the orientation and the commotion he had caused. Once again he had failed.

Lucy noticed Emmanuel's pout. She noticed that he was looking at the ground.

"You, my friend, were magnificent," she said, holding his gaze and taking his hand. "When we're done with the journey, you need to continue your studies. Dig? Today you receive an A for creativity, an A for discernment, and an A+ for independent thinking. You are *university material*."

As her words penetrated Emmanuel's several-week-old crisis in self-confidence, tears welled and she appeared to swim toward him through the salty water. They hugged, and his entire body tingled, until they heard a loud, abrupt announcement.

"SURE I LOVE YOU!"

Lucy spun around and saw the cell phone user. She folded the fingers of her right hand while extending the thumb and pinky. She raised the hand so the thumb touched her right ear.

"*HELLO!*" she shouted into her pinky. "I CAN'T *HEAR* YOU! I LOVE YOU SO MUCH I COULD *PLOTZ! HELLO?* I . . . HELLO? MY CELL PHONE IS . . . *HELLO?* I CAN'T *HEAR* YOU! I LOVE YOU DARLING, I LOVE YOU I LOVE YOU I LOVE YOU! *HELLO*? I AM RIGHT HERE . . . *HELLO?* . . . I AM WALKING . . . *HELLO?* . . . I AM BREATHING . . . *HELLO?*"

The cell phone user glared at Lucy, looked around sheepishly, and continued the conversation in a hushed voice.

Lucy gave him a curt nod and turned to Emmanuel. "Did you know I'm a CPA?"

"A certified public accountant?" he asked.

"No—a cell phone activist."

"What is that?"

"Cell phone users have become more than a nuisance—they've taken over the global airwaves in cities, airports, supermarkets, classrooms, bathrooms, and remote sites in nature. You can't get away from them! Well it's time to stand up for our rights and *take back the airwaves!* It's time to cut out the noise, draw a line between what is public and what is private, and create a world where one can hear silence and do some thinking! We're not going to take it anymore! Join the movement! Be a cell phone activist! Be a CPA!"

"Uh, what should we do?"

"It's simple. When someone is being obnoxious with their cell phone, just pick up your hand—or a stick or banana—and talk into it: "*HELLO!* I CAN'T *HEAR* YOU!" And make up an absurd conversation about completely embarrassing, private things and broadcast it *loudly!* No matter how absurd your make-believe conversation is, it probably won't be as foolish or taboo as the cell phone user's actual conversation."

Lucy scowled at the approaching group of people. Each of them spoke loudly into their respective cell phones.

"I can see it gets worse as we approach the East Coast," Lucy whispered, sizing them up.

"*HELLO?*" the first person shouted into their cell phone.

"*HELLO?*" Lucy shouted into her hand. "I CAN'T *HEAR* YOU—SOMEONE NEARBY IS TALKING ON THEIR CELL PHONE!"

"*HELLO?*" the second person continued. "BAD CONNECTION."

"HANG UP AND DIAL AGAIN!" suggested Lucy.

"OKAY!" the third person shouted and pressed direct dial.

"*HELLO?*" they all shouted, in unison.

"I'M AT THE SUPERMARKET, DARLING," Lucy shouted back. "SHOULD I BUY ONE OR TWO PLY?"

One of the cell phone users noticed and hung up.

"SCENTED OR UNSCENTED?" Lucy continued. "AND BY THE WAY, MY SWEETEST HONEY DARLING, I'M PICKING UP A *MASSIVE* CARTON OF TAMPONS; I CAN FEEL RIGHT AT THIS MOMENT, THIS BLESSED SPECIAL MOMENT, ONE MISSISSIPPI RIVER TORRENT OF A *PERIOD* COMING ON!"

The cell phone users had hung up by now and were scrambling to get away from her.

Lucy followed them. "AND I THINK I'LL PICK UP A FEW BOXES OF IMMODIUM A/D, MY SUGAR HONEY PIE, BECAUSE I GOT A BAD STINKING CASE OF THE SHITS! *HELLO?* ARE YOU THERE? IT'S A TERRIBLE CONNECTION. YES, I SAID THE *SHITS!* I'M TALKING ABOUT A VERITABLE FOUNTAIN, MY SOFT AND CUDDLY SMOOODGINS TEDDY BEAR, A FULL-FLEDGED TOWERING *GEYSER* OF SHIT!"

By now the users had dispersed.

Lucy put down her hand and said, "Click."

— 30 —

"Are we going to a conference in Montreal?" Emmanuel asked Lucy, as they sped north through New York toward Canada.

"Yes," she replied, recalling what she had researched on the Internet. "It's entitled: What Is a Species."

Soothed by the rush of warm air on his face, Emmanuel relaxed in the passenger's seat. It was late at night and he dozed off.

Bright lights shone in his eyes; he blinked a few times and looked around. He noticed they were stopped at the international border.

"Bon soir!" said the broad-shouldered man at the Customs checkpoint.

"Howdy, m'seur," replied Lucy.

"U.S. citizen?"

"Born on the fourth of July!" Lucy beamed.

The official nodded and returned her passport. "And m'seur?"

"Originally from East Timor," Emmanuel said meekly. "But I live in Washington."

"How long will you be staying in Canada?"

Emmanuel thought the official looked like Father.

"A few days," Lucy answered for him. "We're going to a conference."

"I'm sorry," said the Customs official, sizing up Emmanuel, "but we're looking for a point-two GMP and . . ."

"A what?"

"A Genetically Modified Person who is 0.2 percent not human. They're used in terrorist cells, m'seur, surely you read the news. Now please get out of the car."

"But . . ."

"It will only take a moment. Stand here—that's right—and jump to the bar. Good! Now swing from it. C'est bon! Now catch the banana and peel it while you're hanging. Stop! Stay right there and don't move! Pierre come quickly with the gene chip!"

Lucy touched Emmanuel. "Wake up, friend," she said, massaging his shoulder with one hand.

Emmanuel looked around.

"We're seventy miles south of the border," said Lucy. "Nightmare?"

"Yes."

Lucy's approach to physical or psychological pain was to not dwell on it, and she thought it best to change the subject. "I've been thinking about the writing program in Pittsburgh," she mused. "The department had been infested by an extreme form of deconstructionism."

"What is that?"

"The philosophy you had questioned during Rebecca's orientation.

Deconstructionists often claim that there's no such thing as good writing, that there's no difference between fiction and science, and that language mostly fails as a tool for communication."

Emmanuel looked wistfully out the window. "Language may not be perfect, but it is useful. I would not want to lose the genes for human language."

"Nor would I," said Lucy. "If deconstructionists lost the ability to use sophisticated human language and were transported en mass to a harsh, demanding environment, I wonder how many of them would survive."

Emmanuel, nervous about which of his genes had been altered, slouched in the seat and touched his throat. "Maybe . . . Maybe there is a problem here. Maybe not all the human genes are here and . . ."

"I can assure you," said Lucy, "your speech-controlling genes are fully intact. I'll tell you what: I'll give you two language tests. Okay? Ready?"

"Ready," he said, sitting up straight.

"Imagine you're a monkey who, on occasion, needs to communicate the presence of danger to other monkeys. Imagine there's the danger of snakes and of predatory birds. How do you go about signaling the danger?"

"Uh," said Emmanuel, "the monkey should have two different sounds: one for the snake and one for the bird."

"Why?"

"Each danger needs a different response."

"And would death come swiftly if you didn't master the rudimentary form of language that you're now describing?"

"It could."

"You've passed the first test—you're an animal!"

"What is the next test?" he asked nervously.

"Imagine that you and your prehistoric friend, Nork, are horribly hungry and you happen to be standing, with hunting tools in hand, by a herd of deer. Imagine that you had noticed—without Nork noticing—one lovely lady swimming naked in the lake nearby. What would you do?"

"That is easy," said Emmanuel, smiling. "Tell Nork to sneak up behind the deer. Tell him to shout and to try and direct the deer toward a place we agree on. After the deer are caught, tell Nork to go home the long way, *away* from the lake, because of sounds you heard from an angry mother bear. Say good-bye to Nork. Bring dinner to the lady of the lake."

"Could you communicate all that using an absolutely bare-bone language and syntax?"

"Probably not," admitted Emmanuel.

"Brilliant!" exclaimed Lucy. "You pass—you're a manimal!"

"A what?"

"A *manimal,*" explained Lucy, "is an animal that is largely human. Now keep in mind that animals *do* use language—some even use simple syntax—but only manimals and humans convey vast quantities of abstract information with precision. By the way, there's a hitch with the story of Nork and the lady of the lake."

"What is that?"

"Prehistoric gals weren't lounging around while the guys were out hunting for food. In fact, the gals tended to provide the bulk of the food."

Emmanuel did not respond. He was picturing Nork and the lady of the lake.

Lucy noticed that Emmanuel seemed physically and mentally relaxed. He certainly wasn't fidgeting. He seemed to enjoy the discussion and the mental workout and it was a relief to see him lifted out of despair.

"Guess what the opposite of deconstructionism is," he asked, grinning.

"Huh?"

"Guess!"

"Constructionism?"

Emmanuel grinned. "*Cellphonism.*"

"What are you talking about?"

"Deconstruction kills communication but cellphonism—extreme cell phone use—does the opposite."

Lucy slapped his knee hard and his foot responded by kicking forward. "By golly!" she exclaimed, "you're one heck of a smart gorilla! And why do you suppose cell phones are becoming so popular while deconstructionism is headed for the garbage heap of academic fads?"

"Why?"

"One reason is that humans love to talk. Scientists call us babbling apes for good reason: *babbling is what we do best.*"

"You make it sound negative," said Emmanuel.

"Not necessarily," replied Lucy. "Some scientists think our babbling is an important part of the way humans create and maintain social bonds, similar to the way nonhuman apes groom one another. My problem with cell phones is not their use but their abuse."

"If cell phone users had some manners, would you still be against them?"

Lucy regarded the question. "Babbling," she conceded, "is better than the destruction of communication."

She took a deep, slow breath. She was no longer smiling. "Let me tell you a story," she said. "Once upon a time a professor moved from Europe to the United States where he got a job teaching at Yale University. From Yale, he spread deconstructionism, a philosophy in which words have no meaning, communication largely doesn't work, and objective reality doesn't exist. One day it was discovered that the professor had kept a secret—he had never shared the fact that, back in Europe, he had been an outspoken Nazi supporter."

"Is the story true?" asked Emmanuel.

"It is," she replied, frowning. "The professor's name is Paul de Mann. *He* brought deconstructionism to the United States."

"What happened?"

"Some claimed that the words used to expose him have no meaning, that communication hardly works, and that objective reality doesn't exist. Others followed a different path."

"What path was that?"

"They spoke openly about history and they used language to communicate danger."

Emmanuel looked up and squinted at distant lights. "We are approaching the border," he said.

— 31 —

Camped with Lucy by a lonely stretch of wooded road, Emmanuel stayed up late listening to the crickets and thinking about his parents. He was now in Canada, and soon he would be in Africa, yet his parents had no idea where he was or where he was going. He thought of Africa as a dangerous place and he felt certain his parents would worry about him if they knew more about his plans. He knew that he could not tell them. He had to lie to protect them, but the lie did not come easily. His parents had loved and cared for him; they had taught him by example to be open and honest. He missed them, he missed his sisters, and he wondered what had been for dinner tonight. But he had to leave the comfort and safety of their nest and the comfort and safety of the university; he had to go to the jungles of Africa to discover who he really was. If harm came to him he hoped they would understand. He loved them and he would always love them and he did not mean to hurt or disrespect them.

He sighed. Twenty minutes later, he fell asleep.

The following day, Emmanuel and Lucy drove to McGill University, Montreal, where they used the public-access computer terminals to check their e-mails.

Emmanuel recalled a dream from the previous night.

"What is wrong, Maria?"

"It is Emmanuel. He rarely writes and does not call us back."

"The housemates say he is studying or traveling."

"Yes, but . . ."

"He is a good son. We must give him the freedom to discover for himself who he is and who he is not."

"Yes, of course. Good night, dear."

"Good night."

Emmanuel began to compose an e-mail to Father. It had only been a dream but somehow it felt real and he felt grateful for his parents' unconditional love. He wanted to tell them the truth; he wanted to ask them for help. Fighting back the tears, he wrote:

subject: Seattle is nice

Dear Father,

Seattle is nice. I am staying with a friend and studying on my own. I may take a summer course, I am not sure. Thank you for the v-mail, it is good to hear your voice. I am glad everyone is well.

Your son,

Emmanuel

He sent the e-mail, hardened his stomach, and told himself that his parents were only part of his family and that his home was as much the jungle as it was Washington DC.

Lucy sat across the room from Emmanuel and read an e-mail from one of her housemates:

subject: Hi Lucy

There's a bunch of letters and bills here for you, plus a large package for Emmanuel. What to do?

-claire

Lucy responded:

> subject: Re: Hi Lucy
>
> yo Claire! Send it all and address like this: "Hold for Lucy Huxley, Hotel Heureux Singe, 723 Pikine Rue 15, Sendou Plage Bargny, Dakar, Senegal, Africa"
>
> thankx!
>
> -lucy

She then e-mailed the hotel in Senegal and told them she'd soon make a reservation and could they keep a lookout for a package addressed to her. As she typed, she heard three students talking nearby.

"They're at it again, eh Goddess?"

"They have all those guns," replied the Goddess.

"Guns and bombs," said Dave. "What's that aboot?"

"Their dream is to dominate, eh?" said Vilno.

Lucy assumed they were criticizing a right-wing paramilitary group. When it became clear they were criticizing the United States, she stood up and faced them. "Yarrrrrrr," she growled at the one they called the Goddess, "you're talking about *my country!*"

"Ahhh," replied the Goddess, whose soft brown hair framed her expression of concern. "Oui."

"Why?" demanded Lucy, looking up at her.

"Talking about your country is what we Canadians do best. Besides, it's the truth, eh?"

As Lucy defended the United States, she had to acknowledge the irony of the situation.

"Usually *I'm* the one critical of the U.S. government," she admitted. "But it makes me uncomfortable when outsiders agree with me."

When the conversation turned to Canadian and U.S. cultural difference, Lucy wagged her finger at them and said, "You know what? You Canadians are too nice. That's your problem."

"We were weaned on Queen Victoria's transatlantic tit," explained Dave, who towered over Lucy like a bear, "so we were kind of taken care of. We don't have such an independent, violent streak and we believe in the potential goodness of government."

"You've got to be joking," said Lucy incredulously.

"Another difference," said Vilno, who looked to Lucy like the Superman comic character, "is the sense of entitlement. The entire world knows that the United States—love it though we do—is like a big spoiled child."

"While we have a common European heritage," agreed the Goddess, "you could almost say we've evolved into two separate creatures, and yet each nation has competing subcultures, eh, many of which have more in common with *distant* neighbors than local ones."

"That's right," said Dave. "Each country is composed of many nations, culturally and economically speaking."

"Which explains," Lucy extrapolated, "why our peace-loving, tree-huggers are probably more numerous than the entire population of Canada and a few European countries put together. In other words, *many of us agree with you.*"

Vilno smiled. "We know that you do, and we appreciate you saying that."

The tension in Lucy's chest eased. "Shoot me dead but I've got to ask: why are you called the Goddess?"

The Goddess blushed. "It wasn't my idea."

Dave explained. "She has traveled the world living among the poor, giving much, asking for little, not calling attention to herself, without pretensions of greatness."

There was a silence.

Finally the Goddess spoke. "We'll work it out, eh? We're all human."

"Yes," Lucy replied, glancing at Emmanuel, "of course."

Lucy shook hands with the Canadians and fetched Emmanuel.

"Let's go!" Lucy said to Emmanuel, who hesitated as he logged off the computer (Meecha, he had just learned, would not be visiting Montreal anytime soon).

They left the room and walked down the steep hill on Peel Street.

"I'm awfully glad I didn't ask those students the million dollar question," Lucy confessed.

"What question is that?"

"Why they raise their voice at the end of their sentences, even when they're not asking a question."

"Maybe they feel more comfortable asking than telling?" Emmanuel mused. "Or maybe, because of the English and French language wars going on here, people are not so confident."

Lucy, keenly aware of her inclination to step on other people's toes, felt pleased she had not commented on their speech patterns. "*C'est bon,*" she said, smiling as they made their way toward lower campus.

"I did not know you speak French," Emmanuel said.

"*Un peut.* A little. It will be useful in West Africa."

Emmanuel nodded. "Say something in French."

"*Vous êtes mon petit chimpanzee!*"

"Very nice," he said as they climbed the steps to the Redpath Museum where the conference would soon begin. "But with French, I wonder how to tell where one word ends and the other begins."

Inside the museum they walked past skulls and whale bones into a half-circle shaped auditorium with a high ceiling and high wooden benches, where the smell reminded Emmanuel of the old musty Bible in the attic.

It was not difficult in the odd-shaped room for Lucy to imagine monks and masters of science seated in the hard wooden pews, scribbling on scrolls with quill pens.

Emmanuel and Lucy took seats.

A tall man approached sporting a cape and ponytail.

"What are you doing here?" the man asked, speaking quickly.

"I thought the conference was open to the public," countered Lucy.

"I mean in the bigger sense," the man replied.

"Whudd-a-you kidding?" Lucy said, hiding a smile.

"I'm Thurstian."

"And I'm Lucy and here be Emmanuel—won't you sit with us?"

Thurstian gave a low bow and kissed Lucy's hand. "A pleasure."

"He's dashing," said Lucy to Emmanuel.

"Lovely," said Emmanuel.

"Shhhhhh," scolded Thurstian, "the conference is ready to begin!"

While much of the material from the talks went over Emmanuel's head, he nonetheless listened closely.

During an intermission, he wondered aloud about the definition of a species.

"It is a group," explained Thurstian, "whose members can successfully reproduce with individuals from the same group, and whose members can't successfully reproduce with individuals from another group."

"That is Dr. Barr's definition?"

"Correct."

"And Dr. Jean-Danse?"

"According to him, Dr. Barr's definition is not verifiable, nor is it universally valid."

Emmanuel wondered if Jean-Danse's critique had scientific merit.

"Yes," said Thurstian emphatically.

This made Emmanuel feel hopeful. The species concept had inserted a wedge between him and humanity and between him and God, and he welcomed alternative definitions. If it could be said that there was no such thing as a species, he would feel less abandoned and less alone.

Lucy considered the scientists' arguments and wondered if perhaps Jean-Danse was right. After all, she reasoned, how could one verify the accuracy of any species classification using Barr's definition? The offspring producing pairs for the species in question might be spread out across an ocean. How could one test each offspring to see if, eventually, *they* produced healthy offspring? No way! No *way* could such a test be done for one species, no less each of the millions of species! And what about the individuals on the verge of forming new species? Where do *they* fit in the definition? And what about bacteria? They exchange their DNA with other bacteria just by going for a stroll in their little bacterial neighborhoods, as it were. Certainly, it makes no sense to say that *all* bacteria form a single species. And what about the countless forms of life that don't reproduce sexually? So maybe Jean-Danse *was* right. Maybe the species concept primarily exists as an abstraction in the minds of humans and not as a reality in nature.

But maybe, Lucy acknowledged, Dr. Barr is also right. An overwhelming number of large creatures fit the traditional definition: they can successfully reproduce with *some* individuals but not with others, and members of such a reproductive unit, whether verifiable by humans or not, do in fact share genes, behaviors, isolating mechanisms, and history. So why not label such a unit as a unit even if the label is not perfect? And wouldn't conservationists say that despite its imperfections, a species definition is needed so that biodiversity can be labeled, studied, described, and protected? If a population is divided for a million years or more, gene flow between subpopulations *will* eventually cease. And the concept of speciation, central to the Barr definition, is more than an abstraction in the minds of humans. It's an actual process found in habitats the world over.

Later on, Thurstian led Lucy and Emmanuel to one of the refreshment tables and introduced them to Dr. Jean-Danse.

Lucy said, "I agree with you but I also think it's important to have a way to refer to what's out there."

Dr. Jean-Danse smiled. "It's fine to refer to populations as species," he said, "as long as you know the limitations of the definition."

Recalling the deconstructionists in Pittsburgh, Lucy felt relieved that this curly-haired professor with round-rimmed glasses seemed to be reasonable.

"There are several paradigms through which a taxonomist may define a group," said Dr. Jean-Danse. "Each has its pros and cons.

The policy people don't always get this—they get nervous—but the scientists already know it."

Emmanuel felt heartened. "Why not have an identification book with different sections for each way to look at species?"

"That," said Jean-Danse, "is a creative idea. Perhaps such a concept will be possible to implement over the Internet."

During the next set of talks, Lucy considered the species concept and how it might affect Emmanuel. Perhaps it mattered less what he was than what he believed in. It dawned on her that, belief aside, the truth behind Emmanuel's creation *could* very likely be determined based on molecular evidence. By extracting a few of his cells, it should be technically feasible to determine what percentage of his genes were human and what percentage were not. This was not rocket science, nor was it science fiction; it was everyday work for technicians, such as Thurstian, at genetic laboratories around the world.

She had another, more radical, idea and said "Ooooh!" a few times, softly, to herself.

After the talks sandwiches were served, and Emmanuel foraged at the tables as if he had not eaten in days.

When the crowds thinned, Dr. Barr—distinguished scientist, host of the COSEWIC conference, and museum director—championed the cleanup.

Lucy, Emmanuel, and Thurstian offered to help.

Lucy and Thurstian moved tables while Emmanuel and Dr. Barr—recognizable by the touch of gray, the conservative waistcoat, and near-perfect posture—looked for a roll of black plastic garbage bags.

Perhaps it was the dim lighting or perhaps it was a defective roll of bags but, at first, Barr could not find the perforations. He tried pulling the bags apart but that didn't work either.

"Maybe the bags are like species," Emmanuel offered, "and it is not always possible to tell where one starts and another ends."

Barr painstakingly examined the bags until he detected a subtle perforation. "You *can* tell," he said, separating the plastic and handing the clump to Emmanuel. "But sometimes you have to look hard for the break."

Emmanuel noticed, but did not mention, that the eminent biologist had handed him two plastic bags.

— 32 —

Two days after leaving Montreal for Manhattan, Emmanuel felt unnerved at the thought of meeting someone even more famous than Dr. Barr and, so, he suggested that Lucy go ahead without him, which she did. She approached EO, her name for Dr. Edward O. Wilson, a Harvard professor whose ideas on the biological basis of human and animal societies, on principles of ecology, and on the interconnectedness of knowledge placed him among the most influential scientists of his time. Dr. Wilson stood in the aisle, toward the front of the auditorium in the American Museum of Natural History in New York City.

A line of luminaries had already formed, attracted to Wilson like ants to a dollop of honey, and Lucy waited in line, thumping her foot impatiently as Wilson had a word with the director of the National Science Foundation. After fifteen minutes, it was Lucy's turn.

"Hi, Dr. Wilson!" she said. "I wanted to thank you; I'm writing a story and your books inspire me *big time!*"

"It is kind of you to say so," he replied, tilting his head to one side and squinting at her as if he were studying an insect. "What are you writing about?"

"It's the story of creation, of Genesis, told from the biological point of view. You see, in real life I have a friend who discovered—or believes he discovered—that his chromosomes contain nonhuman primate genes, though he doesn't know which ones or how many. Before the so-called discovery, my friend had loved and depended on the Bible, but he now believes that he's not fully human and, therefore, old Bible stories no longer apply to him."

Dr. Wilson looked across the aisle and observed the long armed young man scratching himself. "I see," he said.

"Whether or not the discovery has merit," Lucy continued, "my friend needs to know what he is, how he came to be, and where in the living world he belongs. He needs for the knowledge to resonate with what, genetically speaking, he has evolved to accept. I'm afraid that 'just the facts' will not suffice."

"As you embark on this project for your friend," Wilson said, "and as your research unfolds, you may wish to consider what *you* are, how *you* came to be, and where in the tree of life *you* belong."

Lucy nodded.

"Stories can be powerful," said Wilson. "Write me if you have questions about the science."

The biologist looked at his watch. "Now if you'll excuse me," he said.

As Wilson ambled toward the stage, Lucy returned to her seat and recalled a passage from one of his books: "People need a sacred narrative . . . if the sacred narrative cannot be in the form of a religious cosmology, it will be taken from the material history of the universe . . . " The passage made her think about her writing project for Emmanuel. She hoped that someday what she was writing would comfort Emmanuel, and now she wondered if it might comfort others as well.

"What was EO like?" Emmanuel asked.

"Don't be fooled by his mild-mannered demeanor," she said. "He's a *dynamo!*"

The auditorium became quiet as Dr. Wilson, keynote speaker for the Assembling the Tree of Life symposium, took his place behind the podium.

"There exists on earth an estimated 10 to 100 million species," he began, the white wave of his hair shining in the spotlight, "and yet only about 1.75 million species have been discovered. If we create a global census of earth's species, imagine what new phenomenon will come to light! Imagine what the new data will teach us! Biology is the only scientific field whose subject is vanishing and now is the time for the scientific community to discover and study the millions of unnamed, uncategorized forms of life before they forever disappear. Now is the time for our government and for governments around the world to support such a project and to fund it as though we were sending a man to the moon. Let us embark on such a quest, let us create a freely accessible all-species encyclopedia—*let us discover the tree of life!*"

Spellbound by the talk, Lucy longed to join the taxonomic quest.

Emmanuel listened closely to Wilson and tried to keep his fears of Africa—he would arrive there in two days—from puncturing his curiosity about life forms other than himself.

Later on during the lunch break, Lucy felt drawn to the human biology and evolution exhibits, but as they entered the hall, she worried that these displays of naked, primitive-looking hybrids might feed Emmanuel's fears.

"Let's explore TOL," she announced, turning around.

"What is TOL?" Emmanuel asked.

"It stands for the tree of life."

"Is it an actual tree?" he asked as they meandered past the North American Forests exhibit.

"No—it's a way to describe life on earth. More to the point, it's a way to describe the interconnectedness of all living things."

"Each living thing is related to every other living thing?"

"Yes!"

"Are you sure? How are butterflies related to great apes?"

"In the same way they are related to humans."

"How is that?"

"Through a common ancestor!"

"I do not understand."

She took his hand and led him to a vast room—teeming with people, displays, and large trees in a re-created rain forest—called the Hall of Biodiversity.

"Let me explain. You and your sisters share a common ancestor—your parents. You can trace your lineage back in time to your mom and dad, as can each of your sisters. So far so good?"

"So far."

"Imagine you could go back in time to when your parents were young. Imagine asking: *who will join me?*"

"My sisters would join me?"

"That's right. They would join you because you are joined or related to them, genetically speaking, through a common ancestor: your parents. Now go back another generation in your imagination, to when your grandparents were young, and ask: *who will join me?*"

"My first cousins would join me?"

"Good. Notice that you are more closely related to your sisters than to your first cousins because you share a more recent common ancestor with your sisters. Now go back another generation and ask: *who will join me?*"

"Second cousins."

"And again."

"Third cousins."

"Imagine going back in time millions of years and now ask: *who will join me?*"

"It would be my cousins *many* times removed," guessed Emmanuel.

"Brilliant! Now imagine that you're a chimpanzee and I'm a human."

Emmanuel sighed. "Rub it in."

"Imagine that we've not yet gone back in time. Imagine that it is now, today. Imagine that you, a chimp, and I, a human, are sitting on the top of the tree of life. Since we're not the same type of creature—for instance, your canine teeth would be much larger than mine—we're sitting on different branches of the tree."

Lucy stepped away from Emmanuel.

"We're on separate branches," she continued, "but notice we're not so far apart either. Now let's start to climb, in our imaginations, down from the top branches of the tree of life."

"What does it mean to climb down the tree of life?"

"It means we're going back in time. Now imagine that you—a chimp—go back in time 5 or 6 or so million years. Imagine asking: *who will join me?*"

"All humans who have ever lived?" asked Emmanuel.

"That's right!" Lucy exclaimed, stepping toward him.

"Do you know what that makes chimps and humans?"

"Distant cousins?"

"You're a genius!"

"But wait," said Emmanuel. "Forget the chimps a minute. What if you take a human from Asia and a human from Africa and a human from Australia? Could you do the same thing?"

"You could. You could go back in time, down the branches of the great tree of life and eventually you would find the common ancestor for the three humans. How far back you'd need to go would depend on which three humans you selected. That said, you wouldn't have to go far back to find the common ancestor for *all* living humans."

"How far back would you have to go?"

"Some scientists and statisticians suggest roughly three thousand years."

"Do you mean if you go back around three thousand years, you might find the ancestor to all living humans?"

"Yep."

"So, because of a common ancestor from around three thousand years ago, all living humans are related as close, and not-so-close, cousins."

Lucy beamed. "The understanding is that we're all hundredth cousins or closer, give or take a few."

"And because of a common ancestor from around 5 or 6 million years ago," he continued, "all humans and chimps are related. *All humans and chimps are distant cousins.*"

"Yes! Now let's climb further back in time, farther down the tree of life, to roughly 7 million years ago."

"*Who will join me?*" chimed Emmanuel.

"All gorillas who have ever lived!" replied Lucy.

"Gorillas and chimps and humans are cousins!" he said excitedly.

"Let's climb down to roughly 14 million years."

"*Who will join me?*"

"All orang utans who have ever lived!"

Emmanuel felt special. He was not so far removed from humans after all.

"Let's climb down to roughly 40 million years."

"*Who will join me?*"

"All New World monkeys who have ever lived!"

"New World?"

"The ones found in South America. Let's climb down to roughly 63 million years."

"*Who will join me?*"

"All primates who have ever lived! Incidentally, the classification of primates includes humans and chimps! Let's climb down to roughly 105 million years."

"*Who will join me?*"

"All mammals who have ever lived!"

"It is incredible," said Emmanuel, "that all mammals are related to one another because their—because *our*—common ancestor lived about 105 million years ago!"

"It's incredible and true. Hmmm . . . actually, that would be for placental mammals, and apparently the ancestor was a furry nocturnal shrewlike creature. Pretty wild! Anyway, let's continue. Let's climb down to roughly 310 million years."

"*Who will join me?*"

"All dinosaurs who have ever lived!"

"But dinosaurs are extinct!"

"True, but roughly 310 million years ago all dinosaurs that have ever lived shared an ancestor with all humans and apes who have ever lived."

"What did the common ancestor to all dinosaurs and apes look like?"

"I wish I knew! Let's climb down to roughly 445 million years."

"*Who will join me?*"

"All horseshoe crabs who have ever lived."

Lucy reached into her pocket, gripped the flat rock, and showed it to him.

"Wow—it looks like a fossil!"

"It seems to be ancient artwork of a distant relative. Now let's really take a leap back in time. Let's climb down to roughly 1,300 million years."

"*Who will join me?*"

"All plants!"

"Plants? Chimps are related to plants?"

"Yes and so are humans! But don't hold me to the 1,300 million years. The numbers get *very* shaky when you go so far back in time."

"It is hard to imagine something so old."

"Yea, well, we higher primates aren't particularly good at picturing deep time. We can continue to climb down, *way* down, and we'd be joined, eventually, by all archaea, simple single cells found in acid or extreme temperatures and pressures, such as near hydrothermal vents, at the bottom of the sea. We'd also be joined, eventually, by all bacteria. Bacteria are tricky! There's a heck of a lot we don't know about them. We do know that without bacteria, most life on earth would rapidly cease to exist."

"I had no idea. I wonder if there is a way to thank them."

Lucy agreed. "Perhaps we should create Bacteria Appreciation Day as a national holiday!"

"So," summarized Emmanuel, "all forms of life, from simple cells to chimps, humans, elephants, trees, plants, whales, fish, and bugs—all forms of life are related."

"Yes! That said, there may exist a relatively simple form of life that emerged on its own and that isn't related to other forms of life. But that's unclear. People are still looking."

"What about . . ."

"Go on," she said. "Don't be shy!"

"Could we try climbing down *farther?*"

"Okay."

"*Who will join me?*" Emmanuel asked, cautiously.

"The replicators."

"What are they?"

"Molecules that, by their very nature, happen to encourage the creation of molecules identical to themselves."

"So *that* is what happened!"

"Yep!"

Emmanuel and Lucy held hands as they walked the Hall of Biodiversity and read the displays. Science had long fascinated Emmanuel but had been largely dismissed from the house of the Church, and he had not taken it seriously. Now he considered the story of biological creation, the story of TOL, with interest and need.

"What an honor it is," he told Lucy, "to share thousands of millions of years of history with the ancestors of humans."

"On the contrary," she replied, squeezing his long powerful fingers. "The honor is ours."

— 33 —

During a sermon by Father Forsyth, Evelyn pondered a question that had fascinated her since the trip to England: *could traces of spirituality, however small, be found in animals?* It was a difficult question, particularly as it wasn't clear to her what spiritual capacity in animals even meant. Could a chimpanzee, for instance, have a momentary, rudimentary perception of God? She was certain that a chimp could never perceive God in the ways that humans do, but she was less certain, given God's mysterious countenance, what billions of God's creatures could and couldn't grasp. Nor was it clear that an animal's glimpse of God, should that ever occur, implied spiritual capacity. To further cloud the issue, it was doubtful that humans could ever know an animal's heart or mind. Nonetheless, she sensed that the Church's position on the question, like its position from long ago on Galileo, would come back to haunt it.

She agreed with the Church that humans were created in God's image and likeness but, in contrast with the Church, she sensed that nonhuman primates reflect *some* of God's sacred visage. She agreed that humans have great capacity for spirituality, but she sensed that nonhuman primates have *some* spiritual capacity. She agreed that humans have a value of their own, but she sensed that nonhuman primates have *some* value of their own.

Evelyn wondered how long ago God had granted humans the capacity for spirituality. Had it been four million years ago? If so, would *Australopithecus afarensis, Homo habilis,* and *Homo erectus* have been included? Had it had been five hundred thousand years ago? If so, would Neanderthals have been included? She wondered if the capacity had appeared gradually, perhaps over hundreds of thousands of years, or if it had appeared instantaneously, perhaps in a hundredth or thousandth of a second.

She wondered, too, about the future. Evolution is a continuing process, she recalled from her recent readings in biology, and over long periods of time new species may arise from future human descendents. Which of these descendents, she questioned, will have spiritual capacity three million years from now? All of them? None of them? And what of the various populations of human hybrids three million years from now. Would they have *some* spiritual capacity?

These questions would make church elders uncomfortable, Evelyn realized, and perhaps would encourage them to discredit, directly or indirectly, the theory of evolution. But, she noted, there were dangers inherent in doing so. The theory of evolution was no ordinary theory, she was learning. Rather, it was the central organizing principle for modern biology. Nearly all legitimate scientists think that the evidence for it is overwhelming.

Nor did it seem a wise strategy for the Church to discount science. Doing so in the past, she worried, has lost us credibility and people tire of us being wrong.

It doesn't make sense for us to claim expertise in the physical world, she thought, looking up at Father Forsyth. Our expertise is in the realm of the infinite and the eternal, in the tremendous mystery beyond the physical world. *The infinite and the eternal ought be enough.* If we build airplanes without a system to understand engineering fundamentals, if we treat disease without a system to understand the microbes and their fast-changing ways, if we reach into areas we don't have the tools to understand, we're going to get called on it and it's going to hurt.

To Evelyn, the way forward seemed clear: the Church should fully accept and embrace the foundation of biological science. It should acknowledge that its acceptance of evolution through natural selection, like its acceptance of the force of gravity, in no way diminishes the power and profundity of God.

The Church should focus on its area of expertise and leave science to the scientists. Doing so, she noted, would protect it from humiliation and decreasing membership.

It seemed clear, too, that the Church should reexamine its belief that animals have no spiritual capacity whatsoever. If animals have some spiritual capacity, it hardly leaves humans with less and, besides, claiming the lion's share of God's blessings seemed like such an animal thing to do.

— 34 —

"Am I missing something?" asked Ernesto, scowling at the computer screen.

"What do you mean, dear?" replied Maria.

"Is Emmanuel purposely avoiding talking to us?"

Maria was silent.

"I feel like we're getting the run-around. Seattle is nice, everyone is nice, I'm glad everything is nice, but it would be nice to get to talk with my son."

"Yes, dear. He sounds very busy. I'm sure we'll talk with him soon."

Ernesto took a deep breath. "I hope so. Good night."

"Good night, dear."

— 35 —

After the Assembling the Tree of Life symposium in New York City, Emmanuel and Lucy dropped off the car in New Jersey and caught a flight to London. From there they took a bus to Oxford, where they walked along the River Thames until they no longer heard the sound of cars. Exhausted, they curled up beside one another and fell asleep.

Emmanuel stood by an ocean's edge. A cold wind swept the gray sky. The water receded and he followed the slope to the ocean floor. Horseshoe crabs and rotting fish littered the vast plain. The floor gradually rose and he followed the slope until he came upon a man in tattered clothes sitting in icy mud.

The man had bulging veins and a thick beard that hung like Spanish moss. He chanted, "SEESEEAYTEESEESEEJEE-AYJEE."

The vibrations hummed in Emmanuel's chest like a honey bee's buzz.

"Excuse me," said Emmanuel. "What are you saying?"

"The Word," said the man, "is your name and the Word is your story."

"What does it mean?"

"It means you are unique and there is no one in the world quite like you."

"I do not want to be alone."

"But you are truly, terribly alone, and if you survive the jungles of Africa, if you survive the meeting with your kin, the knowledge you'll have gained shall make matters worse indeed."

"Worse? How could things get worse?"

"How could things get worse?" Emmanuel asked. He woke, scribbled the dream in his journal, and looked up. Lucy pointed to a long flat boat.

"Look," she said. They watched the boat move, slowly and in spurts, powered by a bearded man at the stern, who pushed a pole against the river's bottom.

The British were tough, uncomplaining, and drawn to oddities unaffected by the forces of evolution, she explained to Emmanuel. They'd find comfort in backbreaking, inefficient transport.

But Emmanuel hardly listened. He imagined, instead, the boat pulling away with the man, precariously balanced above the river, clutching the pole. The images came easily because this was how he felt: stuck, precariously balanced, and left behind by the Church and by humanity.

"So monkey boy," Lucy said, interrupting Emmanuel's reverie. "Now that we're in England, are you ready to meet Dawkins?"

"Who is he?"

"Dr. Richard Dawkins, professor of zoology and evolutionary biology, is known as Darwin's rottweiler. This builds on the reputation of T. H. Huxley who, in the mid-1800s, had been known as Darwin's bulldog."

"What do Darwin's rottweilers and bulldogs do?"

"They defend Darwin's theory and rip competing ideas to shreds."

"And the theory is . . ."

"That life evolves by way of variation and natural selection. Dr. Dawkins will explain it to us; he's a wonderful bio-storyteller."

They walked to the university and searched for Dawkins, but he was out of town and would be traveling for several weeks, so they sat outside his office beneath a huge oak tree where Emmanuel picked, and ate bread crumbs from Lucy's sweater while Lucy entertained him with a story.

"Last year," she began, "I learned at a lecture that only 40 percent of North American adults believe in the theory of evolution, whereas in Great Britain *80* percent believe in it."

"Why the difference?"

"Hold that thought! So a week after the lecture, I was listening to a band at a coffeehouse when I got talking to the mom of a friend in the band. The talk drifted from music to churches to belief systems, and I mentioned the statistic from the lecture. You should have seen her expression! *She* had not evolved from a bunch of monkeys!"

"What happened?"

"Her son happened to overhear part of the conversation. 'It doesn't mean we evolved from monkeys, Mom,' he had pointed out. 'It just means that we share a common ancestor.'"

"Her son understands the tree of life?"

"Perhaps, though I'd imagine our common ancestor with Old World or New World monkeys would, by most observers, be called a monkey. But I've been thinking lately about the mom. She also has an understanding of a tree, a different tree no doubt, but . . . I wonder if there's a way to reconcile . . ."

Lucy wanted to tell Emmanuel that her writing project was an attempt at such a reconciliation, but she wanted the gift to be a surprise.

Meanwhile, unbeknownst to Emmanuel and Lucy, a young man had been observing them from a branch above. The man now leapt from the tree and landed beside Lucy.

"Sorry to interrupt the grooming session," said the man, "but I overheard you talking about Richard Dawkins."

Lucy glared at him. "Why heavens *yes!*" she declared. "We're creationists from the *U*-nited States and we *demand* to debate Dawkins on the BBC!"

The man blinked. He had black hair and a half-smile, half-frown.

"Actually," said Lucy, "Emmanuel and I want to learn about evolution; we're here to talk with Dr. Dawkins."

"Have you thought about reading one of Dawkins' books?" asked the man.

"We thought we'd start by *talking* with him," she said, unaware of her own tendency to be drawn to charismatic, older male academic types.

"Perhaps I can help; I am called Zann. I'm a student of zoology at Oxford, and I work for Richard Dawkins."

Lucy grinned. "I guess it makes sense that a zoology student would hang out in trees. Zann, Zann, the *monkey man!*"

"So," said Zann, "what would you like to learn?"

"How evolution works. I've read a bunch of books but don't feel I have a handle on it yet, and Emmanuel is somewhat new to the subject."

"Learning about evolution," said Zann, "is a bit like looking in a mirror; you might not like what you see."

Zann led them to a courtyard surrounded by high walls. At the far end rose a towering mound covered by trees and dense foliage.

"Now," said Zann, scanning the mound, "before the lesson begins, we need to choose a biological object, part of an animal or plant, that is explained by the theory of evolution."

"Like an eye?" asked Lucy.

"Everyone wants to do eyes," said Zann. "Let's choose something else, yeah?"

Zann stared at Emmanuel's hand, which seemed to hang unusually close to the grassy field.

"Let's explain hands," said Zann, leading them to the base of the mound.

"Can you explain hands," asked Emmanuel, "by saying that God created them exactly the way they are?"

"That sort of response," Zann pointed out, "explains the *what* but not the *how*. It's like asking: how does one remove a dangerous tumor, and the surgeon replies that God does all the work. Such a response might obscure significant and helpful information."

Zann stepped on to the gradual slope of the mound. "Studying and accepting the actual *mechanism* of creation," he said, "does not necessarily contradict belief in God."

Lucy took a step toward Zann.

"The mechanism of biological creation," Zann continued, "is about evolution through variation and natural selection, which provides a detailed, scientific explanation of how hands—and *all* bits of life—came about in stunning diversity."

"If variation is key to the theory of evolution," asked Lucy, "does that fly in the face of the belief that we're all the same and that we're all *one?*"

"It does, at least genetically speaking, but that's no reason to start feeling alone in the universe. On the contrary, we'd be a bit lonely *without* variation, because it's essential to the long-term survival of living things."

"Is it good to be different?" asked Emmanuel, stepping onto the gentle slope.

"Yes," said Zann, "and I will tell you a story that explains why this is so. But first, make up fictitious names for yourselves, and the names will be part of the story."

"My name is LucySmallerHands," said Lucy, imagining the way variation works. "And here be EmmanuelLongerHands."

"Pleased to meet you indeed," said Zann, shaking their hands. "Once upon a time there lived SallySameHands and SamSameHands. Due to a copy error in the genetic code of Sally's sex cells, their son—named LukeSlightlyLargerHands—carried Sally's dominant, altered gene in the DNA of each of his cells. DNA contains blueprints for building bodies, and in Luke's case the altered DNA built hands a bit larger than those of his parents. From time to time, Luke's larger hands helped him. For instance, he was better able to grasp a larger spear, which was useful for hunting and for protecting his wife, Renee. Luke and Renee had children, each of whom carried the mutation for slightly larger hands, and in each subsequent generation the larger hands proved to be somewhat useful. After many generations, Sally and Sam's descendents had noticeably longer hands than people in the general population."

Zann took Emmanuel by the hand. "You, EmmanuelLongerHands, are a descendent of Sally and Sam."

"You, LucySmallerHands, are also a descendent of Sally and Sam, though clearly you did not inherit the larger-hand variant from them."

Emmanuel spread his fingers. "How much variation is normal in a species?"

Zann did not reply. He looked worried.

"What's wrong?" asked Lucy.

"My cell phone is buzzing and it's only for emergencies."

Zann read the device and scanned the courtyard.

"What is it?"

"Shhhh! A tiger from the Oxford Zoo is loose and . . . *is heading our way.*"

Lucy bit her lip, bent her knees, and took a quick deep breath.

Emmanuel raised his eyebrows and sniffed the air. "Are you sure . . ."

"Shhhhhhhhhh!" said Zann. "The tiger escaped last month and ate a tourist *right on this mound!*"

"What should we do?"

"Split up! Run! Run as though your life depends on it—*it does!* We'll meet at the top; there's a structure up there we can hide in!"

"But which way is it?" Emmanuel whined.

"Oh dear—I can hear the tiger!" said Zann, forcefully pushing him into the dense trees and shrubs. "It will be here in just a bit—now *GO!*"

Zann pushed Lucy in a different direction. Then he climbed the steep stairs and sat on a bench. After a few minutes, he glanced at his watch.

Emmanuel and Lucy arrived, panting.

"Actually," admitted Zann calmly, "there's no tiger on the prowl. I made that bit up."

"You *lied* to us!" said Lucy angrily.

Zann pointed out that evolutionary processes, particularly those affecting large mammals, are difficult to grasp and that they would learn more if they exercised patience. He asked them to describe their ascent.

"I don't know why we should trust you," retorted Lucy, mumbling about his all-knowing British accent. She did trust Zann, in the way she would trust a schemer and rascal whose pranks intentionally benefit the greater good.

"Anyway," said Lucy, frowning, "it's ridiculous that we fell for your crazy story, but we did, probably because we're exhausted and somewhat sleep deprived, but what the hey. I was really scared. I ran like the dickens up the gradual slope until I came upon a tall wire fence and a gate blocking the path. A single wire ran along the top, which I assumed was electrified, so rather than hopping the fence I tried the gate. It was locked. My hand was shaking and I had the real sense I was about to be mauled but I managed to control myself enough to pick the lock with *this*."

Lucy showed the metal clip attached to a key ring. "Then I closed the gate behind me and followed the incline to the top."

Zann turned to Emmanuel.

"I was scared, too," he said. "I ran hard. Part way up, I had to swing."

"What do you mean you *had to swing?*" asked Lucy.

"There was no path on the ground and there were many bushes, and a tiger would have more trouble following me in a tree, so I took the path through the branches by swinging."

He pressed a bloodstained handkerchief to his wrist.

"What happened?" asked Lucy.

"I got cut."

"I apologize," said Zann, looking slightly remorseful. "I didn't mean for you to get hurt. But imagine, EmmanuelLongerHands and LucyShorterHands, that there *had* been a hungry tiger chasing you. Think about variation, natural selection, and the interplay between the two."

"What do you mean?" asked Lucy, forgetting the anger.

"You explain it to me," instructed Zann. "Define the bit on variation."

"One of us," replied Lucy, "has longer hands than the other."

"Right. Now define the bit on natural selection."

Lucy recalled her hike on Mount Rainier last month. "If the tiger ate me, my genes would not be selected, or passed on, because I don't have kids. Selection is based on successful reproduction."

"Right. Now define the interplay between variation and natural selection."

Emmanuel smiled. "In order to swing in trees to avoid tigers, it is useful to have strong hands and long fingers."

"In order to pick locks and avoid tigers," added Lucy, "it's useful to have small, dexterous hands."

"It was fortunate indeed that each of you took the paths that you did," said Zann, "but what would have happened had you switched? In other words, what would have happened if you, EmmanuelLongerHands, encountered the fence bit and if you, LucyShorterHands, encountered the jungle bit?"

Emmanuel and Lucy looked at each other.

"Lunchtime for tiger," said Lucy.

"Well said," said Zann. "The fence and jungle paths represent different environments. Some variations will do better in certain environments, whereas other variations will not."

"Is the process of evolution *random?*" Emmanuel asked slowly.

Zann reached in his pocket for a coin and threw it several feet above them. "Heads or tails?" he queried.

"Heads!" said Lucy.

"Tails!" said Emmanuel.

The coin struck the ground. Tails.

"*That's* random," said Zann. "Is the process of evolution random? Think back to when you were rushing up the mound. Imagine that you, EmmanuelLongerHands, and you, LucyShorterHands, were being chased by a *real* man-eating tiger and imagine that you both took the jungle path. Who would have been tiger food?"

"Lucy would have been," Emmanuel pointed out, "because shorter hands do not help with swinging through the trees."

"Right," said Zann, "and you, Emmanuel, would have fed the tiger on the fence path because longer hands don't help with picking locks. Evolution is based on a creature's ability to survive within a given environment. Is it random that creatures who are endowed with advantages end up surviving and reproducing? No. Is it random that creatures who are stuck with disadvantages end up getting eaten before reproducing? No. Is evolution random? No."

Emmanuel stared at the coin on the ground and pondered his ability to survive within the African jungle.

Zann offered to take them on a walking tour of Oxford. "Did you know that the great debate on evolution, between T. H. Huxley and Samuel Wilberforce, Bishop of Oxford, occurred near here?"

"Huxley," Emmanuel recalled, "was Darwin's bulldog?"

"That's right," said Zann. "Speaking of which, you might want to read Richard Dawkins' *Climbing Mount Improbable*. He's quite good at explaining things."

As they walked into town, Emmanuel unknowingly dropped the handkerchief with the dried blood on it, and Lucy picked it up with a tissue and stuffed it in a bag.

PART FOUR

Into the Forest

— 36 —

Lucy's nightmares and dizzy spells had begun a week ago, after she and Emmanuel had traveled from Oxford, England, to Senegal, West Africa. Now, drenched in sweat, she swatted a mosquito and missed. "Is it time to take the malaria medicine, isn't it?" she asked drowsily. She badly wanted to be able to take care of herself.

Emmanuel, who now felt protective of Lucy, studied her face. "We took it already," he said.

Crowds, cars, and bicycles sped across Lucy's vision. She focused her dilated pupils on a stationary vendor as a way to steady herself, but her legs grew wobbly and she started to fall.

Emmanuel quickly reached out, wrapped his arms around her, and carried her from the dusty street to an alley, where he placed her in the partial shade of a tree.

She sobbed quietly.

"You are going to be okay," Emmanuel said, holding her hand.

She shut her eyes. "It's like someone's humming in my brain," she whispered, hoarsely, squeezing his hand. "It's like a *drug* trip."

Emmanuel recalled the nurse's caveat back in Seattle about possible side effects from the preventative malaria medicine. It could, the nurse had warned, alter one's dreams, one's mental state, and one's nervous system. But if the medicine was the problem, then why had Lucy suffered no ill effects during the first two weeks of taking it? Perhaps, he hypothesized, it took time for the toxicity to build and for the body to react.

Emmanuel hailed a taxi and asked the driver to take them to a good hotel. During the ride, he looked out the window and noticed a woman helping an elderly man cross the road. He noticed a man supporting an elderly woman. He noticed other people helping one another, and suddenly the city seemed awash in hope and caring and he marveled at the beauty of it all until the taxi stopped by a cramped, red-tiled building.

Emmanuel carried Lucy from the taxi to the hotel room bed, ran to an Internet café, and e-mailed the travel clinic in Seattle. The subject of the message read: "HELP NEEDED NOW!"

The reply came forty-five minutes later: Lucy should immediately stop taking *that* drug and, instead, start taking doxycycline.

Emmanuel returned and explained to Lucy what had happened.

"Your body will cleanse itself," he assured her.

Her face looked pained. She twisted her mouth and tried to smile but ended up looking away. It was horrible being awake; it was worse when she slept.

The next day Lucy felt less dizzy. She sipped water and nibbled on the crackers Emmanuel had brought.

Emmanuel touched her forehead; she had no fever.

She reached for his hand, kissed it, and fell back asleep. This time the nightmares were gone.

Emmanuel returned to the café, e-mailed Father, and reflected on the journey. Though the first two weeks in North America and England had seemed like a blur of highways and airports, he felt pleased that he had learned so much in so little time. In contrast, the past week in Africa felt like a slog through warm, chest-deep molasses. Information seemed frustratingly slow to arrive. A ChimpCorps representative, for instance, was supposed to provide them with an assignment, but Lucy had grown so dizzy that she could not recall whom to meet or where.

The next morning, Lucy managed to whisper, "Kindly, if you please, won't you lift me and bear my wilting corpse to yonder bathroom?"

He bent down to lift and noticed the grin.

She pressed her nose against his and hugged him.

Her strength had started to return.

"Thanks for taking care of me!" she exclaimed, reaching for the sneakers.

"Where are we going?" asked Emmanuel, slipping on sandals.

"To forage," she said, sweeping the tangle of hair from her eyes. "I'm *starving*."

— 37 —

Lucy told Emmanuel that she had received an e-mail from the ChimpCorps representative.

"We will get the assignment in a day or so," she said as they left an Internet café.

"That is fine," said Emmanuel, suggesting that Lucy meet the representative here in Dakar while he goes ahead to search for his ape family.

"Where will you go?" asked Lucy.

"Dillafoullou," he replied, pointing to a map. "It is several hundred kilometers southeast of Dakar, on the border with Guinea. There are chimps, cheap huts for tourists, and a big waterfall."

"Perfect," said Lucy. "Let's meet by the waterfall in five days—August sixth at noon. Deal?"

"Deal."

Lucy liked the idea of traveling separately. She believed in the strengthening effect of independent travel, and she wanted Emmanuel to be strong. And a brief parting of their ways, she figured, would make it easier for her to fabricate a meeting with the fictional ChimpCorps representative.

— 38 —

In a letter to Zann, Lucy explained Emmanuel's genetic confusion and spiritual crisis, and asked him to forward the blood cells on the enclosed handkerchief to a molecular technician, such as Thurstian at McGill, for analysis. As she finished the letter, she felt drawn to Emmanuel. She felt drawn, as well, to know the facts, and she reminded herself that she could uncover his genetic identity by having his children.

The possibility of blending genes brought to mind her bible-writing project in which she had been blending—conceptually at this point—

the story of Genesis with life science cosmology. She had felt the power of her imagination as she experimented with language, rhythm, and ideas and yet, something in her approach to the writing project, something in her psyche, seemed to be missing, and the gap was too great to ignore.

What was missing, she realized, was the world of the spirit and the sacred, of visions and spiritual revelations. She had been hearing no voice from God, nor did she consciously connect, on an emotional or nonphysical basis, with unobservable and immeasurable kingdoms of the Divine. The lack of knowledge of what is beyond human comprehension would surely grow increasingly problematic as the project progressed.

Lucy mailed the packet to Zann from a post office in Dakar and thought about the missing spiritual link. It would be much easier, she noted, to write a fresh, cool, creative bio-story of the *physical* creation but Emmanuel would want—and need—more.

She imagined what Emmanuel would want and need. She imagined it was some kind of religious truth that touched upon the sacred, and while it was unclear to her what religious truth or the sacred actually meant, she sensed that such concepts were used by the intermediaries—the Gobis—to signify a hierarchical system whereby some things are closer to God than others. She sensed that the Gobis, with their powers of interpretation, got to identify who and what was close.

She felt torn. Those who heard, or claimed to hear, voices from above seemed unfit to lead the flock. She was tempted, nonetheless, to create a narrator, a chimp or ape-human hybrid who had visions, who heard voices from God, and who bestowed upon the apes the truth about their morality, creator, and creation. She wanted to avoid the use of hierarchy as a way to guide the primate readers, and yet she knew that Emmanuel and the vast bulk of the public longed—consciously or otherwise—to be manipulated in a hierarchical way. Though the creation myth should be scientifically correct, it had to be compelling and bold in a nonscientific way if it were to create for Emmanuel, and potentially others, a sense of comfort and security.

— 39 —

In southeastern Senegal, near the village of Dillafoullou, a man named Mamadou watched as Emmanuel meandered through the tall grass.

Emmanuel stopped.

Mamadou stepped slowly from behind a tree. He was tall with a gentle, sorrowful look about him. As he approached, his head and neck moved slightly forward and back, reminding Emmanuel of the gait of a giraffe.

"Bonjour."

"Hello," replied Emmanuel.

"At first," said Mamadou, "I thought you were a chimpanzee."

Emmanuel filled his lungs with the hot pungent air. "Close," he said blithely.

Mamadou shrugged. "I am not very good at tracking animals."

Emmanuel looked up at him. "Maybe you are better than you think," he offered.

Mamadou laughed. "Come sit in the shade and have water. I shall tell you a story."

Emmanuel accepted the canteen and took a sip.

Mamadou, whose village lay far to the north, belonged to the griot (pronounced "gree-o") caste, which included singers, musicians, public speakers, and storytellers. Months earlier, Mamadou's village had experienced severe drought and the griot, considered by many in Senegal to be the lowest strata in society, fell on hard times.

"So I have been trying to make money by taking people to the chimpanzees," explained Mamadou.

Emmanuel nodded. "Soon I will be working as an intern at a small organization called ChimpCorps," he said. "But I do not know much about the chimps. Will you introduce me to them?"

"There are few left in Senegal," cautioned Mamadou. "But I will try."

— 40 —

Emmanuel expected to search for chimps in Niokolo-Koba National Park, a reserve 70 kilometers to the northeast, but Mamadou shook his head.

"Very few are left there," he said.

"But the park is huge," protested Emmanuel.

"The park *is* huge," Mamadou agreed, "but we'll have more success looking around here."

They walked an hour south from Dillafoullou to the base of a three hundred foot waterfall where, in three days, Emmanuel and Lucy had planned to meet.

"We'll return here and meet your friend," said Mamadou, "but we don't need to travel far—there are chimpanzees close by. There are tourists close by, too. Should we try to avoid them by walking southeast?"

"Yes," said Emmanuel.

Though it was rainy season, it had not rained in nearly two weeks and the earth was hard and dry.

Emmanuel sipped water from a canteen. "You mentioned that there are few chimps left in Senegal. Are they in danger?"

"They are in danger all over Africa."

"In what way?"

"Thirty years ago there were more than a million chimps in Africa. Now there are less than a hundred thousand, and soon there may be none."

Emmanuel tensed his stomach muscles. He had known from school and from conversations with Lucy that numerous species around the world—including great apes—were threatened but the information had not affected him emotionally. But now his immediate ape family was in danger.

"None?" he asked.

Mamadou sighed. "Soon the wild chimps will probably be gone."

Emmanuel felt dizzy. He gnawed the skin edging his fingernails. He felt as though he were floating above a deep, foggy abyss. "Please," he pleaded. "Would you please explain the problem to me?"

"There are many problems," said Mamadou, pausing to gaze at the hills of Fouta Djalon, "and the problems are difficult. I will tell you what I know."

Mamadou explained how humans hunt chimps as part of the bushmeat trade.

"What do you mean *bushmeat?*" Emmanuel blurted.

"Chimps are killed by local hunters for their meat. In places like Senegal, this is rare because the Muslim religion forbids eating them, but the same cannot be said for other areas in Africa. Then there are the traveling gangs of heavily armed men who shoot the chimps for the trade."

Emmanuel imagined a mother and infant, force-marched toward a human-sized pot of stew and licks of flame. He imagined the shock of scalding water and sweet, putrid smell of burning flesh, the memories of which haunted him from East Timor. "You mean people *eat* chimps?" he cried.

"Some do."

Mamadou spoke about infectious disease, sluggish reproduction rates, and the pet trade in which ten or so chimps die for a single baby to be harvested.

"*Harvested?*" cried Emmanuel. "Do we speak of *corn?*"

Mamadou explained that the loss of females caused by the pet trade dramatically diminishes the reproductive capacity of chimp communities. He described how increased logging, particularly clear-cutting, destroys chimp habitat. Even selective cutting causes problems, such as partial habitat loss, food source modification due to the introduction of exotic trees, and noise, which disrupts chimp communities. He described how chimps are being eaten by increasing numbers of hungry loggers. He described how farms are rapidly replacing chimp habitat throughout Africa and how farms and logging roads are fragmenting chimp territories into increasingly smaller and isolated—and therefore less viable—units.

"Each problem is big," concluded Mamadou, "and the problems are connected, which makes them even bigger."

Emmanuel felt devastated. His new family—the family he came to visit—was slipping rapidly toward extinction. "I cannot let this happen!" he muttered as he bent forward and began to walk.

Mamadou followed.

Emmanuel swung his arms and began to move swiftly. He seemed unaware that Mamadou had to jog to keep up.

After a few minutes, he turned to Mamadou. "What would it take to help the chimps?"

"To help a few chimps?" Mamadou panted. "Or many of them?"

"Many."

"It would not be easy to help many of them."

"What would it take?" asked Emmanuel sternly.

"People around the world would have to change. It would take *hundreds* of millions of American dollars."

"Which problem is the most important?"

"All of them are important, but the separation of groups is a good place to start."

"And the way to fix the problem is . . ."

"To protect and connect chimp habitat."

Emmanuel turned away and began to walk. He swung his powerful arms as he gained momentum.

— 41 —

Over an hour later, Emmanuel stopped and sat down.

Mamadou sat beside him.

"The idea then," said Emmanuel, tracing a finger over the hot red dirt, "is to protect the forests and join protected areas. Is that right?"

"That's right—protect and connect."

"Okay, then," he whispered. "*Fit the need to a strength.*"

Mamadou raised an eyebrow.

"People like to sign their names," beamed Emmanuel.

"As in writing large checks?" asked Mamadou.

"Not exactly. Imagine seeing your own name from an airplane."

"I don't understand."

"There are some nice people who are very rich. Maybe they would like to sign their names."

Mamadou tilted his head to the side.

"To connect chimp populations," Emmanuel explained, "we can plant corridors of forests that match the shape of someone's signature. What millionaire would not want to plant a forest in the shape of their signature to help save the chimps?"

Mamadou slowly nodded.

"And the Church would want to sign the forest!" added Emmanuel.

"The Church could sign," exclaimed Mamadou, "with a cross the height and width of five nations! The cross would protect and connect life across Africa!"

"Each religion would sign with their own symbol!" said Emmanuel.

"And companies would sign with their name!"

"And married couples with their names and a heart!"

"And poets with a poem!"

Emmanuel, arms swinging like hairy pendulums, started walking again, propelled by a rush of ideas and hope. He hoped that the planted forest signatures would be visible from airplanes and, possibly, outer space. He hoped that the signatures—comprised of trees and countless layers of other living things—would last a very long time and would offer the donor, symbolically speaking, a constructive form of immortality. He hoped that the signatures would create viable habitat and, thus, rescue ape relatives, himself included, from extinction.

"And countries would sign with a flag!" he breathed.

Though Mamadou took long strides, he gradually fell behind and didn't notice when Emmanuel, focused on the ideas, took a smaller fork in the path.

Twenty minutes later, Emmanuel stood by the base of a fig tree, hunched over from sharp stomach cramps.

"Mamadou!" he shouted. The shadows grew but there was no response.

— 42 —

An immense pink-red sun edged just above the horizon and bled light on West Africa as Lucy waded naked in the river.

Emmanuel approached, removed his sandals, and stuck his long toe in the river.

Lucy bent over, splashed water to her face, and stood up. Water made its way down her body.

Emmanuel imagined her motioning him toward her. Her breasts, uncensored by the spandex top, brought Meecha's melons to mind, but what stood out was the thick, matted lower hair below. He imagined getting behind her, cupping her bull's-eye breasts, thrusting his bone-shaped tool into folds of flesh . . .

A shot rang out. And another.

Emmanuel felt the blast vibrations in his chest. He saw a blur—it fell from a nearby tree.

He heard the thud. He heard shrieks and rustling in treetops, then the shouts of men. Then silence.

He ran, barefoot, to the fallen chimp: blood flowed from its throat and its hand. A bullet had severed its finger.

Emmanuel touched its long, hairy arms and held its remaining fingers. He had never been so close to a chimp. He raised its eyelids and peered into its eyes.

The chimp spasmed and choked on its blood.

Emmanuel grimaced. He saw them again, the men with machetes, shouting and slashing.

"My family!" cried Emmanuel, cradling the chimp in his arms.

Drenched in sweat, Emmanuel woke the following morning and with shaking hand wrote the dream in his journal. He tried to rise on wobbly legs but dropped back to the ground. He pressed against the tree, curled into a ball, and fell into another dream.

— 43 —

"Buy some," the toothless hunter hissed.

Emmanuel noticed chunks of burnt meat on the yellow tarp. "What is it?"

"Chimpanzee."

Emmanuel, stomach muscles tightening, backed away.

"NO!" he wailed. He turned to run but the hunter caught him.

"Hybrids are next, Mr. Grizzwauld," said the hunter, holding a knife to his throat.

Emmanuel woke, stumbled through the bushes, and relieved himself. Trembling, he returned to the fig tree and drifted in and out of sleep.

"Did you shoot the ape?" Lucy screamed, stomping her foot.

"I did," replied the bioprospector, a stout woman in high leather boots.

Lucy screwed up her face.

"It had been wounded by poachers and was nearly dead," said the woman.

Lucy, mouth agape, stood there shaking.

"I'm sorry," the woman continued, "but I can't let an animal suffer like that. Maybe there are special rules for apes, but I don't know what they are."

Tears streamed down Lucy's face. "Oh my God," she howled, burying her face in her hands, "I love him . . . I can't believe he's gone . . . oh my God it hurts so bad . . ."

Emmanuel sweated, sobbed, and slept intermittently. "Special rules," he moaned. "Special rules for the apes."

— 44 —

Emmanuel stood by an ocean's edge. A cold wind swept the gray sky. The water receded and he followed the slope to the ocean floor. Horseshoe crabs and rotting fish littered the vast plain. The floor gradually rose and he followed the slope until he came upon a man in tattered clothes sitting in icy mud.

The man had bulging veins and a thick beard that hung like Spanish moss. He chanted, "TEESEEJEETEESEEAY-AYJEEAYJEE."

The vibrations hummed in Emmanuel's chest like a honey bee's buzz.

"Excuse me," said Emmanuel. "Will the Word protect my people from death?"

"Your kind shall survive," the man bellowed, "if you follow the rules!"

"I do not understand."

"There are rules for the apes and the rules must be followed!"

"Please, teach me the rules."

"Protect chimpanzees as you would your own kin!"

"But how . . ."

"Sign the forest!"

"I do not want to die . . . my family is dying. . . ."

"Have faith! Have hope! God will teach you to sign!"

"Please help. . . ."

The man stood up and towered above Emmanuel.

Emmanuel gasped.

"Behold your family!" roared the man. "Behold the humble vessels of the Will Divine!"

The man raised his arms and a great light filled the sky and a beam illuminated the chimps in the tree. "Sign the forest and your kind shall survive!" he bellowed, tapping Emmanuel on the head.

— 45 —

Emmanuel woke, wrote the dreams in the journal, and tried to understand what they meant. They had seemed so vivid and real.

He saw a blur in his peripheral vision and turned toward a chimp as it hurled an object at him. He ducked—the object nearly hit his head. He reached over to examine it.

It was a fig.

Emmanuel noticed figs strewn about on the ground. He noticed the taste of figs in his mouth. He had sustained himself through the two-and-a-half day semidelirious state, he realized, with figs thrown from above.

Less than thirty feet away, Emmanuel saw three chimps in the branches, their soft backlit halos illuminated by the early morning light. He observed the dignified way they carried themselves.

Emmanuel slowly rose to his feet. "Thank you," he called to the chimps. "Thank you for the figs. Thank you for helping me."

The nearest chimp to him—Nelson—had been born at a North American university where he had been taught elements of American Sign Language. Though the university eventually provided funds to re-educate him to live in the wild, Nelson continued to use the signs, which, on occasion, he combined in new ways. He did not recognize Emmanuel's scent. He noticed Emmanuel's long arms and posture, and signed, "Man ape."

"You do not understand me," Emmanuel went on, "but . . . I am in your family. You are my cousin. I never saw . . . until now . . . how graceful and giving you are."

Nelson recognized a small number of spoken English words, not with the comprehension of an adult human but with sophisticated mental capabilities nonetheless. Nelson recognized the word *family,* and signed, "Family ape you."

"I have traveled far to see you," Emmanuel said, now crying. "I had to learn about my family and myself. I was scared to look in a mirror and see the ape. I was upset and confused and did not know what to do. But it is no longer scary. It is *wonderful* to be part ape. I am so *proud* to be your relative. But now . . . I am terribly sorry that you are in danger, that we are in danger, *our family is in danger*. We must do something right away or there will be no more of us and . . . I . . . I will work hard to help . . . please have faith, please have hope and pray to God that the forest shall be signed. Please hang on—God will help us to survive."

Nelson signed, "Africa home."

"I need to leave now and find my friends," said Emmanuel. "But I will be back—*I promise.*"

The chimps watched as Emmanuel slowly walked away. A wild-born female, who had observed Nelson for nearly three years, signed, "Man ape go."

— 46 —

Stunned and miserable that his client was lost, Mamadou searched through the night, walking and shouting, but there was no response. In the early morning he slept for three hours before gathering a larger team of volunteers from the village. In the afternoon, he took a break from the rescue effort to find ChimpCorps' Web site and to e-mail a note describing Emmanuel's idea for wildlife conservation. If Emmanuel would not live on, he figured, at least the Sign-the-Forest idea could.

The following day still more villagers joined the search party, but Emmanuel's whereabouts remained a mystery.

Just before midday of the following day, Mamadou slowly tapped his fist against his palm as he approached the waterfall.

Lucy sat by the waterfall. After taking an extra day in Dakar, she had traveled east toward Tambacounda, lurching side-to-side and back-and-forth in the back of a cramped minibus. There had been plenty of time to think about ChimpCorps and now, waiting for Emmanuel, she reminded herself of the ChimpCorps assignment she had made up. They would conduct a survey of Senegalese chimps south of Niokolo-Koba Park. That was it. They'd walk around and count the chimps.

Mamadou assumed that the young white woman was Emmanuel's friend. Introducing himself, he looked at the ground and explained what had happened.

Lucy strained her neck to look up at him and bit her lip. "Thank you for searching," she said grimly.

"We *must* continue to search," said Mamadou.

"Of course."

Hours later, Emmanuel was still missing.

Visualizing what the local poisonous vipers might look like, Lucy recalled Ana's black and red death mask in Seattle.

— 47 —

The following morning, Lucy returned to the waterfall, closed her eyes, and recited a prayer. It was hardly in her nature to seek help—be it from the U.S. embassy or from God—but the situation seemed dire and she had designed the prayer as part of the bible-writing project for Emmanuel.

"Ooo, oo," she said, timidly.

That's not how it's done, she thought.

"Ooooo, oo, oooo, ee," she tried again.

The prayer called for all great apes—chimps, bonobos, orang utans, humans, and gorillas—to call out with a common voice in support of the branches of the spectacular tree of life. Lucy hoped the prayer would call Emmanuel back from darkness, back to life, back to her. She felt moved by a longing, a desire that rose like a primordial tide to her chest from below. Her breathing accelerated. She felt hot.

"OOOOOO! OOOOOO!! EEEEEEE!!! EEEEEEEEEE!!!!!! EEEEEEEEEEEEEEEE!!!!!!" she screeched.

Seconds later, she heard a faint echo.

She looked up and saw him, stooped over, knuckles to the ground. He stumbled and fell.

"*EMMANUEL!*" Lucy cried, rushing to him.

"I have not eaten much," he whispered, recalling the taste of figs.

As he lay on the ground, she protected him from the sun and nursed him with water and candy bars until the better part of an hour passed. His strength gradually returned and he told her what had befallen him.

"My week wasn't nearly as dramatic," she admitted, after he had told his story. "In Dakar, I . . ."

Lucy paused and tried to recall the ChimpCorps assignment she had fabricated. "Uhhh, well, I met with the ChimpCorps rep and . . . uhhh . . . our assignment is, let's see, what was it . . ."

"*Hello!*"

Emmanuel turned and saw Mamadou approaching.

"Oh, I remember now," Lucy said. "We're going to count . . ."

"You're *found!*" Mamadou exclaimed, waving his arms and running toward Emmanuel.

"Lucy was just telling me about the ChimpCorps assignment," said Emmanuel.

"Yes," said Mamadou, whose smile was as large as his face would allow. "I, too, spoke with ChimpCorps."

Lucy rolled her eyes. "You spoke with *who?*"

"ChimpCorps," said Mamadou.

"You mean ChimpCorps in *Seattle?*"

"Yes, of course. Emmanuel told me about your organization."

Lucy looked dazed. She managed a weak smile. "Uhhh, okay then, why don't *you* tell Emmanuel the assignment."

"Sure—we should follow up on Emmanuel's new idea!"

"What idea?" asked Emmanuel.

"Signing the forest."

"You mean putting up signs?" asked Lucy.

Emmanuel explained the concept.

"I had e-mailed Emmanuel's idea to ChimpCorps," explained Mamadou. "Mark loved the concept and started reaching out to people. He reached out to those who can't have children, to those who wish to leave their name as a positive legacy for generations to come, to corporations trying to green their image, to churches trying to change their image for other reasons. He reached out and already has raised a huge amount of U.S. dollars in pledges!"

"Money to sign the forest?" asked Lucy.

"Yes!" beamed Mamadou. "And I've been hired by ChimpCorps to help manage the project. *Thank you,* Emmanuel. Thank you for helping my family!"

"Thank you," said Emmanuel, "for helping mine."

That night, Lucy and Emmanuel slept close together and brushed against one another more than usual. As the cinnamon and musk scents mixed, their faces drew close and they could feel the warmth in each other's breath. Feigning discomfort, Emmanuel shifted and brushed his lips across her cheek; Lucy, who looked to be asleep, turned her head so that their lips met. They kissed with focus and abandon, and after the hands came the pole of the beast and the howling at the moon.

— 48 —

Evelyn's friend Faith was on the phone from Boston.

"Your church is doing what?" asked Evelyn.

"It's a brand new project," said Faith. "We're building a cross, a *huge* cross, in Africa."

"Okay, so how big?"

"Thirty by forty-five miles."

"*What?*"

"Isn't it amazing?" said Faith.

"It's *crazy!* How does it work?"

"With trees. We're planting a corridor of trees, miles of trees, in the shape of a cross."

A shiver traversed along Evelyn's spine and her body tingled, as though brushed by an airy feather.

Faith recalled how her Church, which had been looking for a way to attract youth to its ranks, had been contacted by ChimpCorps' Sign-the-Forest initiative. "Shall I send you more information about the project?" she asked.

— 49 —

"ChimpCorps headquarters, Mark here."

"Lucy in West Africa, reporting for duty!"

"Lucy, it's great to hear your voice! You know, you and Emmanuel are eco-heroes."

"It was Emmanuel's idea," said Lucy.

"Yes, Mamadou told me, but I know a troublemaker when I see one and I'm not surprised to find you mixed up in all this."

"So, hey, how's it going?"

"We're swamped, based on the Sign-the-Forest project, with pledges and donations and, if truth be known, we're trying to learn how to run an organization on short notice."

"Need help?"

"Seriously?"

"That's why I called."

"Can you and Emmanuel get to western Uganda?"

"You can count on it."

"Okay, here's the plan: you and Emmanuel help Mamadou get things rolling in Senegal. In two weeks or so, head to Dakar and fly to Kampala; call me when you . . . wait a second . . . standby . . ."

Mark's voice grew dim and Lucy strained to hear. She thought she heard him mention a vice president at Intel.

Mark returned to the phone. "Okay, Lucy, I'm back. Yes, so there's a massive Sign-the-Forest project in the works in Uganda, and we're ramping up."

"No worries," Lucy replied. "We'll call you from Kampala."

"I really appreciate it. ChimpCorps will reimburse you for . . ."

"Don't sweat it—we've got it covered."

"And Lucy, do me one more favor."

"What's that?"

"If you and Emmanuel have additional wildlife conservation ideas, please write them down."

"Will do."

"Thanks!"

There was a silence.

"Lucy?"

"Yes?"

"It's about Ana."

"What . . ."

"She . . ."

"Ana?"

"Passed on."

"Oh, no."

"Lucy?"

"Oh . . ." Lucy clutched her stomach. It hurt like a punch.

"Ana loved you so much," said Mark. "She never had children. She thought of you as a daughter. She spoke of you at the end."

Lucy crumpled like a rag to the floor. She coughed, gasped for air, and cried into the dirt floor.

"Lucy?"

Lucy recalled Ana's advice. She pictured moose in Canada, bears in the Rockies, snowy owls in Wisconsin, manatees in the Everglades, apes in Africa.

Breathing slowly and deliberately, Mark remained on the line.

— 50 —

It was nearly midnight and the fire crackled, shooting sparks toward the black sky. Emmanuel and Lucy sat among the dozens of villagers who were listening to Mamadou.

"Many years ago," Mamadou was saying, his voice embellished by insect and bird song, "our ancestors could transform themselves into animals, though not all those who made such transformations had the power to reverse it. Today people don't much believe in transformations, but tonight I'll share stories of both ancient and modern transformations, and the stories will help us recall what our ancestors knew so well."

Lucy listened closely, hoping to gain knowledge relevant to her bible-writing project.

Emmanuel wrapped his arms around his legs, pushed his forehead into his knees, and took a deep breath. Soothed by Mamadou's words and phrases, which repeated like soft drumbeats, Emmanuel thought about how genetic change can result in the transformation of a creature. When genes are changed, particularly genes that control other genes, the resulting creature might have an increased abstraction capability and perhaps a greater control over its vocal apparatus . . .

"HELLO?"

Emmanuel lifted his head.

"YA, YA," announced the cell phone user, interrupting Mamadou's story. "TOMORROW FOR CERTAIN."

Mamadou fell silent.

Emmanuel turned to Lucy.

Lucy lifted her hand to her ear. "*REPEAT POR FAVOR—I CAN'T HEAR YOU!*" she shouted into her pinky.

"TOMORROW FOR CERTAIN!" repeated the cell phone user.

Another cell phone announced its ditty and a new voice shouted, "HELLO?"

"*HOUSTON WE HAVE A PROBLEM!*" Lucy barked, lifting her other hand to her other ear.

A third phone went off.

Emmanuel looked worried.

Lucy calmly reached below her belt and lifted a small black device.

Mamadou gazed at the ground.

Lucy pressed one of the buttons on the device.

The three cell phone users said, "HELLO? ARE YOU THERE?"

Silence returned and, gradually, the birds resumed their songs and Mamadou resumed his story, but by then Emmanuel had fallen asleep.

The following morning Emmanuel and Lucy prepared to travel first by bus to Dakar, then by plane to Kampala, Uganda.

"My friend," said Lucy, hugging Mamadou, "we hope to see you soon. Keep up the good fight and here, take this."

She handed him the small black device.

"What is it?"

"A cell phone jammer. I used it last night but be careful—it's illegal in some countries."

Mamadou sighed. "Ever since mobile phones have become popular, I can't tell a story without continuous interruption. I fear it will mean the end of the griot as storytellers."

Lucy pressed her lips together. "It's a serious problem here in Senegal and in every other country. What separates humans from all other animals is that humans, given their druthers, will incessantly babble on."

Mamadou nodded. "For storytelling to work," he said, "you need silence for listening, for reflection. If people are constantly babbling on their cell phones, there's no space for the wisdom of the ancients to sink in."

"There are ways to combat cell phone abuse such as talking into your hand," said Lucy, explaining her work as a CPA—a Cell Phone Activist. "I only use the jammer as a last resort."

Mamadou wondered about the other possible tools for a CPA.

"If you don't want to risk the jammer and you're too embarrassed to talk into your hand *and* you wish to remain anonymous, there's always Cell Phone Rage's album *Tower of Babble-On*."

"How does that work?" asked Mamadou.

"In addition to songs such as 'Goodbye to Mythology,'" explained Lucy, "there are tracks that contain embarrassing cell phone conversations targeting specific situations. There's one for riding the bus, for airports, for supermarkets . . ."

"What do you do?" asked Mamadou.

"You play the appropriate track on a portable music player so loudly that even an oblivious cell phone user will notice that they're behaving badly."

"Who is Cell Phone Rage?"

"They're a defunct band."

"What happened to them?" asked Mamadou.

"Their practice sessions were frequently interrupted by incoming calls on their cell phones. Eventually, the lead guy quit and moved to an area in the Scottish highlands where cell phone reception is poor."

"This is a true story?" asked Emmanuel.

"Scout's honor!" exclaimed Lucy.

— 51 —

It was unclear to Zann what it meant to be genetically confused. Who *wasn't* genetically confused, he wondered. Who wasn't a mix of cells and subcellular structures some of which, such as mitochondria, contain their own DNA? Who couldn't boast of genes shared with cousin species from long ago? But Lucy's genetically confused friend needed help and, so, he searched the Web for Thurstian's address. A thought struck him and a mischievous grin took hold of his face. *He could send Thurstian a different handkerchief with different blood on it!*

But what blood would he use? That of an ostrich? A longnosed bandicoot? A pygmy chimpanzee? A creative mixture?

If word got out about the results of such a prank, he surmised, it would cause quite a public stir. It would raise questions and challenge assumptions and encourage people to think a bit more about the nature of their origins.

The next day, Zann's Ph.D. advisor called to discuss Zann's thesis. Zann sighed. The software he was developing, which modeled the way evolution affects particular biological processes, needed reworking. The workload was daunting; the prank would have to wait. Oblivious to the papercut on his finger, Zann stuffed the bloody handkerchief back in the bag, which he mailed to Thurstian at the Redpath Museum in Montreal, Canada.

— 52 —

On the bus ride to Dakar, Emmanuel asked, "What are you writing?"

Lucy looked out the window and marveled at a distant baobab tree rising out of the dry, brown plain. The immensely thick trunk and sparse branches gave her the disconcerting impression that she was looking at the tree's roots. "An essay," she replied.

"About what?"

"Bio-spirituality."

"What is that?"

"I don't know. I'm trying to figure it out."

Lucy covered the notebook with her elbow. The essay, which in fact was her bible-writing project, had been progressing well—particularly after she had made a habit of studying Emmanuel's dream journal.

"What do you *think* it is?" Emmanuel persisted.

"It's where biology and spirituality intersect. It's where spirituality is presented in stories to help creatures survive."

"Could it help *my* relatives survive?" asked Emmanuel.

"It could. Compelling stories with the right message might encourage my relatives to coexist with yours."

"So the stories would change the way the humans acted?"

"That's the hope."

Emmanuel looked out the window at the women dressed in reds, yellows, and browns selling mangoes on the side of the road. "I do not think so," he said. "Stories are nice but you cannot eat them—so many humans are hungry and poor. Before helping *my* relatives, humans would need to learn to help themselves."

Lucy agreed. "In addition to the stories," she said, "there needs to be financial incentives—sustainable economic models—for humans in remote places to preserve the land and its biodiversity. Otherwise, the wildlife and its habitat will disappear."

"Financial incentive," Emmanuel repeated. "You mean so that the local people can make a living by keeping the place wild?"

"That's right. Protecting the land and the animals has to make economic sense to the locals."

"How about if the locals gave tours?" suggested Emmanuel. "People could come to the forest, stay in huts, and pay to visit my relatives. The extra money could then go to the humans in the remote places. This way there would be less of a need to hunt my people and less of a need to chop down the forest."

"Good idea," said Lucy, "but someone has already thought of it: it's called ecotourism."

"Oh. Should we ask ChimpCorps to create more ecotourism projects?"

Lucy's face soured. "I don't think so."

"Why not?"

"There are problems with ecotourism—too often it causes more damage than good."

"What sort of problems?"

Lucy considered the question. "I can think of several: it overwhelms indigenous human culture by the introduction of Westerner's culture, it overwhelms wild animal populations with introduced human disease, and it has a large carbon footprint, which means a lot of fossil fuel is burned in getting people to remote places. And—perhaps most significantly—it overwhelms wild animal populations by attracting infrastructure."

"Infrastructure?"

"Ecotourists, for the most part, enjoy their creature comforts. Unfortunately, the roads, cars, hotels, stores, power lines, and pollution—the *infrastructure*—damages and often destroys the wildlife habitat."

"Can ecotourism be done in a way that is good for the animals?"

"If it's managed right but that's easier said than done. And don't forget that ecotourism profits don't necessarily flow to the little guy in the bush."

Emmanuel thought about the promise and problems of ecotourism. Surely someone could improve on the way it was done. He thought about his endangered ape relatives. Clearly, *something* had to be done. But what? Ideas flowed. He thought about tours, storytelling, and ways to broadcast a cell phone conversation over the Internet.

"Say, can I borrow a pen?"

Lucy reached into her daypack and gave him one.

"Do you have any paper?"

"Write on your hand," she whispered groggily, and fell back asleep.

Emmanuel wrote on his hand an R and an H. He drew a thick line of two-way arrows, from the R to the H. He surrounded the R with a circle and the H with a square. He wrote WS and drew a rectangle around it and connected it to the H.

"It is *like* ecotourism," he murmured, adding three C's to the network diagram and attaching them to the WS, "but the tourist does not show up."

— 53 —

"Teresa!"

"*Emmanuel!*"

"I am sorry I have not called."

"Are you okay?"

"I am fine."

"We have been so worried."

"I am taking a summer course in anthropology, Teresa. I have been spending a lot of time in the field."

"We miss you, terribly. Where are you? The caller ID is showing a weird number."

"I am calling over Grasp."

"Grasp? What is Grasp?"

"A free phone-over-Internet system. It always shows a weird number."

"We miss you . . ."

"I am learning a lot, Teresa. Seattle is a wonderful place . . ."

"You are my favorite brother, you know."

"I am your only brother, silly!" Emmanual retorted. "Is Mother or Father home?"

"They went to church with Uncle Mateus. Aunt Winnie is at work, praying."

"Is everything okay?"

"Oh, yes, she is praying for her company to get a big fat contract!"

"Do me a favor. Tell Mother and Father that I . . . that now I . . . understand. . ."

Teresa paused. "Emmanuel, are you *okay?* It's early here, it must be terribly early in Seattle. Shouldn't you be sleeping?"

"Listen, Teresa, I have to go now. . . ."

"You sound so far away, Emmanuel. When will you visit?"

"Soon, Teresa, soon."

"I wish Mother and Father were home. They want so much to talk to you."

"Good-bye, Teresa."

"Good-bye, Grizzwauld."

— 54 —

Emmanuel missed his family and it had felt good to talk with Teresa, but he was relieved that his parents had not been home. Lying was easier done over e-mail. He joined Lucy in an Internet café in Dakar where he wrote:

> subject: Re: PHONE HOME, EMMANUEL
>
> Dear Father and Mother,
>
> Seattle continues to be wonderful. I am studying anthropology through a summer program and I am learning a great deal. I am

doing a lot of research in the field and I am not home much. My v-mail is not working lately. Did Teresa mention I called?

Miss you,

Emmanuel

Emmanuel thought about the e-mail before sending it. The details were, once again, misleading, but the essence of the message, that he was okay, was true.

Lucy, meanwhile, read the e-mails in her inbox. "Awww!" she exclaimed.

"What is the matter?" asked Emmanuel.

"I forgot to pick up the mail."

"What mail?"

"My housemate had forwarded some bills and a book to a hotel I thought we'd stay at, but I forgot all about it."

"We are headed for Uganda tonight and we probably do not have time to find the hotel. Why not ask your housemate to send the hotel some money for forwarding the mail to Uganda?"

"Okay," agreed Lucy. "I'm not so sure about the timing of it all but I'm not too worried about it. Who wants bills, anyway? I'll try and have it sent to the International Youth Hostel in Kampala."

Lucy later read an e-mail from Mark, asking her to call him right away—no matter what the time was. Before dialing, she suggested that Emmanuel share his new idea with Mark.

It was early morning in Seattle and Mark was asleep. In his dream he was speaking with a celebrity primatologist.

"Are you sure?" asked the primatologist.

"I'm sure," said Mark.

"That's fine," she said, "but if you change your mind, I'm okay with autographing your adventure hat."

"Thanks so much for the years of inspiration," he said, stepping back, "but it's not needed anymore."

The phone rang and the dream vanished.

"Hello?" said Mark.

"Did I wake you?" asked Lucy. "What time is it over there?"

"The sun has yet to rise, but who has time for sleep?"

"Just got your e-mail. We're in Dakar."

"Thanks for calling," said Mark. "I wanted to talk with you about the Sign-the-Forest project in Uganda before you flew there. As with the project in Senegal, we need to encourage interest in the long-term health of the land. We need to partner with in-country organizations and draw talent from local universities whenever possible. We're not taking control of the signed land, nor are we forcing our agenda on people; rather, we're offering to help communities protect, and gain financial benefit from, their own land. The project in Uganda is being funded by a Roman Catholic diocese in the United States. The sign, a cross, will be miles across."

Lucy bit her lip. "How sensitive is it to plant a massive cross in a Muslim country?"

"It's largely a Christian country," said Mark, "but you're right: the cross will touch the lives of many people from many different faiths. A lot of diplomatic work is required before the project can get off the ground."

"You may not want me as lead negotiator," Lucy laughed.

Mark paused. "I wonder . . ." he said. "I know you have tickets already, but maybe it doesn't make sense for you to go there just yet."

"Emmanuel and I are super flexible."

"We do need your help in Uganda, but things over there are happening in slow motion right now and I wonder if it makes more sense if you show up a few months later."

"Not a worry—if you'd like we can stay here and help Mamadou. We understand you're experimenting and learning as you go. Speaking of experiments, did I mention that Emmanuel has a new idea?"

"Does he?"

"Would you like to talk with him?"

"Sure!"

"Hello?"

"Hi, Emmanuel, how goes it?"

"Fine. I am feeling much better now that we are working to help the chimps."

"It's funny you say that," said Mark. "We are so closely related. I get the uncanny sense that by helping these creatures, we're really helping ourselves."

"I get that feeling, too," said Emmanuel.

"Lucy tells me you have a new idea."

Emmanuel peered at the network diagram on his hand and explained how the R (remote), H (host), WS (Web server), and C's (clients) interrelate. The concept, he pointed out, provides the long-term benefits of ecotourism without the associated risks.

"So it's a kind of high-tech distribution system for traditional storytelling, as well as a sustainable economic model designed to protect wildlife and its habitat?"

"Yes," said Emmanuel.

"What do you call it?" asked Mark.

"vEcotourism."

"And the *v*?"

"Stands for *virtual*."

"Wild! I have a friend in Singapore who is something of a software genius. I'm pretty sure he's between contracts and, if he's willing to help, maybe you and Lucy could put Uganda on hold and instead develop a vEcotourism pilot project with him."

Lucy and Emmanuel agreed that developing a new idea in Asia made more sense than waiting in Africa, and soon after calling several airlines, they found themselves in a taxi en route to the Dakar airport.

"I think about Ana a lot," said Lucy, taking Emmanuel's hand. "I can't believe she's dead."

"Ana Mayd," said Emmanuel, squeezing her hand, "lives on through the creatures she loved. Ana Mayd shall never die."

"She lives on through those of us who love her," said Lucy.

"She encouraged me," added Emmanuel, "to learn from my problems by taking them on a journey. She said I should share what I learn."

Lucy nodded.

Emmanuel glanced out the window at the crowded street and reflected on what he had learned in Africa. When compared with many other life forms, his problems seemed so very small.

PART FIVE

Ebu Gogo

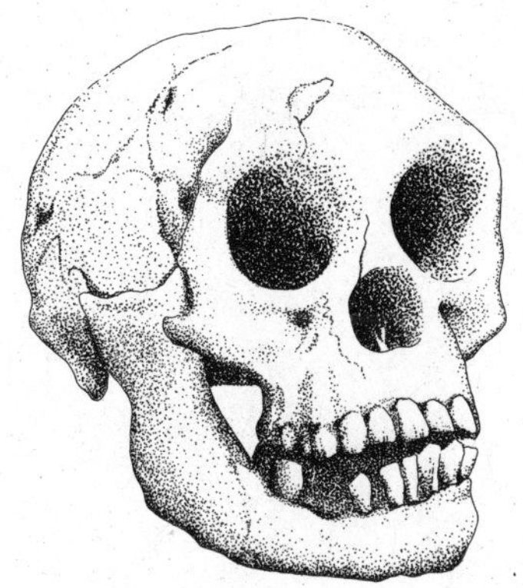

— 55 —

During the flight from Dakar to Singapore, Lucy wondered how one might layer a scientifically accurate, spiritually uplifting creation myth for all great apes. She wondered why some religious narratives survived through the ages while others did not. She sensed it had to do with fear. Fear of death, fear of the unknown, and fear of an angry, vengeful God have been gripping people's minds for thousands of years.

It seemed plausible that some stories survived because they encourage people to kill believers in competing narratives. It seemed plausible that some stories survived because they encourage people to recruit new listeners and because they encourage the creation of large families. It seemed plausible, too, that some stories survived by offering eternal glory, pleasure, power, and self-confidence as a way to make people feel larger than they actually are.

Lucy wondered about the survival rate for narratives that told the truth. A feeling of serenity took hold of her. She closed her eyes, pressed her hands to her chest, and listened.

— 56 —

Hours after the jet took off, Emmanuel fell asleep and found himself gazing down at hundreds of thousands of trees that appeared in the shape of a cross. In the dream, he felt comforted by Evelyn's melodic voice and warm touch as they walked along the spine of the cross. Lowering his knuckles to the ground, he told her who he was and how he came to be and they set out through the woods to save his people.

— 57 —

"Hello?"

"Faith?"

"Yes?"

"It's Evelyn. I'm terribly sorry to call so late but I had a nightmare and . . ."

"You can call anytime. Would you like to talk about it?"

"It was about the Church."

"What about the Church?"

"It was awful."

"Was it about hell?"

"Worse."

"*Worse than hell?*"

"I have fears."

"Of course you do but it was only a dream. Tell me about it."

"Okay," said Evelyn, touching her gold cross. "A Cardinal publicly put down what the former Pope had said about the nature of biology and evolution."

"Publicly?"

"He published the refutation in the Op-Ed page of *The New York Times*."

"My word, you do have dramatic dreams. What did the Cardinal write?"

Evelyn winced. "That the Pope's words on the subject were vague and unimportant."

"That was the nightmare?"

"That's the start of it."

"Then?"

"Then the Cardinal's essay touched off mass protest around the world by Catholics weary of Church revisions, confusion, and contradictions."

"Then?"

"Then the Church elders faltered and the entire hierarchy, like a house of cards, came tumbling down."

"Evelyn, you must not worry—God won't let *that* happen."

"Of course you're right," said Evelyn, "but the image of a top-heavy house of cards . . ."

"Is total and utter nonsense," said Faith. "*The hierarchy is solid!* That said, I can see why the dream upset you."

"Tell me again it could never happen," whispered Evelyn.

"Oh, Evelyn, you poor dear. The Church is in fine shape and will continue to be so! The elders are wise and effective in the ways of God and man; the hierarchy is more powerful than we could ever know. Besides, the Church has long supported the theory of evolution, so I can't see how a Cardinal or Pope or anyone could, realistically, turn back the clock."

"The Cardinal agreed that evolution does, in fact, occur," said Evelyn, recalling the dream, "except for the part about random mutation. He maintained that each and every alteration of DNA is specifically and intentionally designed and directed by the Lord."

"Is that so bad a point of view?" asked Faith. "I can see how, over billions of years and for umteen-trillions of life forms, there would be a staggering number of mutations. But God has infinite love and capacity; He has the power to bring forth each tiny mutation, so that each of His creatures might, over long periods of time, better survive in the ever-changing environments that He Himself creates and maintains. Wouldn't you agree?"

"Yes, of course, but the Cardinal went further: he claimed that no creature could have possibly evolved as a result of the interplay between random mutation and natural selection, and this is where the dream turned into a nightmare."

"Why?" asked Faith.

"I'm fine with the belief that God is the mysterious spark behind the force of gravity, behind the flow of electrons, behind the creation of species. *That's actually what I believe.* But I'm *not* fine with the

Cardinal commenting on what random mutations can or cannot do. I'm *not* fine with the Church dictating science to the scientists. The Church has a long history of doing just that and time and time again we've been *wrong*. Our arrogance in realms we don't understand ends up hurting us and that's *not* acceptable."

"It was a dream, Evelyn—and a nightmare at that. Trust me, no one is going to take the Church back to the days of Galileo."

"That's what I'm worried about."

"Stop worrying," said Faith. "It's not going to happen."

— 58 —

Emmanuel stood by an ocean's edge. A cold wind swept the gray sky. The water receded and he followed the slope to the ocean floor. Horseshoe crabs and rotting fish littered the vast plain. The floor gradually rose and he followed the slope until he came upon a man in tattered clothes sitting in icy mud.

The man had bulging veins and a thick beard that hung like Spanish moss. "JEESEEJEEAYSEEAYTEETEEJEEAYTEEAY," he chanted.

The vibrations hummed in Emmanuel's chest like a honey bee's buzz.

"Excuse me," said Emmanuel. "I have traveled far. I am tired and I long to go home."

"The Word is your home," said the man.

"I do not understand," said Emmanuel.

"Read the Word and the story of your home is revealed!"

"What story of home? Who . . . Who are you?"

"I am the Keeper of the Word—Keeper of the Sacred Memories!"

"I am Emmanuel and I am lost. . . ."

"Here," said the man, "try this on."

"What is it?" asked Emmanuel.

"Googles."

"Goggles?"

"No!" the man thundered. "Googles!"

"What does it do?" asked Emmanuel, peering through the colorful, tilted glasses.

"It can read your DNA and display in detail how you came to be."

"Starting with birth?" asked Emmanuel.

"Starting with the birth," said the Keeper, "of the universe."

"I am tired and I want to go home," cried Emmanuel.

"So be it!" exclaimed the Keeper. "Touch your canines, count to three, and let the googles take you there!"

"Thank you," sighed Emmanuel.

"Now," said the Keeper, "what do you see?"

"Blackness. Total blackness. There is a dot approaching. . . . Now it is like a blue marble. . . . Now it is like a spinning blue and white ball. Now it is like a basketball and look—there are the shapes of the continents! There is Asia and there is all of Indonesia, spread out before me! There is a tiny island—is this my home?"

"You can never go home!" thundered the Keeper. "Not without the Word!"

"There are island creatures," said Emmanuel, pointing. "There are men with long arms and bent-over gaits and one of them, wearing colorful glasses, is touching his canines and pointing. . . ."

"Study the Word," exclaimed the Keeper, "and reveal the story!"

Emmanuel woke and wrote the dream in the journal as the jet flew over the Andaman Sea. He placed his hand on Lucy's leg and less than an hour later, the jet's nose tilted up for a soft landing in Singapore.

— 59 —

The more Lucy wrote and refined the bible, the more she tried to imagine how someone other than herself might read and react to her literary creation. Bibles, it seemed to her, were platforms for ideas and stories; they were doorways for believers. How, she wondered as she and Emmanuel walked in Singapore's Chinatown, could she reach and influence readers if *she* didn't believe in the doorway? Willful suspension of disbelief didn't come naturally to her, and she couldn't bring herself to view the narrative as anything other than an intellectual exercise.

Perhaps she could believe if she encountered an omen, she joked as it started to rain. But what sort of omen? She wasn't sure about the details but it would need to shake her to the bone.

— 60 —

Emmanuel and Lucy recalled Mark's instructions as they entered the Singapore Airport Rain Forest Lounge: look for a tall thin man in his twenties who might be wearing an unusually large hat.

"Excuse me," said Lucy, "but are you Gadget?"

"Before I reply," said the solitary man, "should I set verbosity to low, medium, or high?"

"I don't understand."

"Verbosity," the man explained, "is a way to configure my verbal output; when it is set to low, I keep responses to a minimum."

Lucy nodded slowly. "Can I change your level of verbosity midconversation?"

"I am configurable," offered the man, "during run-time. I also accept zero through nine, if you want a finer degree of granularity."

"Okay," said Lucy, "I'm game. Ready? *Set verbosity to zero!*"

The man stood motionless.

"So," said Lucy. "I assume you are Mark's friend, Gadget—the ChimpCorps tech volunteer."

No response.

"Set verbosity to ten," said Lucy.

"Out of bounds error," said the man.

Lucy frowned.

"Ten causes an error," Emmanuel pointed out, "because the range is zero through nine."

"Good point," agreed Lucy. "Set verbosity to nine."

"Yes, hello, how do you do? I am Gadget, documented, as it were, on my official certificate of birth (the transcript number of which I would be pleased to provide) as Gary Edgar Bitmoore, from Davenport, Iowa, which is part of the Quad Cities vicinity, along the prosperous banks of the mighty Mississippi River, the source of which as you probably already know is in . . ."

"Set verbosity to four," said Lucy.

"Hello. I am Gadget."

"Greetings, Gadget. I'm Lucy, and here be Emmanuel. We understand you're between software contracts and can help us with a ChimpCorps project."

"Yes," said Gadget, removing his hat, "that is correct."

"Excellent! We should describe to you the . . ."

Lucy stopped talking and stared at the blinking, translucent green egg perched on Gadget's head.

"That," explained Gadget, "is a G.E.U.B. version 1.4 wireless peripheral storage device networked to my brain. It stores eighty-five terabytes, which is to say, eighty-five trillion bytes of information."

"And I'm a monkey's uncle," retorted Lucy. "No, really, what's it for?"

"It is an optical backup-up device for my ideas. You see, biologically speaking, I have a terrible memory."

Emmanuel frowned.

"I don't believe you!" Lucy said.

"I do not blame you," admitted Gadget. "I would not believe me either, but I have to because my invention calls for me to believe in it."

"What invention?" asked Emmanuel.

"I truly do have a bad memory," explained Gadget, "so I invented the G.E.U.B. Green Egg Unlimited Believer."

"How does it work?" asked Emmanuel.

"You place it on your head and try to believe it is doing something helpful."

"Helpful, like storing thoughts and memories?"

"That is correct."

"Does it help?" asked Lucy.

"The power of belief is incredible," remarked Gadget. "Once you overcome doubts and enter the flow of belief, you would be amazed at what you can accomplish."

"But does wearing the egg actually *help?*" she persisted.

"I believe that it does."

"Wonderful," said Lucy.

— 61 —

In a grim neighborhood of the Indonesian capital city, Jakarta, Emmanuel, Lucy, and Gadget stayed in a cheap hotel where they refined the vEcotourism system. When the specification's first draft was complete, Gadget began to develop a functional prototype of the vEcotourism software.

"Let's get some dinner," Lucy would say, knocking on the door to Gadget's room.

"I am busy," he would reply.

Lucy and Emmanuel would find dinner in a makeshift *warung* along Jalan Jaksa, after which they would bring him food.

"He just sits in there staring at the computer screen," said Emmanuel. "He hardly blinks and I wonder sometimes if he is even breathing."

"I worry about him, too," said Lucy, "but he sure is focused."

Three weeks after they had arrived, the vEco1.0 system was ready to test. Lucy thought it best if Gadget remained in Jakarta to access the server and refine the software while she and Emmanuel conducted tests from remote sites in Indonesia's far-flung archipelago.

On the day before leaving Jakarta, Emmanuel lay in bed wondering what it would be like to visit East Timor and Sulawesi—the former where he had been born and raised and the latter where his genes had apparently been modified. Lucy had agreed to visit these places with him, and they would start by taking a Pelni ship to Makassar, known as Ujung Pandang, in southern Sulawesi. From there they would take a bus to the Speciation Lab.

Emmanuel pulled the sheets, which smelled of ripe melons, over his head and sensed the weight of his problems. Compared with so many creatures his woes seemed small, and yet he still did not know who or what he was or how he came to be, and he worried about what the journey home might uncover.

With hands pressed to his belly he fell asleep.

Emmanuel ran over familiar hills soaked in pungent smoke. He ran lightly and swiftly. It was not fear or shame that compelled him to hide. He knew the terrain by heart and marveled at the places a boy could hide. He crawled through a familiar passageway where animals had been and the smell reminded him of fish markets from the place of his birth. He began to dig through the soft earth until the moisture gave way to a trickle that opened into a pool of clear still water. He peered at the reflection, covered his eyes, and cried, "NO!"

— 62 —

In the predawn darkness, the Pelni ship sliced the brown waters of the Java Sea bound for Makassar, Sulawesi. As Lucy stepped around the people asleep on the upper deck, she recalled that the ship had a carrying capacity of two thousand, but she reckoned there were twice that many on board.

Too many people, she thought, noticing the rich odor of wet mats.

She imagined a great flood wiping out all the people on the planet, except for the Pelni ship passengers. She imagined mixing her genes with Emmanuel's manimal genes and producing viable offspring. She imagined their descendants sharing new creation stories, such as the one she had been writing, that would help them to survive. She imagined their descendants gradually becoming dominant.

— 63 —

Emmanuel sat on a straw mat on the upper deck of the Pelni and watched the sky gradually come to light. Call to Prayer blared from the speakers. He noticed a Muslim boy, prostrate on a straw mat, offering Fajr, the first of five daily prayers.

He looked past the boy to a freshly painted white staircase. It reminded him of the bright white stairs by the old church back home in East Timor. He fondly recalled the small door frame, blue marble tiles, and gilded statues. He fondly recalled the ornate paintings of Jesus, Mary, and Joseph in black and gold. He dozed off.

Just before sunrise Emmanuel woke and noticed the boy still immersed in prayer. Emmanuel tried to calm himself by breathing deeply, but images from East Timor appeared—images of blood, smoke, and fire. He clenched his fists.

Gradually his breathing slowed and his eyes moistened. He looked again at the staircase. As the sun rose and bathed Asia in brilliant light he saw parallel shimmering spirals with steps in yellow, green, red, and blue. The two spirals seemed to merge into one.

Emmanuel blinked and looked away. He touched the mat with his thick, calloused knuckles, looked to the boy, and loosened his powerful fists.

— 64 —

"Let's get this straight," said Lucy, looking out the bus window at the low gray building. "This is the laboratory where your genes got sliced, diced, and spliced?"

"Yes," whispered Emmanuel.

They stepped off the bus, shouldered their packs, and entered the lobby.

Emmanuel shivered with nervous energy. It was here he hoped to learn the details of how he came to be. In particular, he hoped to learn if the forced insertion had affected part of a gene, several genes, or several hundred genes. And if the affected genes controlled other genes, which ones were they?

Feeling nauseous, he approached the woman behind the reception desk.

After five minutes of rapid-fire gunshot dialogue (Lucy often heard *tidak,* the Bahasa Indonesia word for "no"), Emmanuel returned.

"What did she say?" Lucy asked, following him out of the building.

Emmanuel frowned. "They recently started genetic work on plants and animals," he explained, "but only for purposes of identification."

"What about work on great apes?"

"It would be unethical but she thought it could be done."

"Did you ask about the secret government projects?"

"I did."

"And?"

"She said that those projects, if they existed, were secret."

"Do they give tours?" asked Lucy.

"No," he said, fidgeting.

"Here, let me deal with these people."

"Let it go for now," said Emmanuel. "I do want to know what happened here years ago, and I will return. But right now we should focus on the vEcotourism project."

"Are you sure?" said Lucy. "I'm sure we can sneak into this joint."

Emmanuel badly wanted to learn about his origins, but recently he had become more interested in helping the apes.

"I am sure," he said.

"Then," said Lucy, "we should fly, by way of Bali, to Flores. Flores is remote, exotic, and adventurous. It has human-eating komodo dragons and should be an ideal vEco test site."

"Sounds good," said Emmanuel, noting that Flores was on the way to East Timor.

As they waited by the bus stop, a tall, young woman in her late twenties approached and stood nearby. She had dirty blond hair in a long braid and a tattoo on her right arm.

"Weird!" said Lucy, staring.

"What?" asked Emmanuel.

"Her tattoo."

"What about it?"

"Excuse me!" Lucy called out, "but is that tattoo of a nematode?"

The woman laughed. "Most people don't recognize it."

"That is *so cool,*" said Lucy. "Do you study nematodes?"

"No—I'm a fish person," she said, introducing herself as Annette.

After a minute's silence, Lucy said, "So you work in the lab here?"

"I'm based in the States but I collaborate with scientists here when I do field work."

"I see," said Lucy. "Would you know anything about genetic research being done here? Like research on great apes and humans?"

"Sorry," said Annette. "I'm afraid I've been focused on my own work lately."

The bus arrived and the three of them boarded. During the ride to Makassar, Lucy came up with a few rules and rituals for her bible-writing project, but eventually she could no longer contain her curiosity.

"So why a tattoo of a nematode?" she blurted.

"They are one of the most numerous multicellular creatures on the planet," explained Annette. "They are found in polar regions, in the tropics, on mountain tops, in lakes, and on ocean floors. We people think we're a huge success but, biologically speaking, we're really just one creature out of many sharing the earth."

"Are nematodes like earthworms?" asked Emmanuel, looking at the tattoo.

"Not quite. They're known as roundworms. Most are microscopic, many are parasitic, and some can grow to be over twenty feet long."

"How far back in time," he asked, "were the first nematodes?"

"That's a difficult question to answer," said Annette, "as there is no nematode fossil record to speak of. We have to rely on molecular phylogenies."

When the bus pulled into the central station, Annette said she was headed to a market to look for fish specimens. "Would you like to come along?"

"Sure."

"It's an underground fish market, and it's not for the weak-stomached."

"We're up for adventure!" said Lucy.

Annette led them to a bustling shopping district and into an open-air building. "You mentioned adventure," she said, approaching the stairs at the far end of the building. "I find the science to be interesting, but I wouldn't be pursuing a career in science if it didn't involve physical adventures."

Emmanuel and Lucy followed Annette down the stairs to a huge, dimly lit area the size of a football field. The underground market had a dirt and tile floor. Catchways drained the stalls of excess water, fish blood, guts, and other liquids.

Emmanuel noticed the smell of urine.

Lucy wrinkled her nose and breathed through her mouth.

They slowed their pace.

"Hey, Meeester," a man said.

"I'm not a *mister!*" Lucy retorted. "And for the sake of the children, would you mind not smoking? *Merokok membunuh!*"

"Hey, Meeester," said another man. "*Dari mana?*"

"*Dari America,*" replied Lucy. "And for the sake of the children, would you *mind* . . ."

The man took a drag from the clove cigarette. "*Selamat datang.*"

"*Terimah kasih,*" said Lucy. "Thanks for the welcome."

"*Sama sama,*" said the man.

Annette had meanwhile approached a few of the stalls where her quest for trumpetfish was met with nervous laughter. Dried trumpetfish were used by locals as an aphrodisiac.

Annette approached a stall behind which sat two teenage boys. After laughing nervously, they responded to her question by placing a number of dried fish specimens on the counter.

A crowd gathered.

Emmanuel and Lucy stood at the periphery and watched.

"Hey Meeester," someone said.

Annette picked out two dried trumpetfish from the array.

"*Barapa harga?*" she asked.

"*Satu juta rupiah,*" said one boy.

"*Satu juta? Terlalu banyak!*"

"That is a million rupiah," Emmanuel told Lucy, "or about a hundred U.S. dollars."

The boys puckered their lips.

"*Satu juta untuk satu,*" said the other boy.

"Now they want a million rupiah *per* trumpetfish," explained Emmanuel.

With a trumpetfish in each hand, Annette examined the specimens.

The crowd grew quiet.

Lucy breathed slowly and deliberately, trying not to retch from the stench.

Annette paced by the bloodstained stall.

The crowd stepped back to give her room.

"Poor Annette," Emmanuel whispered. "She is not doing well."

"Why do you say that?" Lucy whispered.

"Look at her fingers. She is twitching. She is nervous and it shows."

Annette cleared her throat and placed the trumpetfish on the counter.

The crowd held their breath.

"*Tidak,*" said Annette. "No thank you."

The boys pouted.

The crowd dispersed.

Lucy and Emmanuel followed Annette to the edge of the market where she transferred scraps of tissue from her fingernails to two tiny tubes.

"Annette had been scratching the specimens," whispered Lucy, "to collect a sample for DNA analysis. Not much material is needed, you know."

— 65 —

Emmanuel hugged his chest, took a deep breath, and stared at the airline's motto embroidered inside the jet: FIFTY YEARS OF CHALLENGE. The motto brought to mind challenges he had faced lately. First he lost his Bible, then he found himself on the wrong side of the line separating humans from spiritually deprived creatures, and then he discovered that his ape family was on the verge of extinction. Then, the other day, the hope of discovering the truth about his genetic makeup seemed to slip from his grasp.

Lucy had observed Emmanuel's self-confidence fall and rise and, since their brief visit to the Speciation Lab, fall again. Noticing the return of his downward-looking pouts, she tried to curtail the backsliding by engaging his intellect. She leaned over him and asked Annette, who was en route to Bali, about the scientific significance of the Wallace Line.

"We are more or less flying over the Wallace Line now," said Annette. "Plants and animals found *east* of here, which you can see out your window, are physically and genetically similar to flora and fauna of Australia and New Guinea.

"Plants and animals found *west* of here, which you can see out my window, are physically and genetically similar to flora and fauna of Asia. In 1858, British naturalist Alfred Russell Wallace noticed that creatures on either side of the divide differ as much as those of South America and Africa. The Line was created millions of years ago when Australia's tectonic plate—and the creatures that had evolved there—collided with Southeast Asia's plate.

"But it's not only geological collisions that make the area biologically fascinating. Due to the Indopacific region's unique geography, it's an ideal place for creating species, which explains its astounding biological diversity."

Emmanuel's curiosity got the better of him. "How are new species made?" he asked.

"One way is through isolation. When parts of a population get isolated from one another for long periods of time, one or more new species arise. Here's an example:

"Imagine a body of shallow water with two deep basins on opposite ends. Imagine a species of trumpetfish living there. It is a single species because any individual male could produce sexually viable offspring with any individual female. Imagine a dramatic drop in the water level so that all the trumpetfish—other than those in the two deep basins—dry up and die.

"Imagine after five hundred years, the water rises so fish in both basins can intermingle once again. All the fish at that point would probably still be part of a single species.

"But imagine the waters did *not* rise after five hundred years. The two populations of trumpetfish would gradually accumulate mutations that would be shared within, but not across, basin populations. After a long time, perhaps a million years, the behavioral and physical differences between individuals across basins would be so great that they would be considered separate species. After such a point, an individual male from one basin could no longer produce sexually viable offspring with a female from the other—even if the waters rose and reconnected the two populations. After such a point, we would have two species where once there was only one.

"When the earth heats up, ice at the poles melts and sea-levels rise. When the earth cools, ice at the poles gathers and sea-levels fall. In certain geographic locations, and in the region around the Wallace Line in particular, the rising and falling of the waters serves as a powerful, isolation-driven speciation engine."

Emmanuel nodded slowly. He visualized a rising sea level that increasingly isolated land-based creatures on mountain tops and that increasingly allowed sea creatures to sexually interact. He visualized a dropping sea level that increasingly isolated sea creatures in deep ocean basins and that increasingly allowed land-based creatures to sexually interact.

"The more we understand about genetics and geography," Annette pointed out, "the more effectively we can determine boundaries for protected underwater parks. So if there is an endangered species that lives in area A, whereas a hugely successful species lives in area B, the protected park ideally would contain area A."

The conversation paused as a flight attendant served fruit dishes.

Emmanuel sniffed at the mangoes as he pictured himself on a mountaintop, isolated and threatened by rising waters. He thought about pathways to Lucy and Evelyn's respective mountaintops and wondered if his genetic differences placed him in a different species.

— 66 —

When the screen at the Internet café finally refreshed, Lucy saw a message from Zann in her inbox. Clicking on the message, she longed for a faster connection. She didn't have much time.

"Holy cow!" she blurted, rereading the e-mail's subject. It read, "Your friend Emmanuel's genetic identity & taxonomical classification results."

Lucy thought of her bible-writing project. Emmanuel might—depending on the content of this e-mail—actually need what she had been writing.

Emmanuel appeared at the door. "Come on," he shouted. "The gates are about to close!"

"Wait!" she shot back.

"We will miss the flight to Labuan Bajo!"

"Damn it—will you give me a minute?"

"*There's NO TIME!*"

Emmanuel spun around, tilted forward, and ran through the Bali airport.

Lucy left 10,000 rupiah on the keyboard and ran after him.

— 67 —

"Blast it," said Lucy at an Internet café in Labuan Bajo. "They're *gone!*"

"What is gone?" asked Emmanuel.

"The e-mails in my *freakin' inbox.*" Her face turned deep red.

Emmanuel took a step back.

"*Jeez,*" she said, inching closer to tears.

Emmanuel recognized the vulnerability, stepped forward, and embraced her.

Chill monkey girl, Lucy told herself, trying to understand the emotions sweeping through her. She wondered if maybe she was getting too wrapped up in trying to help Emmanuel. Her concern for him had, after all, recently triggered frustration and bursts of anger. Then again, she wasn't about to abandon helping him, nor was she about to abandon her bible-writing project, because of some bumps along the way.

"Okay, you handsome brute," she said. "Give me two minutes to send an e-mail and we're outta here."

She wrote to Zann, asking him to resend the e-mail in which he had identified Emmanuel's taxonomic place in the natural world.

"Did you check your e-mail?" asked Lucy as they left the café and stepped into bright sunlight.

"There was not enough time."

"We can go back."

Emmanuel assumed his parents had written and were upset with him for not being in touch. The last thing he wanted was to hurt them, but he needed time and space to explore his roots and identity. Besides, he told himself, he no longer belonged in their nest. It was difficult to distance himself from them, but it was something he had to do.

"Some other time," he said, shifting uncomfortably.

"I think I know what happened to the lost e-mails," said Lucy as they walked through the sparsely populated town. "I never logged out in Bali and whoever used the computer afterward could have deleted them."

"I suppose that is possible," he said, wondering what she had lost.

The phone rang.

Lucy's eyes bulged.

"That is your cell phone," Emmanuel pointed out.

"*My* cell phone?"

"Yes," he said. "Gadget was going to call today to see about testing the virtual ecotourism system."

"It's not *my* cell phone—it's *Gadget's* cell phone! What should I do with this contraption?"

"Answer it?"

"*How?*"

"Press the answer button."

"Hello?" she barked.

"Hi," said Gadget.

"Yo! Gadget, dude, can you hear me? Earth to Gadget, come in Gadget! We're on Flores, heading to a park. Are you ready to test the system today?"

"No," he said.

"No? Did you say no? Hey—wait a second—Emmanuel is trying to tell me something."

Lucy put the phone down. "What is it?"

Emmanuel raised his thumb to his ear and spoke into his pinky. "You are shouting," he said calmly.

Lucy bit her lower lip. "Sorry."

"Gadget," she whispered, "can you hear me?"

"Loud and clear."

"Okay, good. So why can't we test the system today?"

"I am feeling sad."

"Bad connection," said Lucy. "I thought you said you're feeling sad."

"I did."

"Really? Why are you sad?"

"Women do not want to *be* with me," he said, mournfully.

"That's not true."

"You know what I mean."

"Are you saying you're having a rough time attracting a *mate?*"

"Yes."

"Might it have something to do with the luminous green egg strapped to the top of your head?"

Gadget did not reply.

"Have you thought about removing it?"

"It helps me remember things."

After an uneasy silence, Emmanuel decided to join the conversation. He switched on the speaker phone and pointed out that the green egg could, in the long run, help secure the right mate.

"How?" asked Gadget.

"Once you find someone," explained Emmanuel, "you can be sure that she truly loves you."

"Meaning her attraction to me would need to be exceptionally great," said Gadget, "to overcome the egg handicap."

"Yes."

"Perhaps," dreamed Gadget, "I will find a female who is attracted to the egg! Perhaps I will find a female who already wears a G.E.U.B. version 1.4 wireless and our children will be born with such devices. . . ."

"That is not the way it works," Emmanuel explained. "The green egg is a product of your behavior, not your genes. That means your offspring could be *taught* to wear an egg but they would not be born with one."

"That's true," said Lucy, "but remember that behavior influences genes and vice versa. So, in theory, the egg could set off some type of gene-culture pattern of coevolution."

"What do you mean?" asked Gadget.

"The egg could operate as a filter so that only certain types of ladies—mavericks no doubt—would want to mate with you. And maverick parents would likely raise their children as . . ."

"Mavericks!" exclaimed Emmanuel.

"Right! Over time, the maverick descendents might behave so differently that they could find mates only from within their particular group and, over an extraordinarily long time, their genetically isolated population could well be on their way toward the creation of a species."

"The population would achieve isolation based on behavior?" asked Gadget.

"To start with, yes," said Lucy. "But over time shared physical traits within the new population could arise. These traits would be reflected in the groups' genes and could serve as additional isolation mechanisms."

"I see," said Gadget.

"But the mechanisms of evolution aside, I'm sure someone suitable will come along," said Lucy. "So, can we test the vEco system now?"

"You are right," said Gadget, slowly. "It is *extremely* unlikely, but after hundreds of thousands—perhaps millions—of years a new species *could* arise based on a change in behavior. And I now believe, using my G.E.U.B. wireless species initiator device, that I am a genetic pioneer, embarking on a hybrid carbon and silicon-based life experiment! I believe my descendents will one day form a new species!"

Emmanuel looked to Lucy. She looked up and whistled softly.

"Silicon-based life?" said Emmanuel.

"What is life," replied Gadget, "but information systems with embedded self-replication instructions and mechanisms? Computer viruses have that."

"Computer viruses are alive?"

"Some would say yes."

"Can they mutate?" asked Lucy.

"They can be programmed to. They can be programmed to learn from new environments. There is much in the tech kingdom that biologists do not truly understand—such as self-evolving neural networks, computer viruses, and even self-evolving hardware devices! The line separating carbon from silicon-based life forms should not be drawn by the humans with such thickness or confidence!"

"Okay, Gadget," said Lucy quietly.

"Lucy," said Gadget, his voice quivering with excitement. "You are adventuresome! You are creative, intelligent, and attractive! Would you leap into the genetic unknown with me?"

"Sorry," said Lucy, wrapping an arm around Emmanuel, "I've already jumped."

— 68 —

When the project to plant a huge cross in the forests of Uganda stalled due to negotiations with landowners and government officials, Evelyn decided to pursue her idea of recruiting young people into the Church. She shared the idea with Father Forsyth. Making a big splash was not her style, she told him. Her proposed project would move slowly and thoughtfully.

Father Forsyth liked the idea. "Take your time and think it through," he said.

After weeks of thinking about the project, Evelyn decided to use music as a way to reach out to young people. She felt inspired to write the music herself but found herself unable to do so. The problem had to do with her inability to focus. Each time she found herself open to the ideas, melody, and metaphor of inspiration, she was interrupted by gadgets—by bright yellow flashes of her Web updater, by cell phone ringtones, and by vibrations from incoming text messages. Maintaining a creative state of mind, which for her involved a blend of relaxation and motivation, wasn't easy and she felt frustrated. She decided to do something about it. She powered off all her gadgets.

This introduced a new set of problems. Her friends and family grew irritated at her self-imposed isolation and, without the gadgets, she felt disconnected, primitive, and naked. Nonetheless, at certain times during the day and night, the gadgets remained powered off.

The following week, she decided to further her experiment with creativity. Though she felt odd as she drove, gadgetless, to a campground by Chesapeake Bay—she had never gone camping alone—she hoped that a change of environment would encourage her to enter a more expansive state of mind. She set up a tent and as evening fell she listened to the symphony of crickets, birds, and frogs.

It was later that night, nurtured by animal sounds and darkness, when the melody came to her, a simple wordless love song that, in Evelyn's imagination beckoned the very dawn of creation. This, she smiled, could be the first song of a musical, a rock opera of sorts, that she could help write and that could be the cornerstone of the recruitment project. The musical, she thought, could help bridge science and religion by gently encouraging science-oriented people to empathize with, and better understand, the world of religion and by encouraging religious people to empathize with, and better understand, the world of science.

Evelyn loved the idea of creating a musical that blended science and religion. Science may accurately describe what's out there, she thought, but those who dismiss religion and try to stamp it out are turning their backs on Truth they may want and need. I don't think we have evolved to live in a world without protection and comfort, she thought as the melody played in her mind. I don't think we have evolved to survive in a grim, Godless world devoid of higher meaning. Jane Goodall doesn't live like that and I doubt even Charles Darwin lived like that!

That night in a big tent by the water, Evelyn had a vivid dream.

> *In the back of a Church sat a man with a dark waistcoat, bushy white beard, and grim countenance.*
>
> *"I love the music here," Evelyn whispered to him. "Do you?"*
>
> *The man looked up and Evelyn blinked at a large dark tree blowing wildly in the wind.*

— 69 —

"We should do this more often," said Emmanuel.

"Do what?" asked Lucy.

"Relax."

"I'll relax," said Lucy, "when justice prevails, the hungry are fed, and apes live together in peace and harmony."

"Amen," said Emmanuel.

But it was Lucy—bloated and nauseous—who wanted to sit in the beach chair and stare at the sea. She felt weak. Energy seemed to come in bursts lately. She watched divers unload scuba gear from a boat. The labor seemed heavy and cumbersome. She slipped into a haze of chaotic thought and at some point it occurred to her that she had missed a period. She soon fell asleep.

Fifteen minutes later she awoke feeling refreshed. She noticed one of the divers, an Indonesian man, stealing glances at Emmanuel (the man, at first glance, had mistaken Emmanuel for an orang utan).

"*Apa kabar?*" Lucy called out to him.

"*Kabar baik,*" the man replied, approaching with a snorkel, a mask, and fins. "*Saya nama* Wira."

"Hey, Wira. *Saya nama* Lucy and here be Emmanuel."

"You're from United States?" asked Wira.

"How did you know?" asked Lucy.

"Americans wear Canadian flags on their packs to feel safe."

Lucy frowned and asked about Wira's work.

Wira taught scuba diving. The latest set of classes had completed today and now he had a week off.

"Lucky you," said Lucy. "We're just starting our work week."

"What do you do?" asked Wira.

"We're pioneering an interactive, educational, storytelling-based technology called virtual ecotourism—or vEcotourism—which provides an economic incentive for people in remote areas to protect local wildlife and its habitat. In short, we're using storytelling and technology to help animals and currently we're looking for a place to test the vEco system."

"You look for a place here on Flores?"

"Yes."

"What kind of place?"

"A place with wildlife," said Emmanuel.

"A place with stories about the wildlife," added Lucy.

"I know of a place with both," whispered Wira. "*I know of the caves of the Ebu Gogo!*"

Hairs on Emmanuel's chest rose. He had heard of the legend but could not quite place it.

"Who are the Ebu Gogo?" asked Lucy.

"According to the people of Flores," said Wira, "they are little people—about three feet tall—with long arms. They are not monkeys, they are not humans, they are something in between."

Wira stared at Emmanuel.

"You make it sound like they're alive today," Lucy pointed out.

"Many believe that the Ebu Gogo lived with our ancestors on Flores and vanished hundreds or thousands of years ago. Others believe that the Ebu Gogo live here today, hidden in the caves."

"Now there's a novel ideal," said Lucy. "A colony of human-ape hybrids living in caves in Indonesia. What do you make of that, Emmanuel?"

"People have active imaginations," he said.

"Have you ever been to see the Ebu Gogo, Wira?"

"No."

"Why not?"

"Journeys to the caves, locals say, are one-way."

— 70 —

Emmanuel stood by an ocean's edge. A cold wind swept the gray sky. The water receded and he followed the slope to the ocean floor. He crossed the vast plain, which was littered with horseshoe crabs and smelled of rotting fish. The floor gradually rose and he followed the slope until he came upon a man in tattered clothes sitting in icy mud.

The man had bulging veins and a thick beard that hung like Spanish moss. He chanted, "AYJEEJEESEEAYSEEAYAYTEE." The vibrations hummed in Emmanuel's chest like a honey bee's buzz.

"Excuse me," interrupted Emmanuel. "What are you saying?"

"The Word," the man bellowed, "is a sacred code!"

"I do not understand the Word."

"The Word is the code for she who walked the earth some fourteen million years ago, whose offspring begot every chimp, orang utan, gorilla, bonobo, human, and ape hybrid that has or will ever live."

"Why do you chant the Word?"

"The Word is the Source and the Source is blessed by God."

Emmanuel paused. "Apes are blessed by God?"

"Yes."

"All of them? Meaning humans and chimps and gorillas and . . ."

"Yes!"

"Even ape hybrids?"

"I said all of them! Do you doubt me?"

Emmanuel cowered but managed to ask, "All great apes are spiritual beings?"

"Yes," said the man.

"I thought only humans were spiritual."

"Who told you that?"

"The humans."

The man stroked his long white beard and raised a bushy brow.

Emmanuel scratched his head. "So you are saying that all chimps, orang utans, gorillas, bonobos, humans—and even all ape hybrids—are spiritual beings?"

"You doubt me again!" the man boomed.

"I am afraid of you. Are you angry with me?"

"No. I am harsh because apes seek a dominant figure to establish a physical and spiritual pecking order. I am also compassionate and gentle because apes need to be nurtured."

"Who . . . Who are you?"

"I am the Keeper! I keep the stories, rules, and rituals upon which great ape spirituality and survival depends!"

"I do not understand what spirituality has to do with survival."
"Listen carefully," said the Keeper, "and I shall inform thee."

Emmanuel woke and wrote the dream in the journal. He joined Lucy and Wira for breakfast, and they continued the drive to the caves.

— 71 —

"Do you hear that?" whispered Lucy.

"Hear what?" asked Wira.

"Shhhh!"

"It is probably just an animal," said Emmanuel.

"*Listen!*"

The sound of dripping water, then the sound of a ringing cell phone, echoed in the cave.

"Hello?" said Lucy.

It was Gadget. "The vEcotour starts in thirty seconds," he said. "I advertised it on the Web, and quite a few people have signed up."

"What do you mean people have signed up?" Lucy demanded. "I thought we were going to test this thing first. . . ."

"We are—this is the test."

"I mean test it *privately.*"

"Nothing like a little pressure to help iron out the bugs. . . ."

"Gadget you rat fink!"

"Ten seconds," said Gadget. "Nine. Eight. Do not forget to press the video button. Six. Five."

"I'll tar 'n' feather you. . . ."

"Three. Two. One."

Gadget cleared his throat.

"Welcome to ChimpCorps' Indonesian Mystery Virtual Ecotour," he began. "My name is Gadget, and I will be your host and Lucy will be your tour guide. Are you there, Lucy? Or should I ask *where are you?*"

"Thanks Gadget, and hi everyone. I'm here with two friends, crouched in mud, in a limestone cave on an island called Flores."

"Thank you Lucy," said Gadget. "I should mention that proceeds from this and other ChimpCorps vEcotours generate an ongoing financial incentive for people in remote areas to protect wildlife and its habitat. Donations to ChimpCorps are tax-deductible."

"Today's tour," said Lucy, "is an interactive exploration of the cave and, possibly, its legendary inhabitants, the Ebu Gogo."

"Fascinating," said Gadget, searching the Web for *Ebu Gogo*. He highlighted three paragraphs and a photograph of an Indonesian cave and clicked on the Update button. "Perhaps you would like to say a few words about the Ebu Gogo."

"Sure," said Lucy.

A long, eerie wail filled the cave.

Wira dropped to the mud in a fetal position.

Lucy took a quick breath in. "There it is again."

Emmanuel sniffed the damp air and switched the headlamp flashlight to high beam. "Am going deeper into the cave," he whispered, "to find out what is making that sound. Better to meet it down there than up here."

"Lucy," said Gadget, his voice crackling over the cell phone. "Would you please describe to the audience what is going on?"

Emmanuel dropped to his knuckles and disappeared around a bend.

Lucy cleared her throat.

"There's something alive in the cave apart from ourselves," she said, "and Emmanuel, my travel partner, has gone to check it out. I'm here with Wira, who has guided us to this cave."

"Thank you for that, and would Wira like to add a few words?"

"I'm afraid not," said Lucy. "He's shivering too much to talk right now. He thinks we're about to be eaten by the Ebu Gogo."

"Not a problem," said Gadget. "Maybe he can join us later on—

assuming, of course, that he does not get eaten. Now, this just in: one of our vEcotourists, Mike in North Platte, Nebraska, writes, 'Are the Ebu Gogo real or are they mythological creatures?' and, also, 'What is making that frightening sound?'"

"We don't know what's making the sound, Mike," said Lucy, "nor do we know if the Ebu Gogo exist outside the realm of our imagination. What we do know is that we are all affected by stories, particularly those heard repeatedly during childhood. Stories affect the way that we see the world around us. Wira grew up hearing stories about the Ebu Gogo, not just from other children but from local village elders, much the same way many of us were exposed to stories from the Bible. So the Ebu Gogo seem physically real to him even if they are only a myth."

"Thanks for that Lucy and good questions, Mike," said Gadget. "Now Sari in Japan writes, 'Has a vEcotourguide ever been eaten?'"

"Not yet, Sari," offered Lucy. "We should have more on that later today."

"Excellent," said Gadget. "And now, as there do not seem to be any more questions, why not continue with the tour?"

Another wail filled the cave.

A shiver shot up Lucy's spine.

Wira fainted.

"*Holy schist,*" Lucy whispered.

"I hate to be a nag," Gadget pointed out, "but we really should video-enable the vEcotour in case the Ebu Gogo *do* rise from the depths of the cave. One certainly gets the sense that they might do so at any moment. And we should make sure the signal booster is set to maximum."

Lucy heard a shout, a thud, and another wail. She spun around, facing the direction Emmanuel had gone. She didn't want to leave Wira here alone, but Emmanuel might need help. Besides, whatever lurked below would have to get past her before reaching Wira. She switched the headlamp flashlight to high beam, pressed the cell phone's video button, and began to walk. Her torso angled forward due to the low ceiling of the cave.

"Can you still hear me?" she asked.

"Loud and clear," said Gadget. "I am pleased to report that we are now receiving the video stream from your cell phone. Is that a bend in the cave up ahead?"

"That's right," replied Lucy. "Can you see the hanging stalactites?"

"We see them," said Gadget. "They are whizzing by—are you moving quickly?"

"Yes," said Lucy.

Gadget searched the Web for "stalactites" and clicked the Update button.

Lucy rounded another bend and the downward slope grew steeper. The path ended abruptly. She lay on her stomach and peered over the edge. She saw a narrow passageway several feet below that continued to slope steeply downward. She switched off the headlamp and saw light emerging from the passageway.

"You are not thinking of going down *there*, are you?" asked Gadget.

"Emmanuel must have come this way."

"Hold on a moment, Lucy. There are two-hundred-and-seven vEcotourists currently logged in. Let us ask *them* what to do! Okay, everybody, please look on your browser for the Instant Feedback section and click the YES or NO button based on whether Lucy should drop into the dark pit, crawl through the narrow tunnel, and try to rescue her friend. You can also type a comment or question and click SEND."

Lucy took a deep breath.

"Bear with us, Lucy. This will be a wonderful test of the system and will only take a minute—I promise."

Lucy didn't wait. She powered off the cell phone, slid down the slope, and began crawling through the tunnel's warm mud. The light gradually brightened and the ceiling angled upward. Minutes later she switched off the headlight and stood at the edge of a fifteen-foot drop. She marveled at the size and beauty of the cavernous room, with its high vaulted ceilings and gilded mineral formations. A shaft of light from the surface illuminated her muddy black hair. She closed her eyes, pushed her hands deep into her pockets, and squeezed the familiar small flat stone.

"The Tablet of Manimal!" she whispered.

Lucy held it to the light and pondered the two lines and oval etched in gray. She no longer believed that it was prehistoric artwork seeing as how horseshoe crabs, she had learned, never lived near where she had found it. But that didn't matter to her. It still *looked* like a horseshoe crab and it had become a symbol for her. Horseshoe crabs had hardly changed in hundreds of millions of years, and the Tablet had come to represent immensely deep stretches of time during which life had come into being.

She powered on the cell phone and Gadget reestablished the connection. "Are you okay?" he asked.

"Are the tourists still listening?" asked Lucy.

"Yes—and watching."

Lucy gazed at the glowing mineral deposits on the ceiling high above and thought about the "Book of Manimal Revelations" section from her bible-writing project. "I'm back, everybody, and I'd like to tell you a story, a bio-story. This cave is special, because it may contain creatures who are part human and part animal. These creatures are known to some as the Ebu Gogo and to others as manimals."

Lucy's voice rose and echoed in the vast basin as though she were delivering a sermon in a cathedral.

"I have traveled halfway around the planet to learn about such a creature, but today I ask myself: what would it mean if I actually found and observed a living manimal?"

"Lucy?" said Gadget.

"Let me finish, Gadget. Today I ask myself . . ."

"Lucy?"

"*Clam up will you?* Today I ask myself: what would such a discovery tell us about who we are and how we came to be? Would it remind us that humans—like all living things—are subject to the forces of evolution? Would it remind us that so-called hybrids are part of our species' story? Would it remind us of the time, 6 or 7 million years ago, when the ancestors of modern humans and modern chimpanzees knuckle-walked the earth? Would it remind us of how these ancestors, driven by the forces of evolution, began to separate into genetically and behaviorally different creatures, with one group becoming chimps and the other group becoming us? Would it remind us that the separation did not occur overnight and that successful intergroup reproduction occurred *for perhaps a million years after the split began?* Let us be reminded, as we continue to explore the cave, that the fitness of these so-called hybrids may have . . ."

"*Lucy!*"

"What is it, Gadget?"

"*Look down—there is a live manimal!*"

— 72 —

Distracted by the movement of a creature below, Emmanuel lost his footing and fell hard. After he regained consciousness, the sound of dripping water took his mind off the pain. He later crept from the pit, rubbed his canines, and thought about prayer. He felt lightheaded and vulnerable. He wanted to increase his chances of getting out of the cave alive.

He wanted to pray to God, but God sought prayers, he worried, from humans only. And yet with so many different types of creatures on the planet, he theorized, maybe God *is* interested in hearing prayer from hybrids such as himself. Besides, science had not taught that God does not exist, nor had it taught that prayer does not work.

Two months earlier in the Senegalese forest, Emmanuel had implored Nelson, the signing chimpanzee, to have hope and faith and to pray to God. "Please hang on," he had said. "God will help us to survive."

Emmanuel recalled his words to Nelson and felt a wave of joy flow through him.

— 73 —

At the natural history museum the crowd pressed around a computer screen and stared.

"What's going on?" asked Evelyn, approaching.

"It's a live Web tour," said a man, "that apparently is taking place in a cave in Asia. They claim to have found a cross . . ."

"A Christian cross?" asked Evelyn.

"A cross between an ape and a human," said the man.

"But don't scientists think that *that* cross lived a *very* long time ago?" asked Evelyn.

"It's likely a hoax," said the man, "but . . . if not . . . could we have been so wrong about the timing?"

The man approached the keyboard. "Please display a different angle," he typed. "We want to see its face."

He clicked the SEND button.

Evelyn read about the Ebu Gogo on the vEcotourism Webpage and watched the slow, strangely familiar movements of the long-armed creature.

— 74 —

The male primate knuckle-walked around a pool of water. It cupped its hand, took water from the pool, and slowly raised its hands and eyes to the light.

— 75 —

Lucy felt unsafe walking downtown Dili's deserted streets. It was 9:15 p.m. She heard the snap of a twig and spun around. No one was there. Passing a pile of smoldering garbage, she hoped to return to the hotel but the room smelled of decomposing mouse.

So this is Emmanuel's home, she thought. Home is not always pretty.

She passed another burned-out building. "Help me," she whispered, quoting from the book she had been writing that she had named *The Monkey Bible.* "Help me, Protector of All Apes, so my genes may survive."

Lucy heard a cough and she spun around. No one.

She turned and started walking back to the hotel.

Be calm, she thought. Think about something else.

She thought about Emmanuel, who was asleep in the hotel room. Clearly, he needed the rest.

She thought about the journey. They had stopped here, in East Timor's capital, en route to Australia where Mark had recommended they seek medical attention for Emmanuel's leg. Emmanuel had taken a bad fall two weeks ago in the limestone cave, and while the leg seemed to heal quickly, it made sense to have it checked out.

She thought about the creature, the so-called manimal, in the cave. Had it been an Ebu Gogo? Had it been Emmanuel? To confuse matters, Emmanuel could not recall sitting by a pool of water. Was that the truth? Or had the fall disrupted his memories? How could she tell?

Lucy wished that she knew what had happened in the cave. Her own observations there, made from a considerable distance, had been cut short when Wira regained consciousness and started to shout.

Lucy bit her lip and walked faster. She turned the corner and saw the hotel. A wet swollen hand pressed the back of her neck.

The hand let go and she spun around and faced the men with the scars and machetes. One grabbed her arms, another hugged her tightly. She kicked, punched, and screamed. When the barrel of a gun touched her head she grew calm. She could hear herself breathing. The men pushed her to move quickly. They took her to a storefront that they smashed and torched. They robbed her, locked her upstairs, and ran.

— 76 —

Emmanuel woke to the sound of gunshots.

"Lucy?" he said.

No answer.

He looked across the room and saw a man on TV pointing a gun. He switched channels and watched a crowd disperse after it had beaten to death a hit-and-run driver. He switched channels and watched a man, sword in hand, leap from the ground to a rooftop. He switched and watched the commentator discuss tribal violence in remote areas of the far eastern province.

TV, thought Emmanuel. It stands for *tribal violence.*

He picked up a newspaper and read about outbreaks of violence in Halmahara and Irian Jaya. He found an article about chimpanzees in Freetown, Sierra Leone, who had escaped from a sanctuary and had brutally killed a driver and maimed three others.

Emmanuel looked down at his hand and coiled his fingers into a fist.

We are not cute, furry dolls, he thought. We are like you. We are you. *We love to watch TV.*

He heard a scream. His pulse quickened. He switched off the TV. He heard another scream and a window smashing. He rushed outside and smelled the thick smoke.

"Emmanuel *help!*"

"Oh my God," he said, the hair on his back rising.

— 77 —

Following Lucy's shouts, Emmanuel ran two blocks to the smoldering building and leapt up the stairs to a locked door on the third floor.

"Lucy—stand back!"

He threw himself with force against the door, but it did not budge.

He heard Lucy coughing.

"Stay low," he instructed. "Do not panic."

He rushed the door again.

"Listen to me, Lucy. Pick the lock. Do you hear me? Pick the lock."

The smoke grew thick in the hallway.

"Pick the lock of the door," he bellowed. "Do it *now!*"

Emmanuel heard the crackling of the fire. He heard *click.* The door opened slightly.

He pushed past the door and found Lucy on all fours, panting. Flames rose from the center of the room. At the far edge of the room water poured down from a crack in the floor above.

"I can't open my eyes," she cried, gasping for air.

He carried her toward the stairs but quickly leapt back into the room, as flames from the floor below had engulfed the hallway. Here in the room the slow, steady flow of water slowed the spread of the flames. He carried her around the flames toward the open window.

Lucy sensed the light and fresh air. "We're too high," she cried. "We're too high to jump!"

"Trust me, my human friend," he whispered in her ear.

"Wait," she sobbed. "The Bible! Don't leave the Bible! It's in my daypack!"

The daypack had already caught fire.

"The Bible," she gasped. "*Save the Bible!*"

"We do not need it!" he exclaimed.

"We *do* need it! We *all* need it! We need it to *survive!*"

Emmanuel thought she was delirious, but she spoke with such fervor that he put her down, rushed toward the center of the room, and kicked the pack from the larger flames. He leapt back from the searing heat, stamped on the pack, and stuffed the charred book into his own pack. He lifted Lucy and stepped through the window to the edge of the sill.

"Hold on tight," he said and he jumped.

Lucy's arms and legs tightened around him.

Emmanuel's powerful hands reached out and gripped a branch of the tree and there they swung, catching their breath, in the tropical breeze.

— 78 —

Emmanuel marveled at the news. "You mean I am going to be a . . ."

"*Daddy,*" Lucy whispered.

They rushed into each other's arms.

Lucy had been so taken by the news that her giddiness seemed to cover up the loss of *The Monkey Bible* that, except for the section she had copied, had been rendered unreadable in the East Timor fire.

"A daddy?" he gushed. "That is wonderful! Do you know for certain?"

She told him about the mood swings, the morning sickness, the missed period; she reminded him about the unprotected sex.

Emmanuel beamed. He loved the idea of raising a helpless little creature, and he loved the idea that, in a sense, he already was a father. After all, the baby was alive right now.

Lucy breathed easier when she saw Emmanuel's reaction to the news and in her mind she began to converse with the life in her womb. Hey groovy little life form, it's me, Mom! You and me, kid. Are we going to have fun or what! This is so cool. Don't you worry, everything is going to be fine, hey?

Lucy wondered how the baby would affect her relationship with Emmanuel. She hoped it would solidify her position with him. She wondered how the baby would affect her life at the University of Washington, where she planned to continue her studies and build a baby-support network.

It occurred to Lucy that she hadn't heard back from Zann. While she had spent months entertaining possible outcomes for Emmanuel's genetic identity, she had done so from a lighthearted, intellectual perspective. Now the possibilities seemed real and potentially ominous. What would it mean, for instance, if he *wasn't* fully human? While she wouldn't be returning from the hospital with the ultrasound image of a chimp fetus, it wasn't clear what the image would look like.

Lucy set aside her reflections as she and Emmanuel, in a flurry of activity, made plans to purchase tickets to Seattle. They felt disappointed to be leaving Australia and Asia so soon, but the fine print on their medical insurance suggested that they return to the United States right away. They reassured each other that they'd be back.

When they arrived at the Sydney airport, Lucy checked her e-mail and noticed a message from Zann.

"We should probably get moving," said Emmanuel.

"Ya, ya," said Lucy. "I'll be right there."

She began to read the message.

subject: Genetic identity a bit messy

Lucy,

I am resending the previous e-mail, per your request.

I sent the handkerchief to Thurstian who apparently spent quite a bit of time sequencing various areas of the genome. I now have the results. Analysis shows that your friend shares approximately 99.9% of his genes with the broad populations of humans.

The .1% difference is not a cause for alarm and could be due to errors in either the sequencing process or impurities in the blood sample. Keep in mind that any creature's genetic identity tends to be a bit messy and it may be that some of what makes your friend "unique" can largely be explained by the natural variation found among populations.

Additional testing and analysis would be useful. To be honest,

"We should get going," said Emmanuel, fidgeting. "If we are not at the gate in . . ."

"Give me another second!" Lucy demanded and kept reading.

To be honest, I don't have the time right now to help but here's a list (attached) of scientists and technicians whom you might wish to contact.

In summary, an unusual percentage of your friend's DNA sequences do seem more closely related to apes than to other humans, but clearly more research is required. You should let your friend know that genetic variation—the foundation of evolution—is entirely natural.

Zann

"I am *going!*" exclaimed Emmanuel.

"We'll go together," said Lucy, holding her belly.

PART SIX

Unlikely God

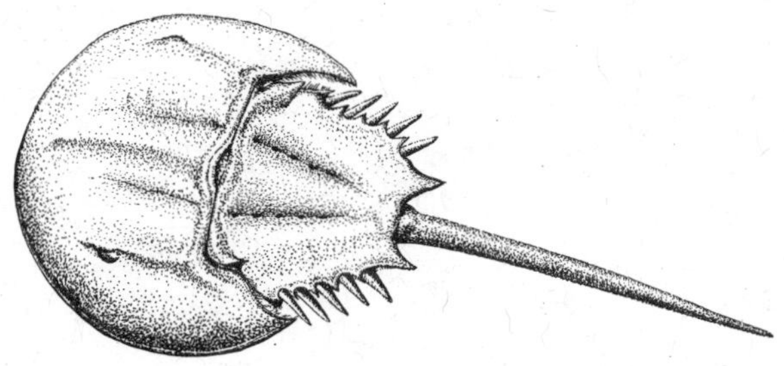

— 79 —

In the back of a Church sat a man with a dark waistcoat, bushy white beard, and grim countenance.

"I feel at home here," Evelyn whispered to him. "Do you?"

The man looked up and Evelyn blinked at the large tree blowing in the wind.

Evelyn woke and replayed the dream in her mind. The grim, bearded man looked familiar, and it bothered her that she couldn't place him.

— 80 —

In Seattle, Emmanuel and Lucy sat by the condiment section of a fast food restaurant and watched a man approach the napkin dispenser.

"What do you predict?" asked Emmanuel.

"I'd say a two-forker, two-spooner, and two-knifer."

"Napkins?"

"A ten-grabber," said Lucy. "At *least* a ten-grabber."

"Okay—here goes!"

"Here's the approach!"

"The reach!"

"And . . . it's a two-fisted grabber! *We're talking fifteen or more in each hand!*"

"And a fist full of forks!"

"And a fist full of spoons!"

"But no knives."

"Maybe he's trying to conserve."

Emmanuel and Lucy broke out laughing.

"Here's someone returning their tray," said Lucy. "It sure looks like a stacker!"

"Yes—there is the stack of napkins and there is the stack of cutlery!"

"Were any actually *used?*"

"None that I can see!"

"Okay—here goes!"

"The approach!"

"The push!"

"The angling of the tray!"

"The nation's glorious trash container burps with delight!"

Emmanuel and Lucy discussed, as they ate burritos, how the wasteful behavior seemed to be particular to the United States. They wondered, as they tried to explain the behavior, if Americans grabbed stacks of napkins from a fear of spilled drink, but this theory didn't explain piles of unused plastic forks, spoons, and knives. They wondered if the surplus napkins and cutlery, like material goods in general, provided a measure of comfort and emotional support.

Lucy put down the burrito, looked around the seating area, and noted that there were many ways by which to identify and classify behaviors. She recalled from *The Monkey Bible* the Gobis, Moos, and Flatlanders. Picking her right canine tooth with the nail of her right thumb, she recalled the aaoa, which stood for *apes aware of apeness*. She recalled other categories including the Manimals, which presumably included Emmanuel, but right now she didn't want to devise a system of boxes into which all of creation could be pigeonholed.

Emmanuel put down the burrito and looked up. "Here comes someone!"

"I wonder how many square feet of napkins *he* has consumed lately!" exclaimed Lucy.

"What do you think?"

"I'd say he's off the scale!"

"We will see! Okay, here is the approach!"

"The reach!"

"And . . ."

"Look at that!"

"Can you believe it?"

The napkin dispenser was empty.

— 81 —

"Lucy—what a nice surprise," said Dr. Feynmore. "I heard you've been taking time off to travel."

"That's right, but I may return in winter quarter and I was wondering what courses you'll be teaching."

"The usual lower division ones, which I presume you know about."

Lucy nodded.

"Additionally, I'll oversee an independent study seminar and teach two upper division courses: one about the use of facial expressions across human cultures and one about current events, or shall we say recent finds, in anthropology."

"Sounds interesting. I've been out of touch the past few months and could use a refresher course on current events."

"One topic we shall cover in depth is ID."

"Meaning intelligent design, as in neo-creationism?"

"Correct. And, yes, the movement has aligned itself with creationism."

"I thought ID affected the teaching of biology—not anthropology."

"ID has the potential to affect the way any science is taught," said the professor.

"What do you mean?"

"ID looks to an intelligent designer, which is to say *God,* to explain complex scientific problems for which there are no clear answers."

"So ID associates God with what is not 100 percent understood by today's science?" asked Lucy.

"Yes and many people of faith think the approach is unsound."

"Why?"

"Because the Kingdom of the Divine shrinks as scientific knowledge continues to grow."

"I take it the scientific community isn't thrilled with ID either?"

"Correct," said Dr. Feynmore. "In the face of complexity, scientists don't throw up their hands and stop looking for answers, nor do they offer explanations based on the unfathomable, the immeasurable, and the unrepeatable."

"It's weird," said Lucy. "It's like you have two universes. The first is defined by what you can see, measure, and understand. The second is defined by what you can't see, measure, or understand."

"Correct, and ID proponents are attempting to introduce the second universe into the first."

"Isn't it good to bridge the universes?"

"It depends on where and how it's done. ID proponents discount the first universe, the universe of science, and try to save people from inhabiting it. For instance, ID proponents want students in biology courses to be taught that the foundation of modern biological science—evolution through natural selection—is only one of many credible theories."

"What other theories would they want taught?"

"The theory of intelligent design, for one."

"So if ID takes root, biology might increasingly be removed from biology classes?"

"Bridging universes can be tricky."

"Sounds competitive."

"It is," said Dr. Feynmore, "and this is exactly the sort of discussion I'd like to encourage in the course. Another topic we'll cover is the recent proto-hominid discovery in Indonesia."

"Which discovery was that?" asked Lucy.

"Where have *you* been?" asked the professor. "It was on the island of Flores and it is believed to be . . ."

"Flores?"

"Yes. In a limestone cave by the . . ."

"In a cave?"

"Yes. I'm surprised you haven't heard about it. It's big."

"Big?"

"It made front page of *Nature*, *Science*, *National Geographic*, *The New York Times*. . . ."

"I had no idea," said Lucy. "Did you see actual images from the cave?"

"No. Mind you, the so-called discovery is controversial. Some scientists think it is a new species of human, *Homo floresiensis*. Some think it is the most important anthropological discovery in fifty years. Others think it is nothing more than a case of modern humans suffering from microcephaly, a type of disease that affects brain size and stature."

"What do you think?" asked Lucy.

"Recent computer simulations suggest it is a new proto-human species that lived much more recently than anyone had expected," said the professor. "But I don't really know."

— 82 —

The wind outside the three-and-a-half-foot-high cave swirled the snow into chaotic frenzy but Lucy, wrapped in a thick sleeping bag, kept warm and dry. She had food, fuel, and candles to last for days. She had returned alone to the mountain sanctuary near Mount Rainier to grapple with the news from the clinic. They had told her that she wasn't pregnant.

"Of course I'm pregnant!" she had exclaimed. "I'm as pregnant as they come!"

"Sorry, ma'am," they said, shaking their heads.

After the initial denial, Lucy tried to soften the loss by making a list of indignities that she could now avoid. She wouldn't have to attend a baby shower, waddle like a duck, or dress like a whale. She wouldn't have to face labor pain, sleep deprivation, or time restrictions on her projects and social life. She wouldn't have to grow intimate with the output of someone else's bodily functions, nor would she need babysitters.

She had tried joking about the news but, to her amazement, the laughter transformed into a genuine longing to have a baby and, in particular, Emmanuel's baby. It didn't matter that he might not be 100 percent human. She loved who and what he was, and she believed unequivocally that his unique genetic identity was just right for her.

Here in the cave she gazed at the candle and tried to make sense of the longing. It occurred to her that having a baby was a way to pass along stories from long ago, stories embedded in the genes, stories about how to survive and reproduce in countless changing environments. Having a baby was a way to share stories, potentially forever, with future generations. Not having one was a way for the stories to die.

Listening to the howling wind, Lucy thought about her baby that never was and about the nature of being and not being. The universe, she noted, was 14 or so billion years old, which meant roughly 14 billion years had ticked by before her parents' egg and sperm cells had managed to come into existence and merge. Had she been associated with consciousness during those many years? If so, what type of consciousness?

Something had been going on before she had become "herself" and whatever it had been, she concluded, it had not been so bad. The innumerable aeons, after all, had gone by pretty quickly. She had no bad memories of it, and there must have been countless diverse and interesting things to be. Death, she figured, was a way to continue with what each of us had been doing for roughly 14 billion years. In contrast, being alive and limited, being awash with self-consciousness, was the tricky part, particularly for those worried silly about the inevitable return to the norm.

The soft candlelight illuminated her long black hair like a halo. She relaxed and imagined what she had been, physically, before she had been conceived. She imagined a cluster of nitrogen. She imagined volcanic ash and dust on the back of an elephant. She imagined rocks, bacteria, worms, soil, trees, clouds, and oceans. She imagined parts of beetles, jellyfish, ferns, crawdads, and horseshoe crabs. So compelling were the visualizations that she lost awareness of being confined in a body. She lost awareness of the passing of time.

Moments later, she regained self-consciousness as she enjoyed the buzz that accompanied the altered state of mind.

She sensed that she had undergone a mini-mystical experience, but without sophisticated neurological imaging tools—tools that likely didn't yet exist—she felt unable to measure, and was reluctant to interpret, what had just happened to her. Without such tools, she figured, interpretation of such a subjective experience would be vulnerable to distortions of whim and fancy and certainly wasn't science.

Lucy dwelt on the word "science." It carried enormous weight for her. She recalled how, when she was a little girl, Uncle Simon took her to the museum by Seattle's Space Needle.

"Science!" he would say, his bald head reflecting light like an orb. "Science is real! It's how the real world works! *Isn't it amazing?*"

Then he'd tell her how electrons spinning around a nucleus at different energy levels affected the world in which we live. Uncle Simon never stopped sharing with Lucy his interest in science and, last year, wowed her with tantalizing stories about the Large Hadron Collider and the elusive Higgs boson, known in scientific circles as the God particle.

Lucy wondered how Uncle Simon's stories and enthusiasm had affected the way she viewed the world. She had learned to inhabit the world of science, the fundamental nature of which is observable, measurable, and understandable through repeated experimentation. It was a world with which she was both intimate and comfortable.

She recognized a separate world, the world of religion and mystical experience, the fundamental nature of which is invisible, immeasurable, unrepeatable, and unfathomable. This world made her uneasy, and yet the experience of traveling with Emmanuel and of writing *The Monkey Bible* had encouraged her to explore the world of belief. Over the course of the past four months, she had come to understand that science describes what is, religion describes what is needed, and both are intertwined with survival.

— 83 —

Lucy sat in the cave, pen in hand, and pondered her charred, largely unreadable gift to Emmanuel, *The Monkey Bible*. Emmanuel would have appreciated the ideas in the book but now, based on the recent revelations of his genetic identity, he would actually need them. She recalled the ideas.

She recalled the section on rules and rituals.

The section had been narrated by UG, the Unlikely God, who helps all ape and human species to survive. According to *The Monkey Bible,* UG is as likely to exist as any other ape's view of the unknown and unknowable.

She recalled the section's various parts. There was the part about biodiversity loss.

Destroy the diversity, UG had said, and life shall renew itself largely in the form of rats and cockroaches. It shall do so because the genetic blueprint of whales and albatross and the like shall long be extinct.

Biodiversity, UG had said, defines avenues for future cells and consciousness, and if creatures go out of their way to preserve biodiversity, their genes are more likely to live forever.

In protecting biodiversity, UG had said, protect your closest kin, for they share most of your genes, but don't place all your eggs in one basket, for doing so has failed countless times over the aeons. Rather, protect your more distant kin as well, for they share quite a few of your genes.

Biodiversity is essential for the survival of all higher primates, UG said. Without the support of countless creatures, without the support of a sophisticated web of life, extinction for most creatures shall arrive in the blink of a planetary eye.

Lucy recalled the part about death and the line.

What does it mean, UG asked, for individual human apes to die? Are their deaths different than those of other creatures?

Yes, UG replied. Human apes, unlike all other creatures, spend significant amounts of time fearing the great transformation. The fear stems in part from their sense of superiority. They are not keen to transform into other creatures and they tend to bolster their sense of worth by drawing a thick, imaginary line that separates them physically, emotionally, intellectually, and spiritually from other forms of life.

Lessen the line, said UG, and the fear lessens, too. Lessen the line and the pain and burden of self-awareness shall be healed and kissed by the mists of ten thousand gentle rains. Lessen the line and life shall rise like blue-black butterflies above green mountain cathedrals. Lessen the line and life shall live on.

What does it mean, UG asked, for extinction to be imposed on an entire human or nonhuman ape species?

This must not happen, UG replied, and yet it *is* happening. It is happening with my beloved bonobos, mountain gorillas, and orang utans, each one of which are, right now, rapidly being pushed to the brink by the humans.

Never again, said UG. Never again shall human apes be allowed to eat and out-compete cousin species to the point of extinction. If they do it again it shall serve as a grave indication of their own self-destructive demise.

And so, UG said, human apes must change their behavior. They must change their attitude toward the life that surrounds them. They must learn about and alter their relationship with the multitudes of creatures, both large and small, whose indirect support gives rise to their continued existence.

Human apes, UG said, shall therefore celebrate Bacteria Appreciation Day.

On this day, UG decreed, human apes shall give thanks to bacteria, mitochondria, and other tiny creatures and subcellular structures.

On this day, UG said, human apes shall recognize that their ancestors had partnered with tiny life forms for over a billion years.

On this day, UG said, human apes shall appreciate that without the tiny life form partnership humans could not last a single day.

On this day, human apes shall vow not to wash themselves or others with antibacterial soap, unless so directed by a nurse, doctor, or other health practitioner, for doing so encourages the spread of antibiotic-resistant bacteria.

While having sex on this day, UG said, human apes shall visualize their ancestors—going back hundreds of millions of years—having sex. Human apes shall, after the sex, pick their right canine tooth with the nail of their right thumb, imagine the tooth as being larger, and, imperceptibly, say, "Aaoa," which stands for apes aware of apeness.

She recalled the part about biodiversity and genetic engineering.

Before human apes can create or manipulate life, UG said, they must explore, describe, and protect the life that already exists.

Lucy recalled the part about biodiversity and motor vehicles.

Human apes who can avoid buying a car, UG said, shall do so. Those who must purchase a car shall, if at all possible, buy a small one. *Let not the human apes purchase gas-guzzling vehicles, particularly SUVs, unless absolutely necessary.*

She recalled the part about biodiversity and pollution.

Human apes shall bring two or three reusable canvas bags when shopping, UG said, and purchased goods shall be so carried. In this way, said UG, my beloved creatures, such as marine mammals, shall not swallow the humans' plastic bags. *Let not human ape purchases be placed in throw-away plastic bags unless absolutely necessary.*

She recalled the part about biodiversity and charitable donations.

Human apes shall donate generously, UG said, to protect wildlife and its habitat. While it is fine for human apes to support large organizations, middle and small tier operations shall not be forsaken.

Human apes, UG said, shall give money for habitat preservation. Human scientists are nowhere near capable of creating sustainable environments that multiple species need to exist. *Vast no-human wildlife zones that interconnect land and sea must be created and enforced.*

Human apes, UG said, may give generously to churches that protect biodiversity. If a church supports no such project, and has no intention of doing so, then money for it shall be withheld. Human apes shall encourage churches to support carbon neutral policies and wildlife corridors.

Projects that protect biodiversity, UG said, shall be designed to help humans, too. *Helping wildlife without helping humans isn't a good idea.*

Above all, UG said, let money flow in great measure to protect my beloved great apes, for they are *right now* peering down into the abyss of extinction.

Lucy felt pleased with how much she was remembering from *The Monkey Bible*. She decided to take a break and put down the pen. It was peaceful here in the cave. Basking in the glow of the candle, she relaxed and listened to the wind.

Then she heard the ringing.

She looked up, startled.

"Hello?" shouted the hiker. "Can you hear me?"

Lucy's heart rate shot up. "Great babbling apes!" she cried.

"I'm on the mountain," the hiker continued.

Lucy shook her head incredulously.

"There's a *terrible* storm here," the hiker shouted. "That's right! No. I . . . hello? I can't hear you! I . . . okay. Yes, I'll pick up toilet paper on the way down. Of course two-ply, darling. Would we have it any other way? I love you, too. Hello? I can't *hear* you? I . . ."

"UG!" Lucy cried. She plugged her ears with her index fingers, recalled a song from *Tower of Babble-On*, and began to sing:

I'm sick of all the cell phones,
I'm sick of all the noise,
I'm sick of all the morons,
With their Web-enabled toys,
I've got *cell phone rage!*

The hiker interrupted, "Hello? Can you hear me?"

Cell phone rage!

"I can't *heeeear* you!"

Cell phone *RAGE!*

"Hello?"

Cell phone *RAGE!*
I'm on a sacred mountain,
I'm buffered from below,
But peace of mind eludes me here,
There's nowhere left to go,
I've got *cell phone rage!*

"Hello? Can you hear me?"

Cell phone rage!

"I can't *heeeear* you!"

Cell phone *RAGE!*

"Hello?"

Cell phone *RAGE!*

Lucy imagined herself singing with a choir of angels:

We don't care what you're buying,
Selfish humans be quiet,
You're adding to heaven,
Your personal hell,
Someone will teach you silence,
Someone will teach you silence.
A vision has come over me,
The way is manifest,
I'll teach the people not to abuse,
Their latest wireless.

She shifted keys and sang:

I'll be a CPA,
I'll be a cell phone activist,
I'll be a CPA,
I'll be a cell phone activist!
I'll fold and raise my right hand,
Extend the pinky and the thumb,
Shout words into the pinky,
That are private, rude, and dumb,
I'll make up conversation,
'Til the airwaves I have won,
I'll make up conversation,
'Til the airwaves I have won!

Lucy unplugged her ears and listened to the sound of the wind.

— 84 —

The storm outside the cave subsided as Lucy, well-fed and warm, continued to recall and to document the rules and rituals section from *The Monkey Bible.*

She recalled the part about secular and religious apes.

Secular human apes shall not look down upon religious apes, UG said, nor shall religious apes reciprocate a sense of superiority. Both systems are valid. To interpret the world around them, secular apes measure the physical world through their senses and instruments, whereas religious apes measure the nonphysical world through their belief in the Truth.

There is nothing, said UG, in the secular world capable of proving that an Unlikely God does not exist, and secular apes shall not assume that what is measurable in the physical universe is all that there is.

There is nothing, said UG, in the religious world capable of proving that a particular belief is correct, and religious apes shall be cautious about which unlikely story they choose to believe.

The two camps, said UG, shall set aside their differences and work together to protect my greatest gift, the diversity of life on earth.

Lucy recalled the part about energy conservation and survival.

Human apes shall use their clothes dryer, UG said, not for drying clothes but for storage. Instead, they shall dry their clothes on a line. In doing so, they shall worry not what the neighbors think, nor shall they worry about the extra time it may take. In inclement weather, they shall dry the clothes indoors, which is a good way to humidify the air inside.

Human apes shall embrace the use of nuclear power, said UG, for it has excellent potential of reducing the potentially devastating carbon build-up in the atmosphere—but only if the nuclear power is generated off-planet. *Humans must never ever generate nuclear power, fission or fusion or whatever, on earth or in earth's orbit.*

Human apes must pursue massively large-scale energy conservation and renewable energy production opportunities as soon as possible, in a way that is compatible with the complex web of living things.

She recalled the part about politics and environmental strategy.

Human apes shall vote, UG said, on an ongoing basis and they shall help environmentally-friendly legislators rise to power. *Above all else, they shall never be moved to such despair by the political process that they don't get out and vote in each and every election.*

It is not about party affiliation, said UG. It is about long-term biological survival.

Lucy recalled the part about the sneeze, the rebels, and the mountain gorillas.

Human apes have endangered mountain gorillas in the wild, said UG, to the point where a single virus infestation, or a small group of armed rebels, could wipe out the entire population. *The sad fact that these intelligent, beloved beasts are devastatingly close to extinction shall move human apes the world over to fully fund initiatives such as the Mountain Gorilla Project.*

She recalled the part about coltan and the gorillas.

Human apes shall not use cell phones or other electronic devices built with the mineral coltan, UG said, because the mining operation puts the future of central African apes at grave risk. In the short-term, human ape consumers shall pressure manufacturers to ensure that the coltan is from a safe source. In the long-term, human ape consumers shall pressure manufacturers to find an alternative to coltan.

She recalled the part about palm oil and the orang utans.

Human apes shall purchase palm oil, palm kernel, palmitrate, and other palm oil products (including lipstick, moisturizing lotions, candy, and baked goods) only if sold by a member of the Round Table on Sustainable Palm Oil (RSPO). Human apes shall learn more about the palm oil initiative through organizations such as the Orangutan Conservancy. *If human apes do not protect the orang utans' rain forest homes—which increasingly are being converted to palm oil plantations—orang utans shall face extinction in the wild within the decade.*

She recalled the part about endangered species and aphrodisiacs.

Human apes using endangered animal parts as an aphrodisiac, UG said, shall, alas, perform poorly during intercourse.

She recalled the part about zoos.

Human apes should go to the zoo, UG said, and observe one another. They should imagine that the zoo is run by animals. It is.

She recalled the part about respecting family values.

Human apes shall not destroy the fabric of other animals' societies, UG said, lest the animals descend into a pattern of chaos and destruction. Through poaching, culling, and habitat loss, human apes have created a situation where elephant family structure throughout Africa and Asia is falling apart, causing "unsupervised" male adolescent elephants to gang rape rhinos and to kill humans.

There had been more to the *The Monkey Bible*'s rules and rituals but other thoughts came to mind. Lucy recalled the section on gene mixing and why it was fundamental to the evolution of life. The point of the section had been to help Emmanuel, and all higher primates, better accept what they are and how they came to be.

She recalled the Ape Bill of Rights that protected individual chimpanzees, gorillas, humans, hybrids, bonobos, and orang utans from extreme hierarchy, closed information systems, physical and psychological abuse, and extinction.

She recalled how many sections of the book were an exploration, both scientific and mythological, of the line that separates humans from nonhuman animals. She recalled how this exploration resulted in a set of moral principles that encouraged the acceptance of racial, religious, and biological diversity, and that encouraged the acceptance of both scientific and religious paradigms.

Lucy put down the pen and packed the food and equipment in preparation to leave the cave. She glanced at the stack of notes that had accumulated over the past two days. She had assumed she'd summarize these notes and present them as a gift to Emmanuel but now, for the first time, she realized that she didn't want to be overly prescriptive.

— 85 —

"Welcome to the Traveler's Circle," Mark began, adjusting the wire-rimmed glasses on his nose. "This is the part of the gathering where we share stories as a group. Before we begin, are there any announcements?"

The thirty or so people remained silent.

"The Traveler's Circle," Mark continued, "is sponsored by Chimp-Corps Wildlife Conservation Fund. For information about our projects here and abroad, check out our Web site, www.chimpcorps.net, or talk with me later.

"The Traveler's Circle is a way to hang out, meet folks, and share stories about travel, culture, and the natural world.

"For those of you who are new or passing through we have a guest book. Add your poetry, your artwork, your wit and wisdom from the road, and, if you'd like to receive our free e-mail newsletter excerpting stories from around the world, add your e-mail address.

"Here's how the group storytelling works: someone starts by telling a story that hopefully triggers memories and stories in others. Subsequent stories are often affected, subtly or otherwise, by the previous ones and, over the course of an evening, themes evolve.

"Now, as for tonight, a few possible themes have been mentioned, including: kayaking with whales, getting kicked out of Peace Corps, and culture shock. Would anyone like to start?"

Emmanuel had a personal story that included his experiences during the past four months in North America, England, Africa, and Asia. His story included culture shock and a lot of other shocks. His story included all the elements that Ana would have wanted him to share at the end of the journey, but now he hesitated. It was not clear to him how to share with family and friends, not to mention with the public, the part about him not being fully human. Then there was the shock of him not being a father. The news was recent, the feelings raw, and he sensed that his words would get stuck in his throat.

"I got a story," said a squat man with grease stains on his shirt. "It's about culture shock. At least I think it's about culture shock. Anyway, it started a few years ago, not far from here, in my shop. You see, I fix cars. So a hippie-looking guy walks in, points to a Volkswagon bus outside, and says he needs a new transmission and wants to know how much it will cost.

"I give him an estimate and he looks at me like maybe that's too much. 'Don't worry,' I tell him. 'I'm not going to Jew you.'

"The guy gets upset. It turns out he's a Jew. *Jeez.* Anyway, he keeps his cool but looks me right in the eye and says I got it wrong.

"'I'm generous,' he tells me. 'And so are my people—as much as any other people. No more, no less.'

"And he walks out of the shop.

"I felt bad afterwards. I didn't mean to hurt the guy. It just slipped out.

"Anyway, that night I went to my uncle's house for dinner and told him about the hippie Jew and the van.

"My uncle swigged his beer and got real quiet. I thought maybe he's mad at me or something. Finally, he starts telling me about my family history, going back to before World War II.

"'Why are you telling me this?' I said to him.

"'Your mother never told you,' he says. 'She wanted to protect you.'"

"'So what are you *saying* here?' I said.

"'She had your best interests at heart, Mel.'

"'You're telling me . . . are you telling me I'm a . . . *freakin' Jew?'*

"My uncle doesn't answer. He just looks me in the eye.

"At first, I didn't believe him but the more he told me the family history the more it made sense, and . . . it turns out he was right. Later that year I went to New York—to Brooklyn—to meet the family I never knew I had. It was the strangest thing I've ever done in my life.

"These are my people? I thought when I met some of them. You got to be kidding.

"I stayed with them a few months and saw how they lived and saw what kind of problems they had. A lot of them weren't doing so well and I wanted to help, which I did, but eventually I had to get home.

"When I got back to Seattle, things were different. They've been different ever since. I see things differently now. I don't know if it's from culture shock or what. Does anyone get what I'm talking about?"

Emmanuel nodded.

— 86 —

After the Traveler's Circle, Emmanuel remained on the rug as the people and dogs dispersed. He looked around the Treasure Room at the colorful rugs, paintings, and shelves of books, shells, and rocks.

The room, he realized, had not changed, but he had.

"I miss you, Ana," he said, looking to the red and black mask. "You encouraged me to discover my larger family. You encouraged me to learn what it means to be an ape.

"As I traveled the world and learned about humans and apes, I learned that we are part of one closely knit family. I learned that there is important work to do and that I can help and make a difference.

"I have taken my story on a journey and the story has changed along the way. I am a type of ape, true, but I am a good ape, and I am proud to be me."

— 87 —

After the Traveler's Circle, Lucy wanted to talk with Emmanuel about their next steps together. Would they take courses, she wondered, at the University of Washington? Would they return to East Timor? Would they continue to help with wildlife conservation projects? She hoped they would do all three, and Mark had expressed a strong interest in their continued involvement with ChimpCorps, but right now Emmanuel seemed lost in thought so she went upstairs and spoke with Mark.

"Need help with the dishes?" she asked.

"Sure."

"How's it going?"

"Really good and sort of good."

"What do you mean?"

Running ChimpCorps, Mark explained, left little time for innovation. The ever-growing list of administrative tasks—tax forms, reports, receipts, accounting systems, lawyers, bookkeepers, CPAs, board of directors, board meetings, and fund-raisers—took precious time away from the Sign-the-Forest and vEcotourism projects. The tasks took time away from new ideas such as Peace Corps Storytelling at the Hostel and the Interactive Creature Environment (ICE), a cross-species, metaphor-driven Web-based communication system. Mark wondered aloud how he could better share the organizational burden.

"I wish I could offer advice," said Lucy, picking up a sponge, "but I know nothing about running an organization. What I do know is that I enjoyed the storytelling gathering tonight. Serving pasta beforehand is a good idea. I'm wondering, though, about the connection between storytelling and ChimpCorps."

"The Traveler's Circle," Mark replied, "gives us firsthand knowledge of storytelling that we can apply to wildlife conservation projects."

Lucy nodded.

"There's another reason why I run the gatherings. Ana used to invite people from around the world to share food, friendship, and stories in an informal setting. The Traveler's Circle is a way to keep the light burning."

"That's special," whispered Lucy. "How long can we meet here?"

"For as long as we want. Ana left the house to ChimpCorps."

Lucy looked out the window at the garden Ana had planted.

— 88 —

In the back of a Church sat a man with a dark waistcoat, bushy white beard, and grim countenance.

"Can I remain in the House of the Lord," Evelyn whispered to him, "and still grasp the tree of life?"

The man looked up and Evelyn blinked at the large tree bathed by the soft light of the coming dawn.

Evelyn woke and smiled as she recognized the grim bearded man from the dream. It was Charles Darwin, and she felt a deep certainty and relief that he would be welcomed and accepted, along with the tree of life, inside the walls of the Church.

— 89 —

"Why did he do it?" asked Ernesto.

"He told us, dear," replied Maria. "He was confused and needed time to think."

Ernesto frowned. "He lied to us."

"He has come home and he is safe," said Maria. "What more could we ask for?"

"For a son who honors his parents."

"It is less important how we fall, dear, than how we pick ourselves up."

Ernesto took a deep breath. "Yes, I suppose it was not easy for him to return home and apologize. In his own way, he is becoming a man."

"He does have a difficult past. One day we will tell him what really happened."

"In due time."

"Of course."

"Good night."

"Oh, did you give Emmanuel the package from Seattle?"

"Yes."

"Good night, dear."

— 90 —

Few people inhabited the walkways of the National Zoo at this early hour.

No one here but us animals, thought Emmanuel, approaching the Malayan tapirs. He observed them forage in the enclosure and he mimicked their high-pitch squeals ("eeeeeee!") and low-pitch grunts ("nckuhnkkunkh"). He could not help but think that these creatures—which looked like huge black-and-white pigs with oversized snouts—were the result of a genetic experiment.

Emmanuel scratched his head and recalled Zann's lesson. Subtle and not-so-subtle differences among living things *are* the result of genetic experiments, he realized. The experiments occur over thousands if not millions of years based on variation and natural selection.

He marveled at how the forces of evolution had sculpted, and continue to sculpt, the Malayan tapirs and the rest of the lowly creatures. *And not just us lowly creatures,* he thought. *Humans, too!*

As Emmanuel continued the walk, he noticed that groups of animals from different species share traits with one another. Each of these groups share a recent branch of TOL (the tree of life), he recalled from Lucy's lesson. He could see that rheas, emus, and cassowaries—large flightless birds that look like ostriches—share a recent branch, as do seals and sea lions, as do Mexican Gray Wolves and New Guinea Singing Dogs. It occurred to him that orang utans, ape-human hybrids, humans, and gorillas share a recent branch.

In a *recent* branch, Emmanuel recalled, members share a relatively recent common ancestor, whereas *distant* branch members share a relatively distant common ancestor. He wondered if recent branch members tended to see the world in similar ways. In particular, he wondered if he saw the world in similar ways to humans.

Emmanuel wondered about God and the branches of the tree of life. Was the rhea-emu-cassowary branch closer to God than, say, the wolf-dog branch? Were emus closer to God than cassowaries? Were *some* emus closer to God than *other* emus? If closeness to God was based on behavioral differences, then what types of behavior does God prefer? Aggressive? Arrogant? Destructive? Powerful? Does God favor sections of genetic code containing ACCTTGATTA? Or is GGCTACGCGA preferable?

Emmanuel sauntered to the edge of the elephant yard where an Asian elephant observed a zoo volunteer shoveling its dung.

"Excuse me," said Emmanuel.

"Morning!" said the volunteer, walking over. "My name's Chig, how can I help you?"

"Oh, no," said Emmanuel. "I wanted to talk with the elephant."

Chig raised an eyebrow.

"Only kidding," said Emmanuel. "I was wondering, have you ever seen elephants in the wild?"

"Many times."

"What is it like?"

"It's a humbling experience. The physical strength of an adult elephant is difficult to fathom, but it's more than that. Elephants mourn their dead. They have deep culture, powerful memories, and sophisticated communication skills. They have an intelligence and self-awareness that I've only seen in humans and great apes and, so, when you encounter an elephant, particularly in their natural environment, there's a sense you are encountering a sentient being, a kind of equal if you will."

"I have always been interested in elephants," said Emmanuel. "Now I really want to learn more."

"Last week," said Chig, "a friend e-mailed me an article about how humans are the only creatures with intuition. Clearly the author has never spent much time with animals, certainly not with elephants, and certainly not elephants in the wild. If he had, and he still believed what he wrote, then it would seem to me that the elephants I've encountered have greater observation skills—and intuition—than the author."

Emmanuel thanked the volunteer and continued down the hill. As he approached the Think Tank, he looked up at the O Line and caught the scent of orang utan urine, but it was too cold for the orang utans to be out today. He noticed across from the macaque enclosure a small, partially hidden display area. Inside were seven life-size chimpanzee statues that represented seven different roles within chimp society: youth, explorer, matriarch, servant, ally, observer, and alpha.

He looked to the powerful alpha ape and scratched his head. Did he have it in him to be a leader? But what choice did he have? His family was being slaughtered, their habitat was being destroyed, and within a few short years they would be forever gone.

But even if he could assume such a role, what could *he* do? He was but a young, inexperienced individual hybrid ape—a manimal at the intersection of humans and apes. How could he counter the momentum of several billion highly intelligent, creative, hungry human apes?

Emmanuel surveyed the statues in the garden.

He would do more than volunteer at ChimpCorps, he decided. He would be an ape leader and help his family. He would go public with who he was and how he came to be. He would get himself on radio and TV and explain to the humans that his family has been pushed to the edge of extinction. He would ask them for help before it is too late.

— 91 —

Ernesto knocked on Emmanuel's door and waited. No reply. He entered the room and noticed a small book on the bed. Its cover indicated it was Emmanuel's diary.

Ernesto felt compelled to read the book. Its contents were clearly private, but he felt overwhelmed by the need to know why his son had lied to him.

He tensed his stomach muscles and left the room.

He quickly returned, his muscles still tense, and opened the book.

He recognized his son's handwriting in the bold heading: "The Story of My Creation."

He started to read: "I am not who I thought I was. The story of my creation was forbidden and hidden to protect me but I wanted to know. Now I know I am the result of a prolonged molecular . . ."

"ERNEHHHHHHSTO!" called his wife from the story below. "*MAKANLAH*—let's eat!"

Ernesto closed the book, laid it on the bed, and left the room.

By the time breakfast was over, Emmanuel had not come home yet and Ernesto found himself back in Emmanuel's room.

— 92 —

"Our youth are leaving us en masse," said Father Forsyth, glancing at the grim, wizened faces of the Catholic priests. "Is it from an ongoing scandal within? From a rapid expansion of scientific knowledge? Or from a view of sexuality that is at odds with popular culture? While these issues *do* affect the Church, there is a far more important, compelling reason for the exodus.

"The key reason, I believe, is inheritance. Our youth are concerned about the world—the *physical* world—they shall one day inherit. They are concerned about the quality of the water and the air. They are concerned about shrinking green spaces, growing ozone holes, and a loss of biodiversity on a scale of Biblical proportions. They are concerned about global warming, and they are gravely concerned about society's chilling response overall toward each of these issues.

"Our youth say God's creatures are sacred. They say physical life on earth is a direct reflection of *Him*.

"They say human destruction of life on earth is accelerating at a dizzying pace and they point to numerous examples. They say, for instance, that humans have weakened the mountain gorilla population to such an extent that a simple outbreak of a virus such as ebola could, and likely will, extinguish the species forever. They say this is on the verge of happening.

"They say we have been called upon not to dominate but to protect the Creation. They say the Church should initiate and innovate projects that will mitigate the current destruction. They say the Church should help shift society's attitude and direction. They say the Church as a whole should step up and make a difference. They say each individual congregation should strive to be carbon neutral. They say the Church should lead the call for a shared, global sacrifice."

Father Forsyth paused.

"This is what our youth say," he said, "but it is not what *we* say. *We* are not tree huggers. Our focus is on the eternal Kingdom of God—not on the physical, temporal world of slime and mud and things that slither and crawl. Thus, we rightly ignore what our youth are saying."

Father Forsyth cleared his throat and continued.

"But there are consequences. Our youth do not appreciate being ignored. Disheartened, they leave us and strike out on their own.

"I have spent many hours thinking about the exodus and recruitment crisis. I have been working with a young, thoughtful member of the congregation who believes, as do I, that the way for the Church to survive is not through radical transformation or alarmist tactics but, rather, through tiny steps and gradual shifts.

"I therefore propose that congregations initiate and fund a number of small environmental and wildlife conservation projects. I am highly motivated to help make this happen. If we do not reach out to protect

God's physical creation around the globe, our youth shall continue to leave us in droves, and without them we, like the mighty mountain gorilla, may soon wither and die."

In the back of the chapel, Evelyn touched the gold pendant, thought about the musical, and prayed.

— 93 —

"I read parts of your diary," Ernesto confessed. "I wanted to know—I needed to know—why you lied to me. Now I understand."

Emmanuel fidgeted.

"It was wrong for me to read it. I am sorry for not respecting your privacy. I am sorry for the terrible misunderstanding."

Emmanuel looked down.

"Months ago," Ernesto continued, "you discovered a story in the old family Bible in the attic. You came to believe the story was some kind of official document. You came to believe the story was true. Now listen closely, my son. *I invented that story for a class in creative writing.*"

Tears welled in Emmanuel's dark brown eyes.

"Now I understand what was behind your travels. Now I understand why you believed that you shared genetics with the lowly animals. *But you have been looking for Truth in a work of fiction.*"

Emmanuel dropped to the ground, sobbing.

Ernesto squatted beside him. "Welcome back home, Emmanuel. Welcome back to the loving care of our eternal savior, Lord Jesus Christ."

"I lost the Bible, Father," Emmanuel moaned softly.

"May God comfort you, my child," said Ernesto. "Have faith that God shall bring you what you need."

Emmanuel longed to hold the childhood Bible. He longed to be taken care of by a higher authority. He longed to live forever. Stooped over, he buried his face in his large, powerful hands and gnawed at his palms with his canines.

— 94 —

In the Think Tank building in the National Zoo, Emmanuel sat by the orang utans and opened the package from Seattle. Inside were two subpackages, one larger than the other, and a note that read:

dear emmanuel,

months ago the large package had been mailed to you in Seattle and then it got forwarded to West Africa and then to East Africa but we had been running too fast for it to catch us. here it is!

the small package is a gift from me. it's a bible that includes and embraces all great apes, without discriminating against genetic variation, written by yours truly. it had been a thick tome until it caught fire in East Timor but the remaining words, along with my own life, owe their survival to you.

i had started to re-create the bulk of what had been lost but instead inserted blank pages. i encourage you to add passages and gather meaning without undue influence.

love ya,
lucy

p.s. the enclosed rescued edition contains photos which Mark discovered in Ana Mayd's basement. is photoshop awesome or what!

p.p.s. i'm wondering how you be (!) and i'm way looking forward to our next adventure. may it be as meaningful as the last one . . .

Emmanuel opened the large package and removed a heavy old book. It was a Bible. He pulled back its thick cover and let its feathery yellowed pages brush against his wrists. He found a note inserted toward the beginning of the volume.

> *Dear Emmanuel,*
> *May the weight of the Bible brighten the spirit and lighten the load!*
> *With love,*
> *Evelyn*

Emmanuel opened the smaller package and removed a thin book that smelled of smoke. Its cover showed an abstract photograph of two humanlike figures and its title read *The Monkey Bible.* He thought about humans and nonhuman animals and the line that separates them. He had once considered this line to be thick and deep but now, after what he had learned during the past several months, it seemed flexible and porous, translucent in places, transparent in others. So flexible and porous was the line, he realized, that a few genes here or there could determine whether someone—even a believer in Jesus Christ—was indeed who they thought they were. So flexible and porous was the line that it seemed reasonable and wise to keep both Bibles, large and small, on hand.

Emmanuel put the small book down and picked up the large, well-worn Bible from Evelyn. He placed it on his lap and pulled back the cover, causing the pages to part at the gap in the binding. He recognized the story spread out before him in which God created humans in His own image and granted them dominion over all the animals. After reading a few paragraphs, Emmanuel could see how this story might empower humans to destroy animals and their habitat. Recalling his mission to protect great apes from extinction, he reached for *The Monkey Bible,* fit it snugly in the gap of the larger Bible's binding, and began to read.

— 95 —

Evelyn waited for Emmanuel by the orang utans and thought about his recent phone call. He had apologized for not contacting her over the past few months. He was back home now and hoped to see her soon.

Evelyn wasn't upset with Emmanuel. She had stopped writing to him because he had stopped writing to her. I hope he's okay, she thought, recalling his appearance on the zoo's Webcam for apes.

When Emmanuel arrived they hugged and Evelyn relaxed, comforted by his presence, his physical strength, and the scent of musk.

After a moment of silence, Emmanuel motioned for them to sit across from the orang utans.

"There is much to tell you," Emmanuel said, "but where to begin?"

"Where to begin?" mused Evelyn. "Why not at the beginning?"

Emmanuel started with the journey into the attic. He described, in part, the adventures in Washington DC, San Diego, Seattle, Ellensburg, Pittsburgh, New York City, Oxford, Senegal, Jakarta, Flores, East Timor, and back in Seattle. He spoke of Dean, Lucy, Ana Mayd, Rebecca, Thurstian, Zann, Mamadou, Wira, Annette, Mark, and his parents. He spoke of what he had learned about himself and about his distant relatives. As he shared his story he felt supported by Evelyn's attentive gaze. When he was done talking he sensed a lightness in him that he had not felt in months.

Now there was silence and Evelyn looked at the crowd that was staring at the orang utan.

"And how have things been for you?" Emmanuel asked.

Evelyn wanted to share the story of her journey to England, where she had first come across the book on humans and their place in nature. She wanted to share the story of her journey to the zoo and to the Jane Goodall Institute. She wanted to share her thoughts about spiritual capacity in nonhuman animals. She wanted to share her interest in recruiting young people into the Church. She wanted to share songs she had written for the musical, as well as the ones her songwriter friend, Eric, had written. She wanted to share her reaction to what Emmanuel had experienced the past few months, which was to say that she was sorry he had been through a tough time, but it sounded like he had learned a great deal about himself and the world around him. She wanted to say that from her point of view a few genes here or there wouldn't have affected her interest in him as a friend and maybe as something more. She wanted, too, to learn more about Emmanuel's new friend, Lucy, but there would be plenty of time to catch up.

"In a way," she said, taking him by the hand and leading him toward the exit, "I've been on my own journey. Shall we go for a walk?"

Evelyn paused in the bright sunlight, opened her daypack, and removed a bottle of grape juice.

"Want some?" she asked.

Emmanuel studied Evelyn. For years their friendship had nurtured feelings of comfort, security, and warmth, but lately he had been through so much that it seemed like he hardly knew her. Searching her large brown eyes, he felt shy yet intrigued by possibility, as if meeting her for the first time.

"I do," he said, as the sun's radiant energy showered millions of his cells.

EPILOGUE

It was a cold night in Montreal. Typically, Thurstian cleared his mind at this late hour by walking alone on the mountain, just north of campus. Tonight was so cold that it hurt to breathe, but he didn't mind—he found it invigorating, particularly after such a long, frustrating day at the laboratory.

There had been yet another mix-up at the lab. So much for a smooth transition to the new system. He couldn't tell with certainty, but it now looked as if a batch of genetic material from roughly three months ago had gotten confused with another batch. So much for the transition team.

He tried to remember what they had been working on back then. There was the reptile batch. There was the random North American human batch. There was the handkerchief from England.

He wondered what the mix-up meant. Perhaps the 99.9 percent human results were associated not with the handkerchief, as he originally had thought, but with the North American human batch.

He quickened the pace and pictured the players on the transition team. Bunch of Neanderthals, he thought.

The Monkey Bible

"tell your story, take it far, find a part of who you are.
tell it loud, let it be heard, in the beginning is your word."
~ ana mayd

Table of Contents

Book of Genetisis

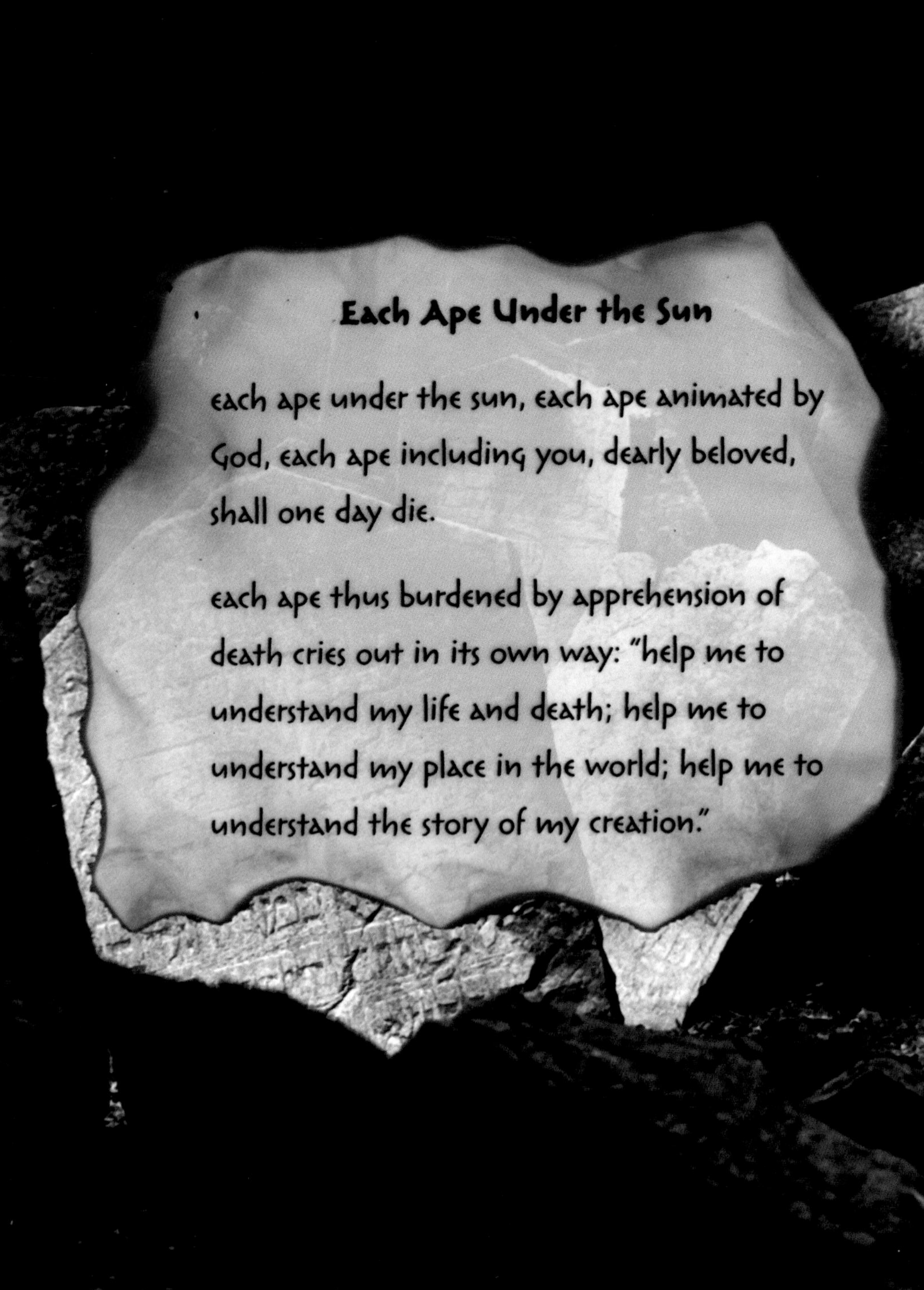

Each Ape Under the Sun

each ape under the sun, each ape animated by God, each ape including you, dearly beloved, shall one day die.

each ape thus burdened by apprehension of death cries out in its own way: "help me to understand my life and death; help me to understand my place in the world; help me to understand the story of my creation."

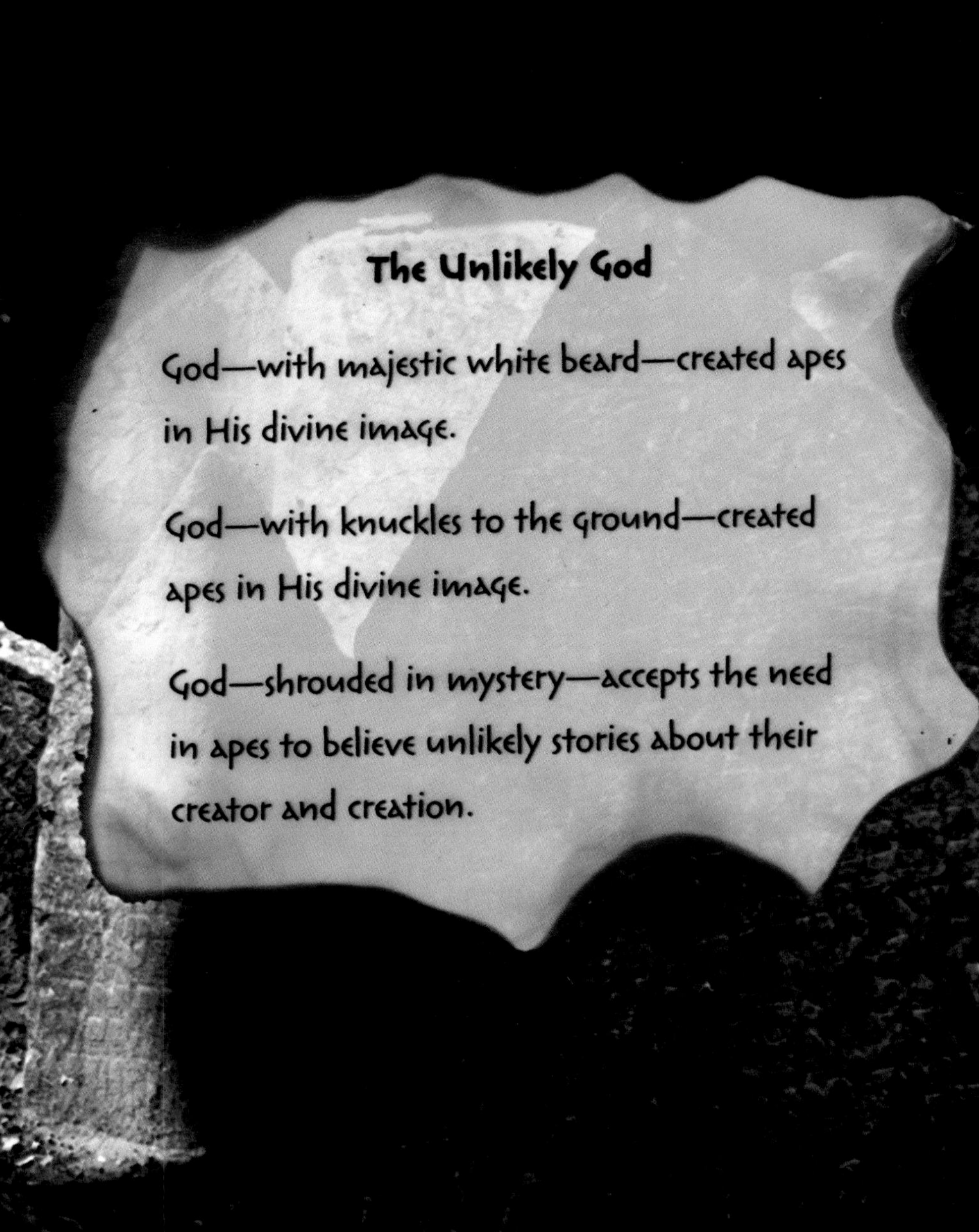
The Unlikely God
God—with majestic white beard—created apes in His divine image.
God—with knuckles to the ground—created apes in His divine image.
God—shrouded in mystery—accepts the need in apes to believe unlikely stories about their creator and creation.

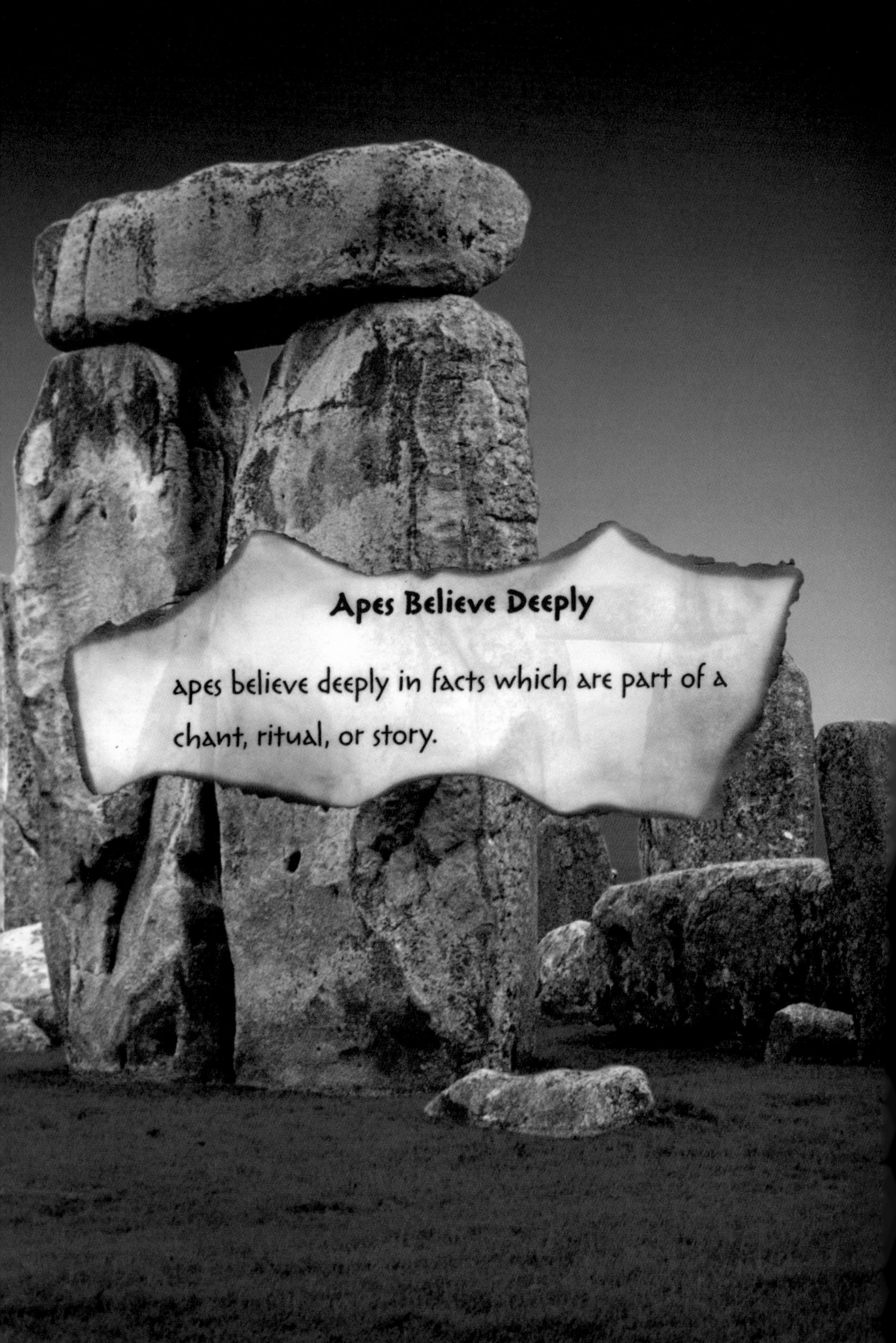
Apes Believe Deeply
apes believe deeply in facts which are part of a chant, ritual, or story.

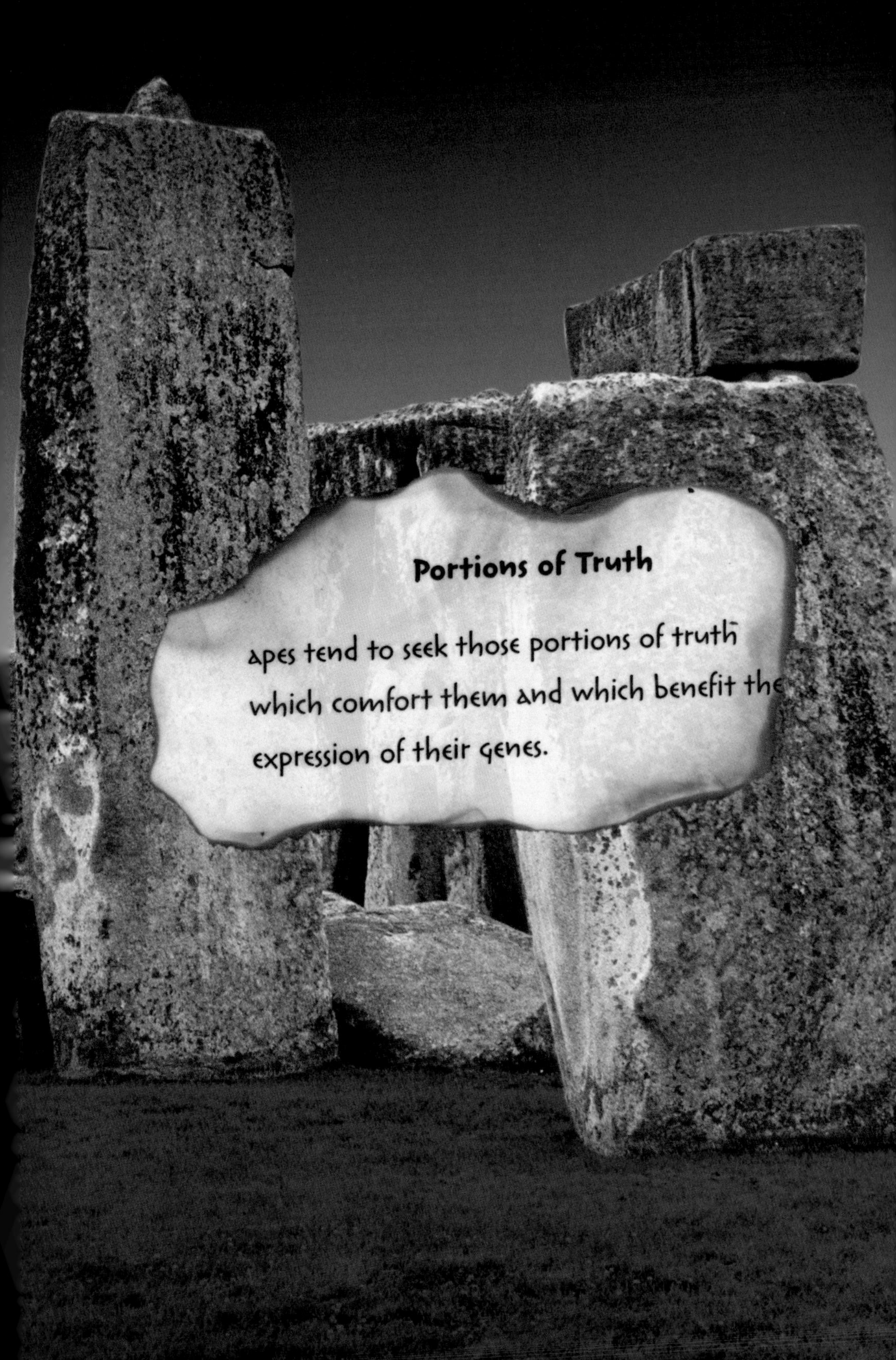
Portions of Truth
apes tend to seek those portions of truth
which comfort them and which benefit the
expression of their genes.

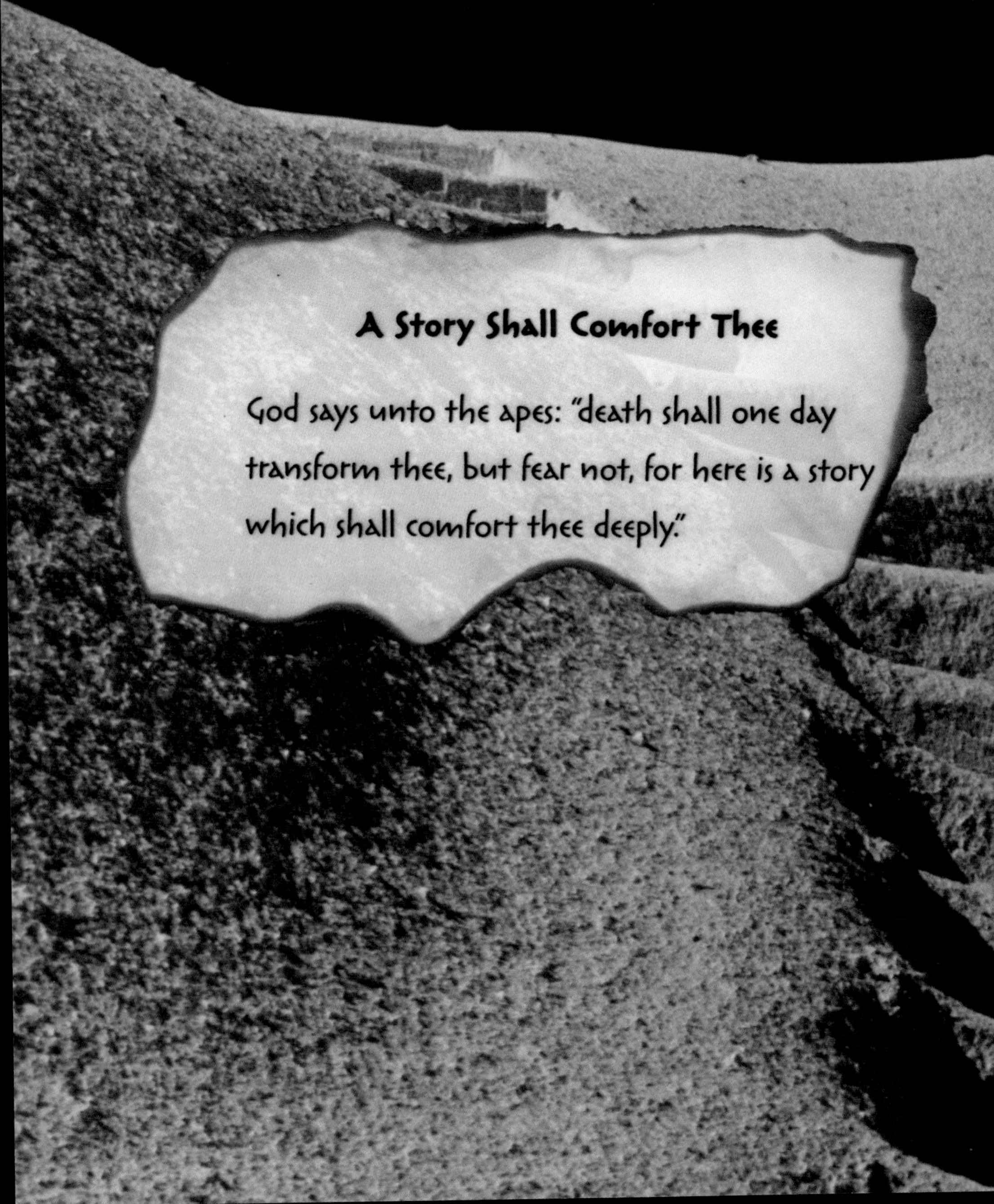
A Story Shall Comfort Thee
God says unto the apes: "death shall one day transform thee, but fear not, for here is a story which shall comfort thee deeply."

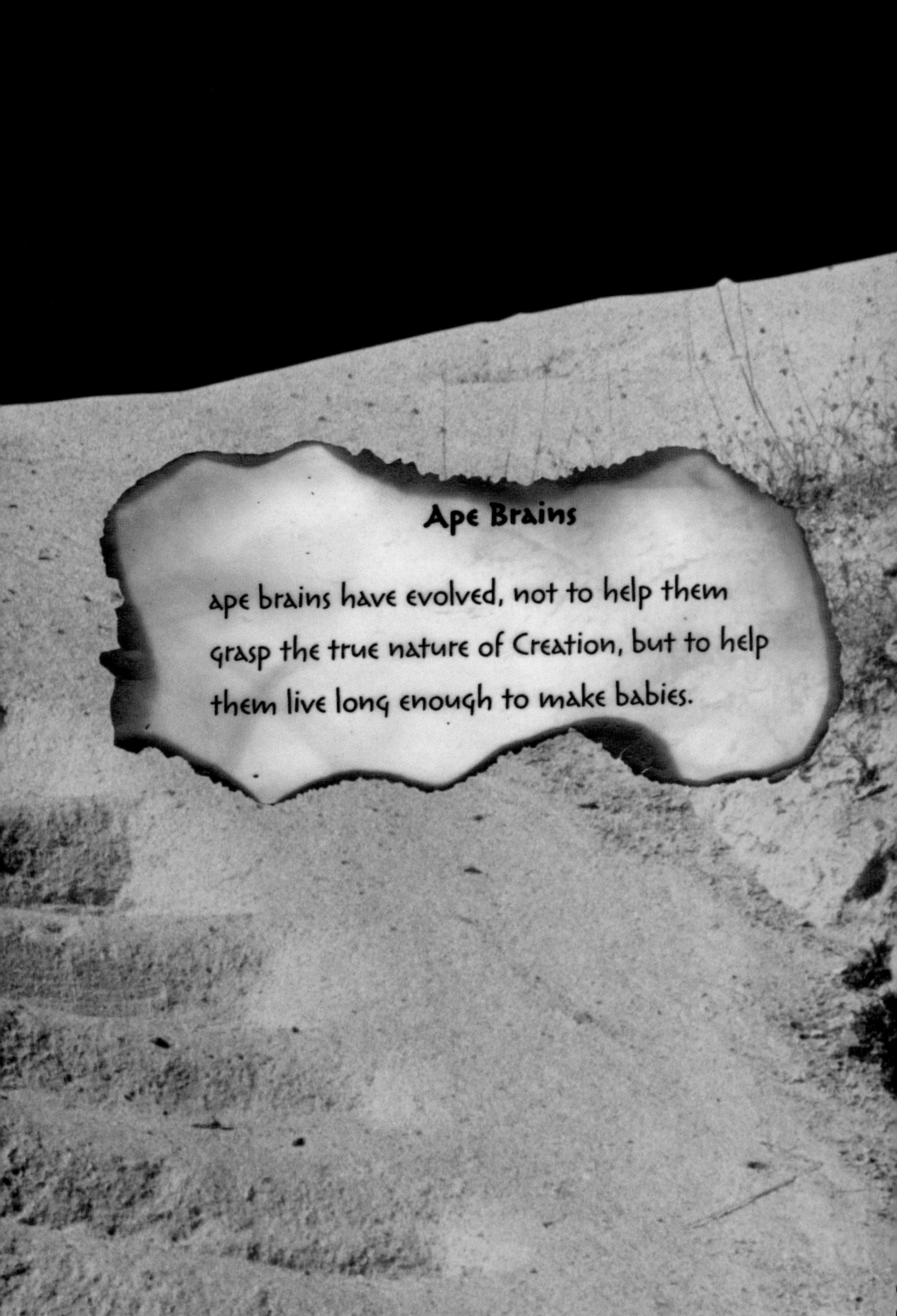
Ape Brains
ape brains have evolved, not to help them grasp the true nature of Creation, but to help them live long enough to make babies.

God says unto the apes: "in the beginning there was great darkness and upon My command a pure and powerful light permeated the universe."

An Explosion

fourteen or so billion years ago there came an explosion, the energy and particles from which warped space.

Heaven and Earth

God says unto the apes: "and I created the heaven and earth, and I swung them forth into motion."

particles combined to form molecules, and some molecules—based on charge, shape, and size—attracted and bound new particles in such a way as to replicate themselves. some crystals, for instance, attracted and bound particles into identical crystals.

as new generations of molecules self-replicated, copying errors occurred. such errors were inheritable when they happened to affect an offspring particle's charge, shape, or size. a newly formed crystal molecule could thus acquire, and share with successive generations of crystals, certain characteristics not found in its ancestors.

when inherited errors happened to increase the efficiency of self-replication processes, the mutated particles rapidly spread and often dominated their environment.

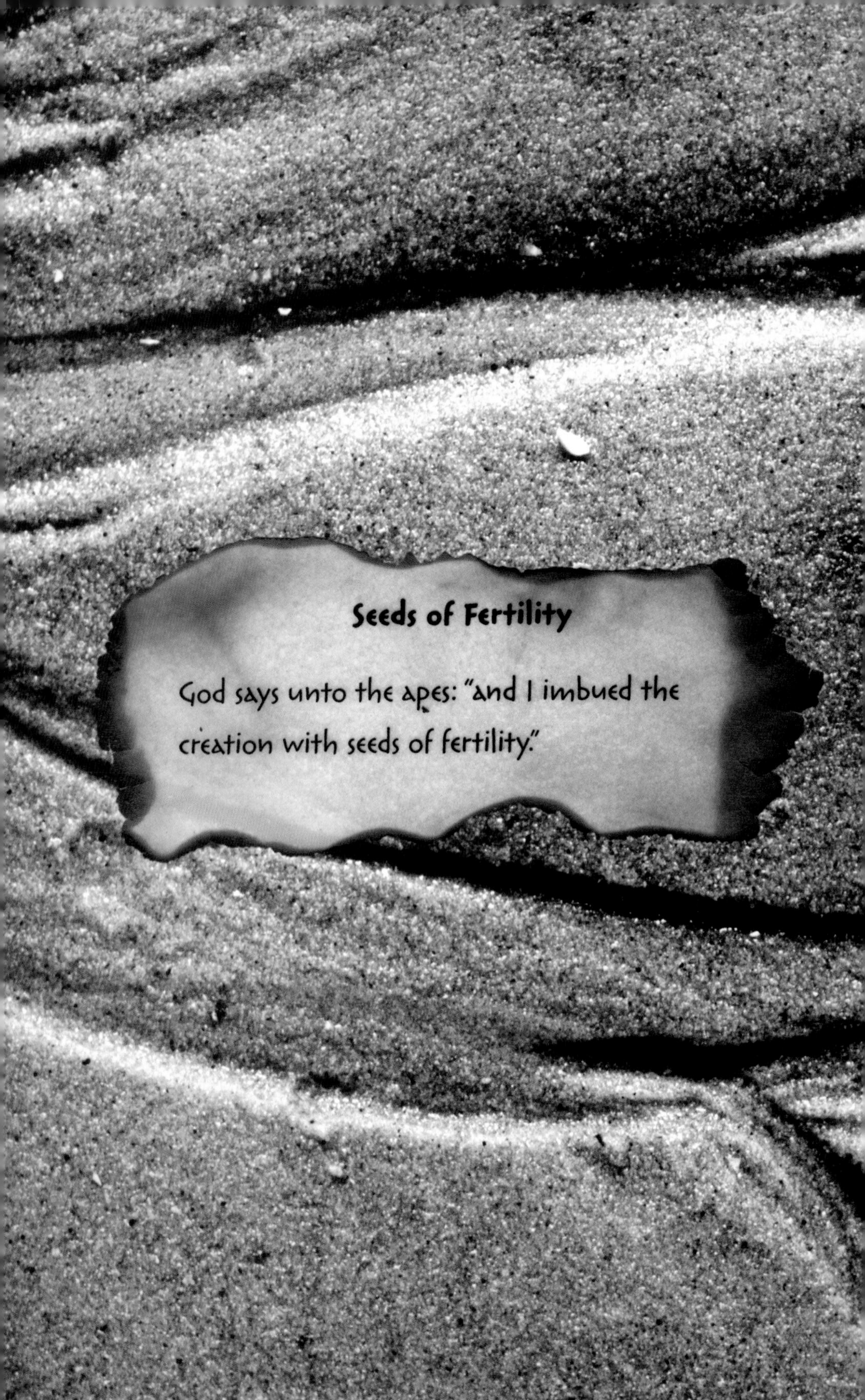
Seeds of Fertility
God says unto the apes: "and I imbued the creation with seeds of fertility."

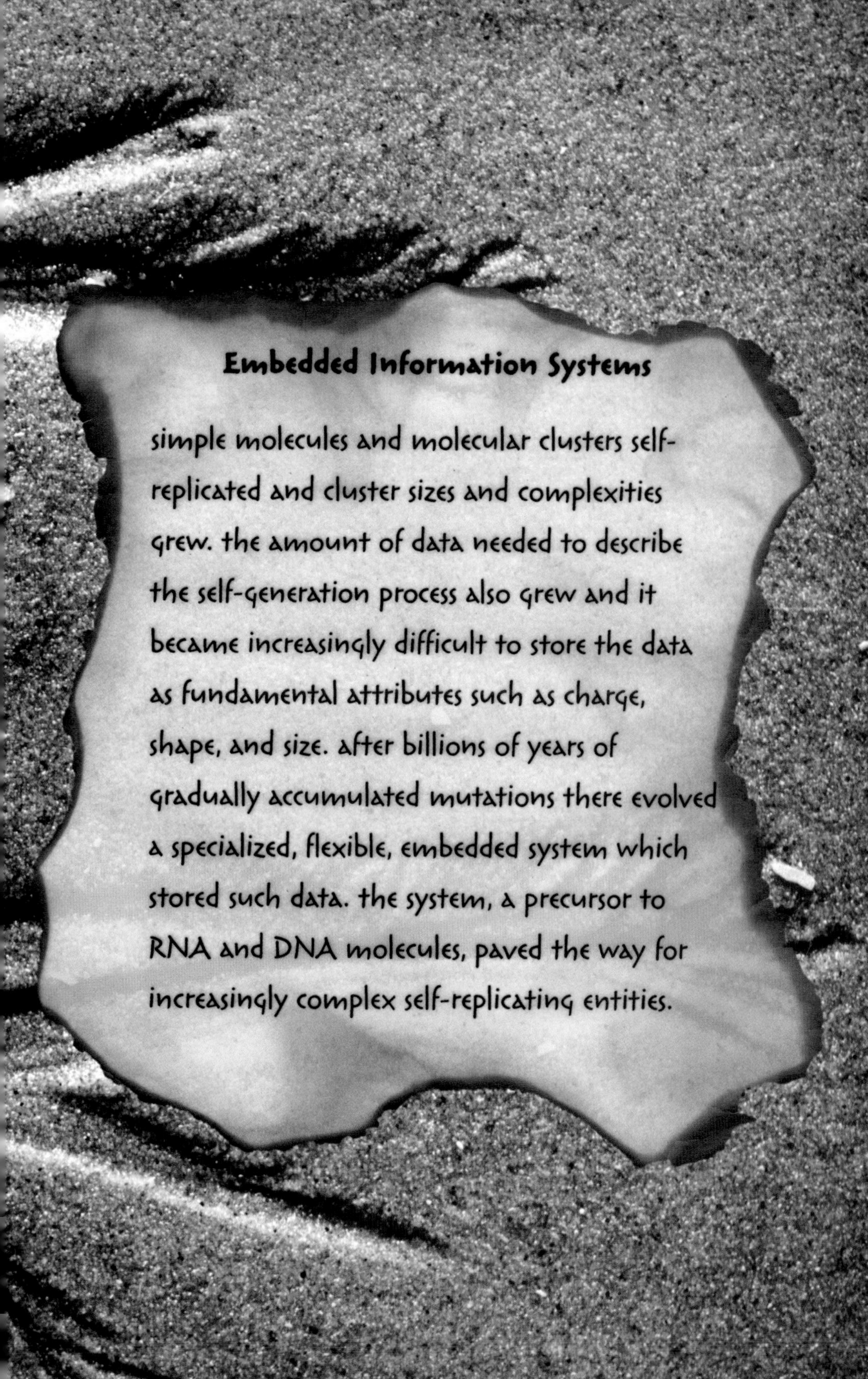

Embedded Information Systems

simple molecules and molecular clusters self-replicated and cluster sizes and complexities grew. the amount of data needed to describe the self-generation process also grew and it became increasingly difficult to store the data as fundamental attributes such as charge, shape, and size. after billions of years of gradually accumulated mutations there evolved a specialized, flexible, embedded system which stored such data. the system, a precursor to RNA and DNA molecules, paved the way for increasingly complex self-replicating entities.

Arise
God says unto the apes: "and I commanded the dust and the clay to arise."

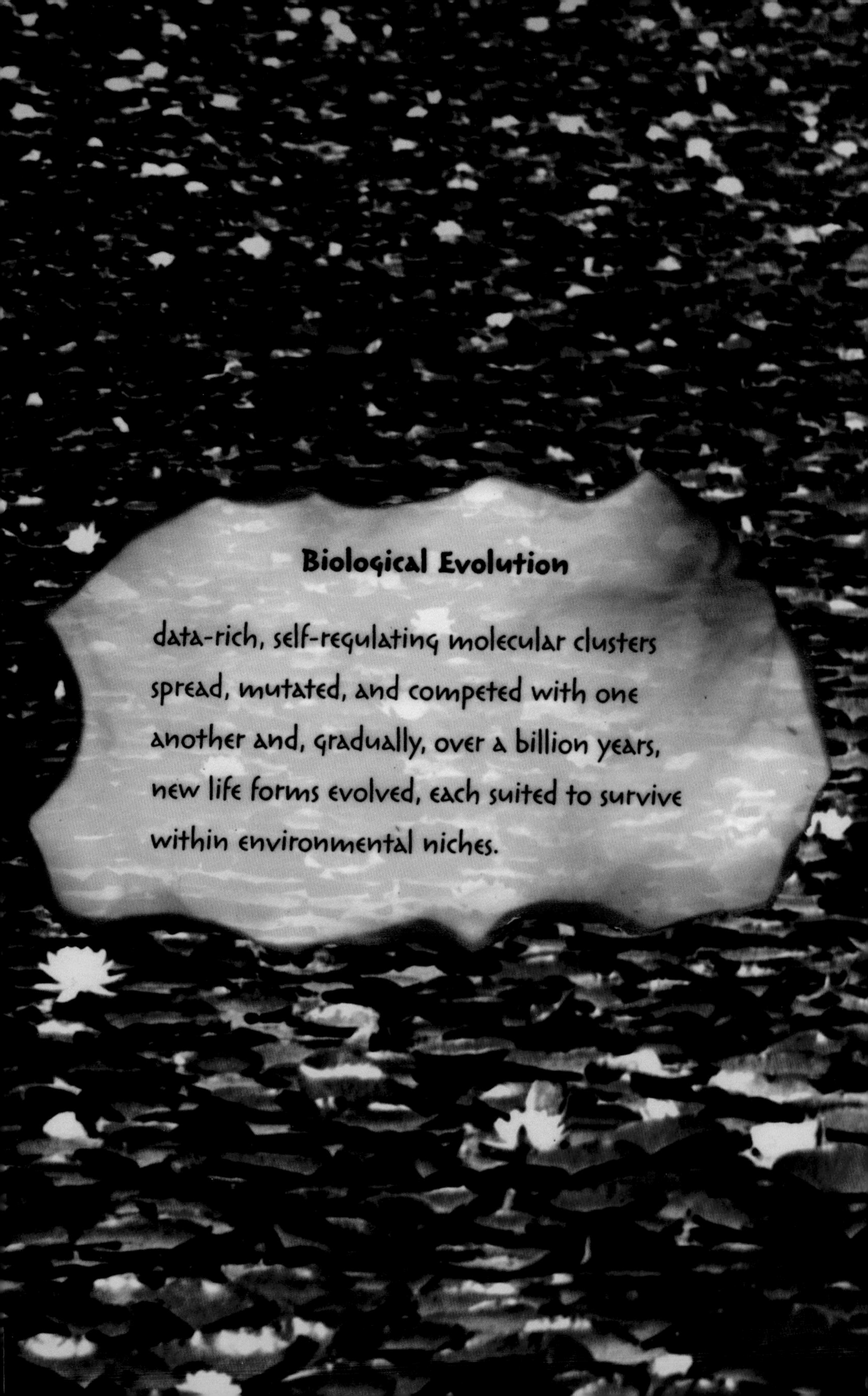

Biological Evolution

data-rich, self-regulating molecular clusters spread, mutated, and competed with one another and, gradually, over a billion years, new life forms evolved, each suited to survive within environmental niches.

Creatures

God says unto the apes: "and I called forth a multitude of creatures."

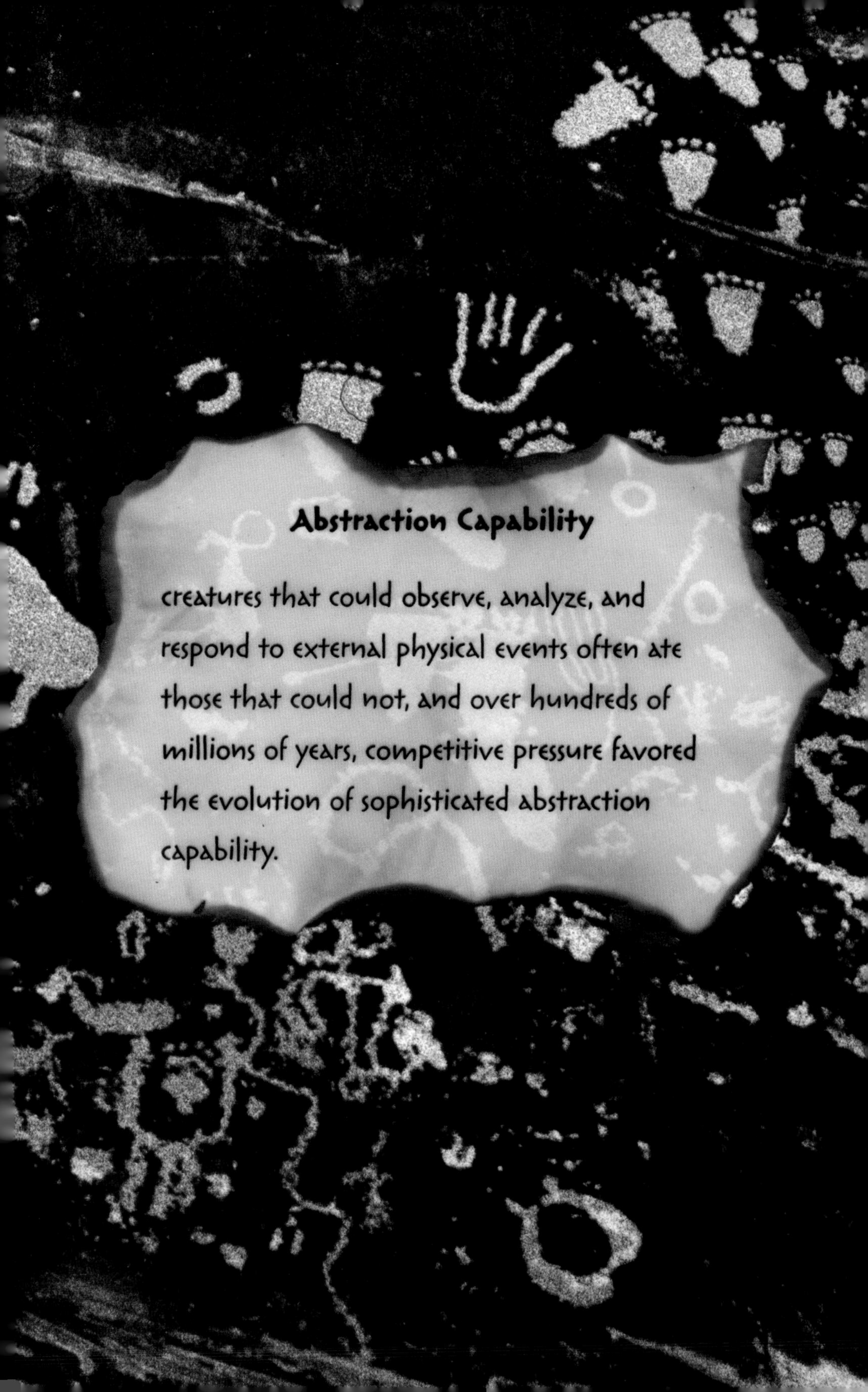

Abstraction Capability

creatures that could observe, analyze, and respond to external physical events often ate those that could not, and over hundreds of millions of years, competitive pressure favored the evolution of sophisticated abstraction capability.

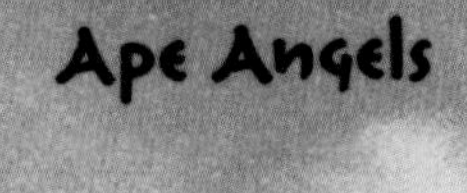

Ape Angels

God says unto the apes: "and I made you in My image and likeness."

Codified Self-Destruction

armed with abstraction capabilities, the apes created stories, rules, and rituals to help them understand their place in the universe. their newfound system of beliefs contained ample justification for them to conquer each creature and environment they encountered. at first, their domineering behavior, coupled with advanced tool and language use, helped them to survive but gradually it triggered a chain reaction of extinctions and put their own survival at risk.

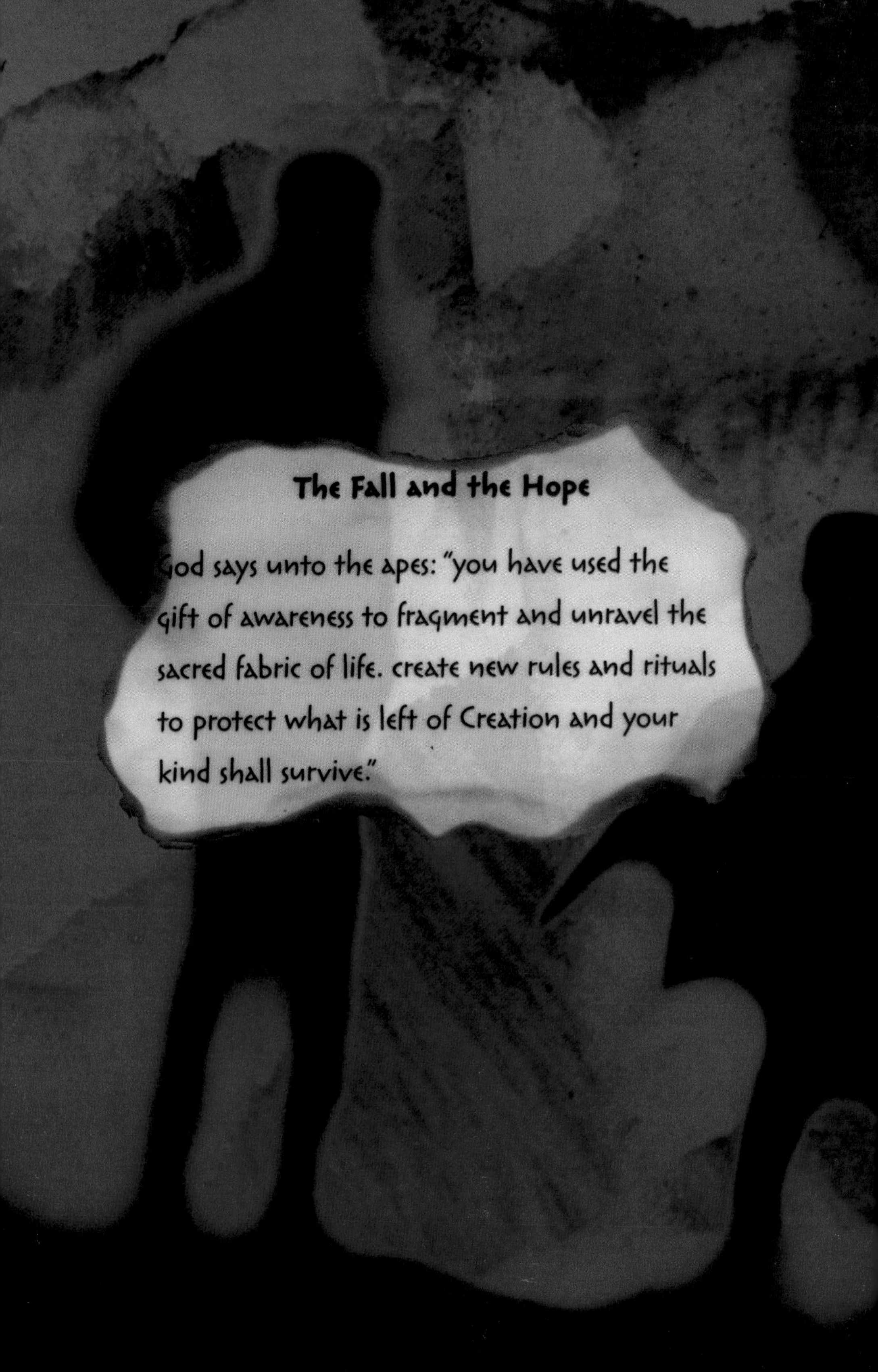
The Fall and the Hope
God says unto the apes: "you have used the gift of awareness to fragment and unravel the sacred fabric of life. create new rules and rituals to protect what is left of Creation and your kind shall survive."

Book of Change and Survival

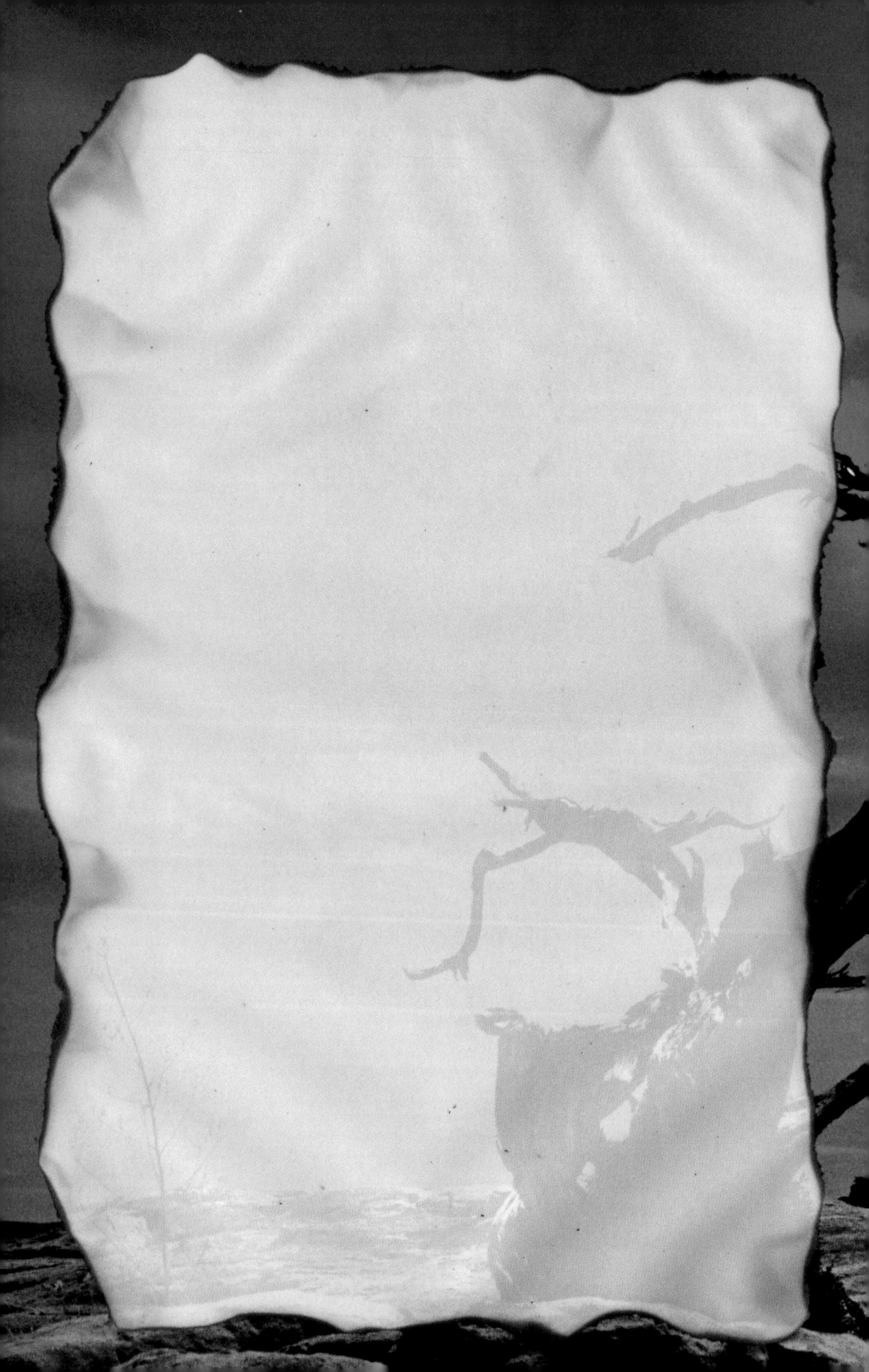

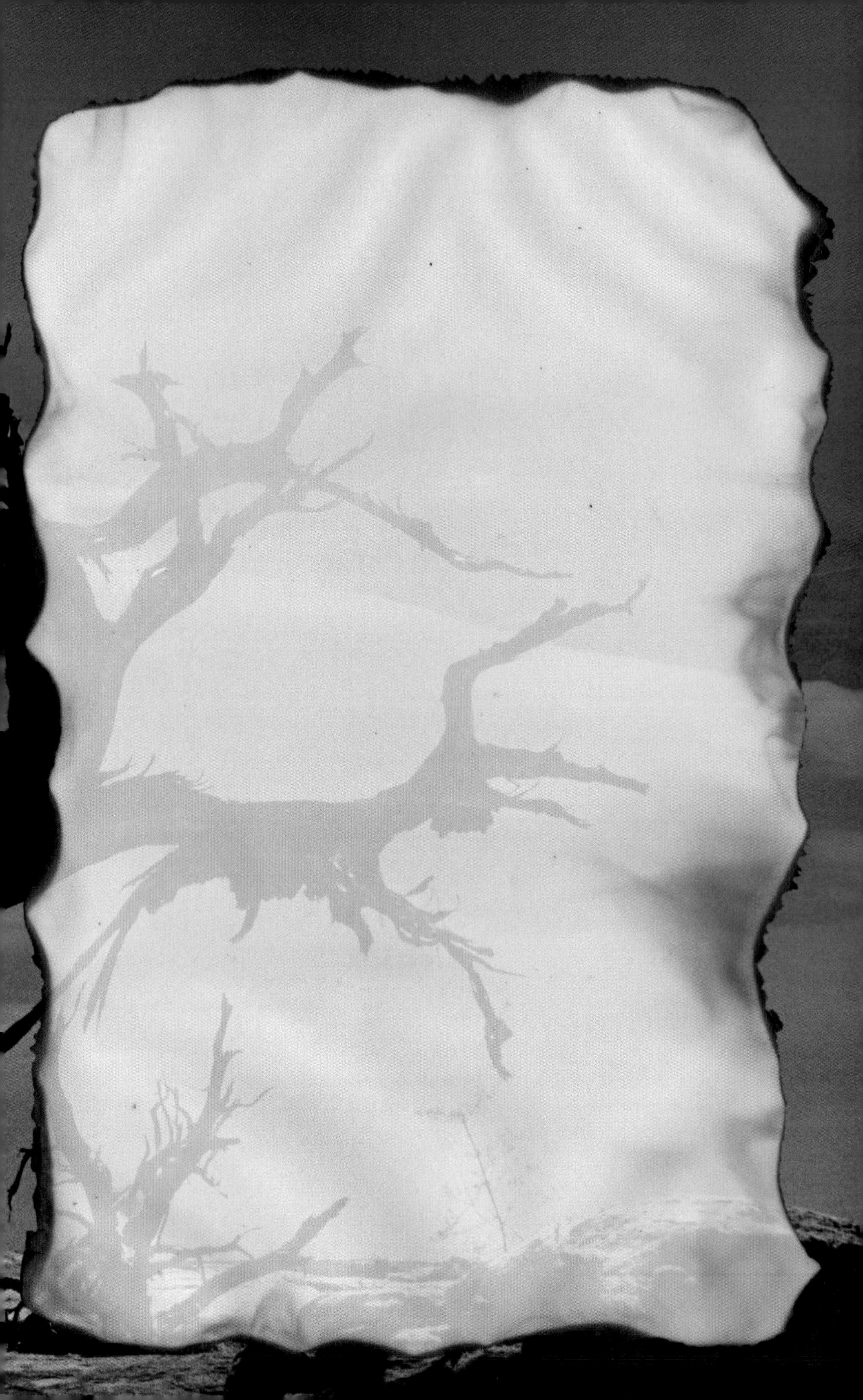

Book of Manimal Revelations

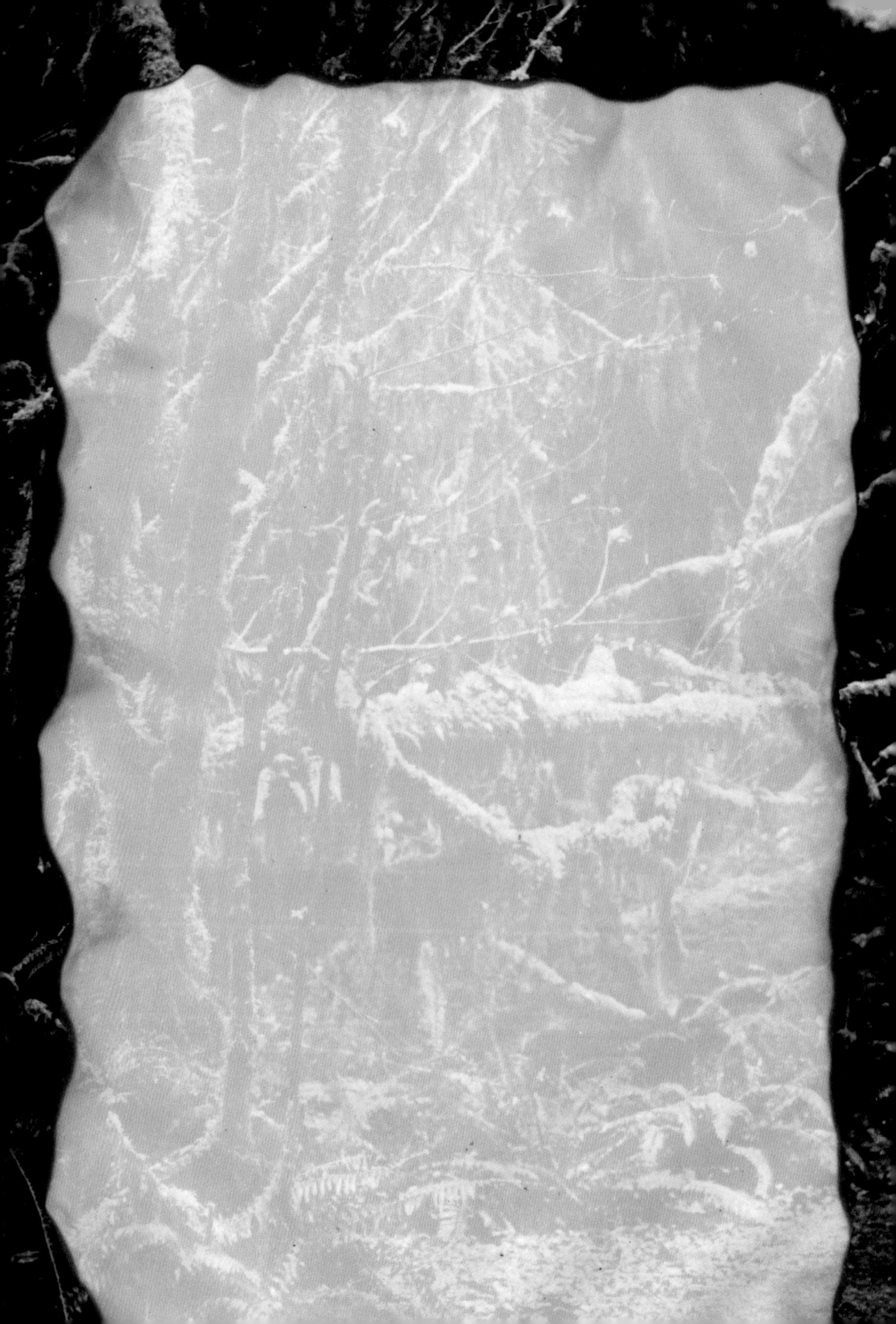

Book of Truth and Need

It was later that night, nurtured by the animal sounds and darkness, when the melody came to her, a simple wordless love song that, in Evelyn's imagination, beckoned the very dawn of creation . . .

ERIC MARING

THE LINE

COMPANION MUSIC CD TO *The Monkey Bible*, A NOVEL BY MARK LAXER

Music and lyrics by Eric Maring | Recorded at Bias Studios, Springfield, VA and Studio 270, Montreal, Canada | Additional recording at Asparagus Medio Studios, Takoma Park, MD | Engineers: Mike Fisher, Jim Robeson, Robert Langloi | Mixed by Jim Robeson | Additional engineering by Mike Monseur and Steve Steckler | Mastered by Bill Wolf at Wolf Productions, Arlington, VA

Eric Maring / Guitar, Vocals, Tabla
Amikaeyla / Vocals, Djembe
Greg Heelan / Vocals
Matt Jones / Piano, Bongos
Matt Grason / Bass
Jerry Busher / Drums
John Lee / Electric Guitar
Will Rast / Organ
Elin Soderstrom / Viola da Gamba
Sara Lourie / Recorders, Accordion
Sari Tsuji / Violin
Rachel Jones / Violin
Matt Jennejohn / Cornetto
Zaccai Free / Spoken words in "Ana Mayd" and "Reprise"
Mark Laxer, Ray Thibodeaux / Voices in "Reprise"

Orchestral arrangements by Eric Maring | Additional arrangement contributions by Elin Soderstrom, Sara Lourie, Sari Tsuji, and Rachel Jones | Song arrangements by Eric Maring, with additional assistance by Betsy Wright

The Line cover design by Peter Holm and Sara Lourie

PRELUDE

WELCOME TO THE LINE

Welcome to the line
between two points,
between two hearts and minds
The line that defines
your place in time,
it's a matter of us, it's a matter of
design, welcome to the line

Lean back, let it flow right in,
the sound of the old,
the song from within
What we know, what we don't,
what we will, what we won't,
Welcome to the line

Lines defend, lines define
I'll cross yours if you cross mine
Lines divide, lines connect
Lines make us wait, lines direct
Lines grow thin
or thick with time
I'll cross yours if you cross mine

Freewill and fate, love and hate,
the open road, the open gate
The line in the sand,
or is it your hand,
that points to the place where we
must stand?
Welcome to the line

The scene plays out,
do we shout out?
Getting a grip on
possibility and doubt
What will and will not
spin out of control
Is tracing a line through
the soul of the day
Asking if it may,
"How much does
humanity weigh?"
Welcome to the line

INTO THE ATTIC

Into the attic, the forest I spilled
Was I the hunter or
the one to be killed?
Either way my fate willed me ever
forward
I saw the tree of life
burning through time
And the vision was like
a glass of wine
That holds sacrament,
time well spent
Lines twisted and bent
through fate and accident

If it's raining here,
is it raining elsewhere?
Is everything tied up in a knot?
Then come what may
'cause some will say
We can't be sure what we got
We can't be sure what we got

Under cover of darkness
with smoke to guide the way
I peered into the night and moved
ever forward
I saw the light of day
burning through time
And a figure with a face like mine
That held sacrament,
time well spent

Lives twisted and bent through fate
and accident

If it's raining here,
is it raining elsewhere?
Is everything tied up in a knot?
Then come what may
'cause some will say
We can't be sure what we got
We can't be sure what we got

WIDE AS A WAVE

I've been on a road and
I'm carrying a mighty load
With my senses open wide,
look at how they glowed
This here's one cat
curiosity cannot kill
Fast as a lightning blast
and I guess I always will
Try to understand the best I can
Not to give in when the temptation
is to slide,
so much to know, the sky aglow
and my heart as wide as a wave

What joy, a canopy of rain
Who we are, I've got
a need to explain
Up and down left and right,
What is God? What is light?
Every answer alive,
every being in sight
And I'm trying to understand the
best I can
Not to give in when the temptation
is to slide,
so much to know, my heart aglow
and the sky as wide as a wave

Or is my heart as thin as the line
That weaves around
and around
and around
like a vine through time?
Then winds its way to the wide-
eyed mystery
What's driven into stardust is driven
into me
And I'm trying to understand the
best I can
Not to give in when the temptation
is to slide,
so much to know, the sky aglow
and my heart as wide as a wave

FARE THEE WELL, ANA MAYD

Deep time in the heart and mind
Woven into the web of life
in the air, the land, the sea,
everything's a part of me
Ana Mayd, she had a dream,
Somewhere standing
in a stream
The stream grew high and touched
the sky
Ana Mayd she did not cry

Fair thee well where you dwell,
Ana Mayd
Cross the line, all is fine,
Ana Mayd

Tell your story, take it far
Find a part of who you are
tell it loud let it be heard
in the beginning is your word

Do not look look for me here,
for I'm long long gone from fear
No longer shall an eye cry
For Ana Mayd shall never die

Fading fade fade into the shade
The moment done,
  the moment made
to the form to the form
  that is the norm
Wade into the water, wade

Fair thee well where you dwell,
  Ana Mayd
Cross the line, all is fine,
  Ana Mayd

Tell your story, take it far
Find a part of who you are
tell it loud let it be heard
in the beginning is your word

MONKEY SEE, MONKEY DO

I've heard the music
  of the monkey
and the language
  that they spoke
They said, "Hedge your bets,
  no regrets,
train your eyes on
  that line of smoke,
of desire, of the raging fire"
A wire from the other side,
some of them lived,
  some of them died
As we watched the curtain close

Monkey see, Monkey do,
I'm no monkey how 'bout you?
To learn to live
  you gotta live a lot
Time is a train
  and it's hot to trot
Monkey see, Monkey do,
I'm no monkey how 'bout you?
Gotta live, you gotta give a lot
Time is a train right to this spot

The music of the monkey is old
Some say it's as old as the hills
No regrets, hedge your bets,
train your eyes on
  that battle of wills
On fire that can inspire
A wire from the other side,
some of them lived,
  some of them died
As we watched the curtain close

Monkey see, Monkey do,
I'm part monkey how 'bout you?
To learn to live
  you gotta live a lot
Time is a train
  and it's hot to trot
Monkey see, Monkey do,
I'm part monkey how 'bout you?
Gotta live you gotta live a lot
Time is a train right to this spot

As you stare afar at a star,
are we who we think we are?
100%, 99%, the secret's
 locked up in a secret jar
or a box out on the rocks
on the sand of a shore
 we don't know anymore
as we watch the curtain close

Monkey see, Monkey do,
I'm that monkey how 'bout you?
To learn to live you
 gotta live a lot
Time is a train
 and it's hot to trot
Monkey see, Monkey do,
I'm that monkey how 'bout you?
Gotta live you gotta give a lot
Time is a train . . .

SAD, TIRED, BEAUTIFUL WORLD

Evelyn's perched on a bench
 in a church
and the bell is ringing she can
 hardly do the work
in her hands, in her heart, or the
 hole in her soul that grows
and takes these
 two worlds apart

The man does preach,
 what will he teach us?
Are we god's and god's alone?
Are we man or beast
 or a bit of each?
Someone's ringing on the phone

Sad, tired, beautiful world
 I'm making a deal with you
Come on here inside
 we've got some talking to do
Now the moment's right . . .
 you can turn off all the lights
and speak the truth
 I need to hear,
c'mon tell me the truth
 I need to hear,
c'mon tell me the truth
Let it ring in my ear

Oh, the organ plays,
 plays through our days
and the leaves turn
 brown to dust
Heel and toe through
 the ice and snow,
what can I know or trust?
This headlong nature,
 relentless nomenclature,
pinning one against the rest?
What does it mean to have a human
 heart and brain?
Does it mean I am the best?

Sad, tired, beautiful world
 I'm making a deal with you
Come on here inside
 we've got some talking to do
Now the moment's right . . .
 you can turn off all the lights
and speak the truth
 I need to hear,
c'mon tell me the truth
 I need to hear,
c'mon tell me the truth
Let it ring in my ear

It's the spirit that matters
and the soul is something
 you can't see

Close your eyes . . . there, that's
enough, you gotta trust me
She crouched and shivered
and listened to the
roar of the wind
Time crushed seconds into minutes
into where to begin, where to
begin?

Well, a long time ago
God created man
and man's ability to see
A long time ago
God created man
and man's dominion over
everything
The soft candlelight illuminated her
long black hair
She fell out of her time
and out of her mind
out of who really cares
Who really cares? Who really
cares? Who really cares?

Sad, tired, beautiful world I'm
making a deal with you
Come on here inside we've got
some talking to do
Now the moment's right . . . you
can turn off all the lights and
speak the truth
I need to hear, c'mon tell me
the truth I need to hear,
c'mon tell me the truth

INTERLUDE

A MATTER OF DESIGN

The telltale signs built in like
designs to remind us of where
we go wrong
The song that belongs on and on
that keeps us in balance and keeps
us strong
It seems again the purchase of
our wills,
the sharper the sword,
the craftier the kills
'Til before us it spills or cuts down
the hills and finds us flinching
after the fact

Are we all here as a
matter of design?
Or a scattering of minds shattering
the smattering of flattering
reminders
'Til we all see the grain
of truth behind us

Are we all really
any different today?
Are we getting our answers?
Is thunder
any less of a wonder?
Or do we just ponder it less
when we've got our wireless?

Bottled up rage
can never be bought out
It's as sure as rent control
And the role we all play
to our own dismay
Sets the pace at the limit and
increases the toll

a matter of design?
r a scattering of minds shattering
the smattering of flattering
reminders
il we all see the towers of truth
behind us

there any song
hat can go so deep
nd touch all of humanity
urn us away from our struggles
and their cost
nd make us gaze
at the glaciers
nd species we've lost?

oetry, the great mystery
here the ancients
tell their tale
nd speak through us
so we'll discuss
anger and what is dangerous

y mind is open,
pour it all inside
his moment shall in each
of us reside
nd if a circle that's wide should
be our design
e may end up with
a greater chance
o continue this dance
or a time

re we all here as
a matter of design?

Or a scattering of minds shattering
the smattering of flattering
reminders
'Til we all see the mountain
of truth
'Til we all see the mountain
of truth behind us

IN MY OWN SKIN

The Bible is gone, the moon is gone
and we're still hangin' on
The answers aren't free, but they'll
be what they'll be
like the words of this song
Whatever justifies our need to
compromise
these consecrated ways
We'll breathe in deep and welcome
the coming days

I am in, in, in my own skin
Talking 'bout the world
and origin
We listen to the song and
where it's headed, can't we listen
to where it's been?
In, in, in our own skin

We hold on to answers,
we hold on strong
We hold on and on and on and on
for so long
With no idea why we're singing that
song or
if it's possible to amend

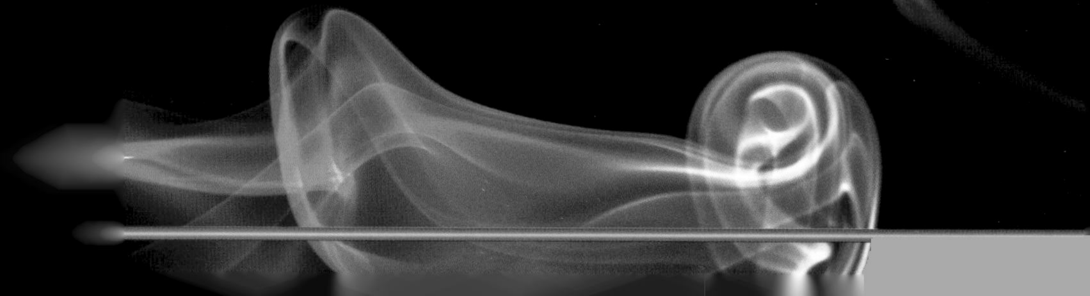

But to sit and wait will take us
straight to the end

I am in, in, in my own skin
Talking 'bout the world
and origin
We listen to the song
and where it's headed,
can't we listen to
where it's been?
In, in, in our own skin

The Bible is gone, the moon is gone
and we're still hanging on
The answers aren't free but they'll
be what they'll be like the words
of this song
Why don't you grab a cup of tea
while we wait,
come watch the stars shine
And if the line's too long, you can
have some of mine

THE END OF THE LINE

This is the end of the line,
this is the end of the line
It's not the end of time,
it's just the end of the line

This is the end of the line,
this is the end of the line
It's not the end of
yours and mine,
it's just the end of the line

This is the end of the line,
this is the end of the line
It's not the end of
your heart and mind,
it's just the end of the line

This is the end of the line,
this is the end of the line
It's not the end of humankind,
it's just the end of the line

POSTLUDE

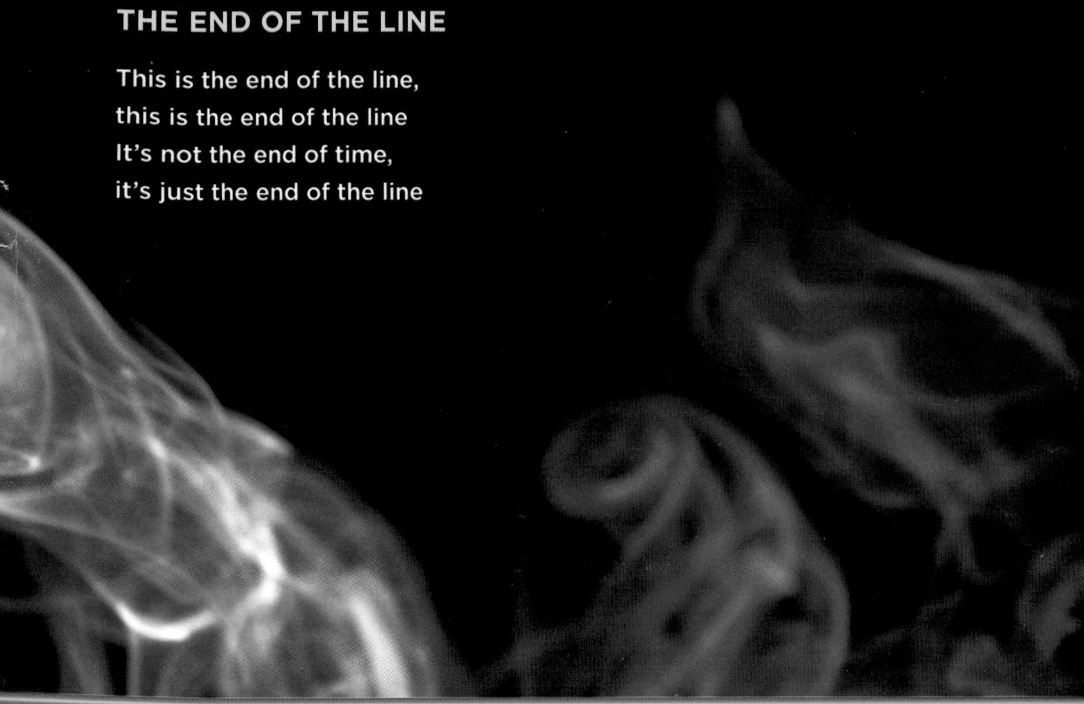